I0460392

Freaks

Under Fire

Also by Maree Anderson:

Freaks Under Fire

Book Three of the Freaks series

Maree Anderson

ISBN-13: 978-0-9941160-3-1
ISBN-10: 0-9941160-3-9

FREAKS UNDER FIRE
Copyright © 2015 by Maree Anderson
First print edition, 2015

Publisher: Maree Anderson

Cover Design: Rob Anderson

PROLOGUE

THE GUARD AT THE GATE flashed a cursory glance at her ID badge before waving her through. She kept her expression pleasantly neutral, while inwardly sneering at his incompetence. At the very least he should have phoned through to Reception to verify that she was expected. The "hiding in plain sight" tactic meant there were a number of storage units available to carefully vetted members of the public, and if one of those carefully vetted people discovered what was in Unit Twenty-Six there'd be hell and all its minions to pay.

Before she'd even released the handbrake, the guard had resumed The Position—planting his substantial ass back in his chair and propping his boots on the desk, exactly as he'd been lounging when she approached the facility. Considering she'd had to blast the horn twice to get his attention, she suspected he'd been napping as well as lounging.

She drove off at a crawl, keeping her speed to a minimum until a glance in the rearview mirror confirmed the guard had remembered to lower the barrier arm. Hah. If Average-height Balding 'n Forgettable back there was an indicator of the caliber of the rest of the staff, just as well she'd been dispatched sooner rather than later. The whole place was a security leak waiting to happen.

Her stomach performed a lazy roll, acknowledging the true nature of the task she'd been dispatched to complete... and the toll it would take on what remained of her principles. She'd been required to do some distasteful things for Evan Caine—highly illegal things that would get her locked up for the term of her natural life if she were caught doing them. Some of those things bothered her in the dead of night when she drifted on the edge of sleep, but in the bright, uncompromising light of day, she found she could live with them. She could get out of bed each morning and stare unflinching at her reflection in the bathroom mirror, because she'd not crossed a personal line drawn in the metaphorical sand: the line that involved harming kids.

Until now.

She gave herself a mental smack upside the head, followed by a mini-lecture. Distance yourself from the task. Stop letting your emotions get in the way. Quit personalizing the target, and thinking of her as a kid.

The target wasn't a child—wasn't even human. "It" was a potentially dangerous machine that was incapable of empathy, didn't have a conscience, and operated on severely flawed logic... if that recent display from Caine's current pride and joy was any indication of typical core programming.

She stomped on the brake pedal, jerking the sedan to a halt alongside the main storage complex. Ingrained caution had prompted her to park where her vehicle couldn't be seen from the reception area, and now she was thankful for the privacy the spot afforded while she took a moment to get her shit together. Her hands tightened on the steering wheel until her knuckles whitened. Bill had been a decent guy, one of the rare colleagues she'd wholeheartedly respected. In a rare moment, he'd confided to her that he was contemplating retiring because he was "getting to old for this fucking crap". And then, against the advice of his techs, Caine had unleashed his shiny new pride and joy upon Bill and his team, and in the space of seconds it'd been all over bar the agonized screams of dying men.

That unholy *thing* had ripped through six men—Caine's most experienced security unit—like a knife through butter, leaving them broken and bleeding. Poor bastards. A shitty way to die—and for what? To prove a fucking point?

She quashed that thought before it took root, forcing herself to relax and focus. She had a job to do. But she would miss Bill's gruff manner and monosyllabic responses. Not to mention their sparring sessions. None of the other men had the guts to go one-on-one with her a second time after she'd wiped the floor with them, but Bill hadn't given a shit about being bested by a female. He'd never fully recovered his peak fitness after being injured in the field, but he'd still taught her a thing or two.

Yep, she told herself, you'll be doing the world a favor. This girl—*it*—is a ticking bomb, and it's your job to defuse it before someone else gets killed.

Exiting the car, she grabbed her kitbag from the trunk and slammed it shut with unnecessary force.

She knew from security footage that the cyborg they called *Beta* was defective—incapable of moving, let alone defending itself. Beta could swallow food, but couldn't feed itself. It responded to aural stimulation with a blink, but otherwise stared fixedly at nothing until one of its minders got around to closing its eyelids. It was the cyborg equivalent of a vegetable. And, according to Caine's latest stable of techs, today's task was simple: play the digital recording that Caine had entrusted to her, and get rid of the evidence.

She scowled, recalling how her boss hadn't even bothered

with a convincing lie. As he'd handed over the recording he'd looked her in the eye, curled his lip, and said, "I trust you implicitly."

Yeah, right. They'd both known that was a crock of shit. The recording was of Caine's voice speaking a command sequence to permanently shut the cyborg down. "Trust" had nothing remotely to do with anything, because it wasn't like that recorded command could be scrambled to, say, recalibrate the cyborg's programming so it would respond solely to someone else's voice pattern.

Not that she would consider attempting such a double-cross—

Well, that wasn't entirely true. If this cyborg *had* been functional, and she'd been handed the means to control it, she would have given serious thought to commanding it to locate Caine's fully functioning killer cyborg and have at it. With any luck, both cyborgs would have destroyed each other beyond resurrection, and the world would be a much safer place....

Until Caine built another one of the godforsaken things.

Gravel crunched beneath her boots as she marched to the entrance. Putting on her "Don't fuck with me" face, she shouldered through the doors into the small reception area.

No one was manning the desk. Voices drifted from a room out back—the break room, at a guess. Huh. Why did it not surprise her that security was so lax? Not that it mattered. She had a duplicate key to the unit, so there was no need to hang around waiting for someone to escort her.

Get in, do your job, get out—good advice for people of her ilk. It was better this way, without any witnesses to her dismantling a thing that looked like a helpless young girl.

A helpfully marked "This Way to Storage Units" sign on a

side door led her to a concrete path running alongside each row of units. She took a right at the third row and halted in front of Unit Twenty-Six. A decent-sized sturdy padlock secured its roller door. At least some effort at security had been made.

Her key stuck in the padlock, and she had to wrestle with it to get it to turn… and then fiddle with the lock mechanism to coax it open. Hmm. Anyone could be forgiven for believing this unit hadn't been accessed in a while.

She pocketed the padlock. Only idiots left an opened lock hanging outside a storage unit—it was just asking for some asshole to lock you in. She heaved the roller door up and squinted, adjusting her eyesight to the interior gloom.

Strangely, the unit was bare save for a large canvas bag dumped in the corner by the right wall. And from what she could see, both security cams were down. Whoever had set up the feeds reckoned there was no further need to monitor this unit.

She snatched a scant moment to dampen growing unease before fishing a flashlight from a side pocket of her kitbag. And she was about to thumb the switch when some deep-seated instinct prompted her to pivot on her heel and close the roller door behind her, blanketing the interior of the unit in darkness again. She'd learned to trust her gut, and if her gut told her it was prudent not to advertise the fact she was here, then so be it.

Switching the flashlight to the lowest setting, she approached the bag, playing the beam over the stained canvas.

Not empty. Whatever had been stored inside was lumpy, and took up the whole interior of the bag. The fine hairs on the back of her neck rose. Damn, but she was getting a bad feeling about this.

She reached for the zipper and, in one swift, decisive movement, opened the bag.

Her torch beam limned chalk-white, almost skeletal features, haloed with a tangle of limp dark curls. It—the cyborg—lay on its side, stick-thin limbs curled tight against its torso.

She swallowed the bile that had surged up her throat and flicked the flashlight beam over that gaunt face again, both hoping for and dreading a response.

Nothing. Not even the merest twitch of an eyelid.

Her hand shook as she reached out to check for a pulse. And the instant she pressed the cyborg's carotid artery, those paper-thin eyelids opened.

Whoa. She had never seen such incredibly blue eyes—eyes that sucked her in and ripped through her defenses.

Horror warred with a wave of hot fury that stained her vision a bloody red... and all possibility of professional detachment died. The hollow emptiness she'd endured for so long it was now a part of her, filled with steely resolve, because she knew without a doubt that Beta wasn't like Caine's current pet. And there was no longer an "it" lying at her feet—some inhuman "thing" to be "dealt with". There was only a defenseless, disabled *child*.

Sweet God Almighty. Beta was conscious and sentient and they'd zipped her into a bag, tossed her in a corner, and left her there to waste away, helpless, trapped in some nightmarish half-life. What they'd done to her.... It was unimaginably cruel. And Beta had suffered. Terribly.

Who were the inhuman monsters here?

Speaking the command that would shut this miraculous but flawed creation down, reducing this child to a lifeless machine, might be construed a mercy. But in this moment, *right now*, it smacked of murder....

And this time she didn't have it in her to commit murder.

She stroked the cyborg's hair. "Well, Beta, looks like it's just you and me, and we're up shit-creek without a paddle because that bastard Caine is gonna pin big-ass targets on both our backs."

Her soft bark of derisive laughter bounced off the walls. And when the echoes of it had faded, she started making plans.

CHAPTER ONE

THE CAB DRIVER PERFORMED an inept three-point turn and zoomed off with a wince-inducing screech of tires, leaving Sam Ross in Nowheresville. The jury of his peers was still out as to whether this was a good career move, but right now, as the sky blushed rosy pink with the birth of a new day, and some nearby feathered denizen warbled a cheery welcome, Sam told himself he didn't give a crap what his colleagues thought of his decision. No one had said respite care was going to be easy and he'd gone into it with eyes wide open. But lately, the chinks in his armor had become gaping holes and he'd not been able to maintain the distance he felt he needed to perform his job. He was burned out.

Bottom line? When you glanced at yourself in the shaving mirror each morning and barely recognized the hollow-eyed stranger staring back at you, it was time for a change of pace.

He hoisted his pack onto his shoulder, inhaling crisp country air deep into his lungs, holding it until tiny glowing sparks zinged through his headspace. And, as he exhaled, he cast off the last of his doubts. He'd been right to make this change—he felt it in his gut and his heart and his soul.

Coarse seal shifted beneath his feet as he approached the gate barring the cobbled entranceway. He pressed the buzzer on the speaker and leaned in to announce his arrival. "Samuel Ross."

As he straightened, a flash caught his eye. A tiny security camera, barely noticeable amid the thick foliage poking through the gaps in the fence bordering the property. Which drew his attention to the fence itself, its sturdy metal palings colored a shade so close to the deep greens of the hedge plantings, he hadn't even noticed a fence until now.

The gates *shooshed* smoothly, almost noiselessly, apart.

Disquiet feathered Sam's spine but damned if he'd turn back now. He walked briskly through the gates... and fought the impulse to glance over his shoulder as they shut behind him. It was hardly unusual for an affluent property-owner living in relative isolation to install some stringent security measures, right?

Rolling the tension from his shoulders, he marched up the meandering pathway, determinedly admiring the freshly mown grass and bright flowerbeds with their neatly clipped borders. He passed two bent figures, diligently plying secateurs to a bed of standard rose bushes. Fulltime gardeners, perhaps? Not surprising given the extent of these grounds. Right now, he could be forgiven for imagining he was taking a stroll through carefully maintained public gardens. Fingers crossed the house wasn't some drafty old mansion full of dusty antiques, with generations of stern ancestors glaring down their noses at him from the walls. Still, given the salary he'd been offered, he could put up with small inconveniences like OTT security measures, clanking plumbing and uninviting décor.

Besides, money hadn't been his primary motive for accepting this position—though it'd certainly helped when he'd weighed the pros and cons. This placement was long-term. His patient was young and healthy—physically at least. And if her mental state left a lot to be desired, well, he could deal with that. So far as he'd been able to ascertain she wasn't suffering. And for Sam, that was pretty much a win any way he looked at it.

He blinked as he caught sight of the house.

Nice. More than nice, in fact. Another win, for sure. The modest two-story, built of cream brick with a red tiled roof, was almost eclipsed by the addition of a huge conservatory. Bi-folding doors had been pushed back to take advantage of the balmy temperature, revealing a substantial swimming pool. An undercover pool—heated, too, at a guess. With a bit of luck he could wangle permission to use it on his days off.

Sam's gaze lingered on what he guessed was the garage. He'd bet his next paycheck it housed some seriously sweet cars. But as much as curiosity pricked him to be nosy and peer through the side windows, he ignored the impulse and continued up the path to the front door. There were bound to be cameras secreted here, too, their feeds manned by someone noting his every move, and it wasn't a good look to be caught nosing around on his first day.

He was reaching for the plain brass doorknocker when the door was yanked open, leaving him confronting a tall woman with short-cropped white hair and cold gray eyes. She wore light, flowing black pants, a loose black tunic, and black sneakers. Sam estimated her age as anywhere between forty and fifty—a polar opposite to the housekeeper-cum-guardian who'd interviewed him a month ago, and professed herself delighted to offer him the position. That woman, one Sally Bridges, had been short and plump, with dimples and a kind smile. She'd worn a floral dress, a pink cardigan and matching pink low-heeled pumps. She'd chatted away, immediately putting him at ease. She'd appeared friendly and harmless, the kind of woman who would sit you down in the kitchen with a plate of fresh-baked cookies and a glass of milk.

This woman? She was all lean muscle and coiled strength. She possessed the sort of watchful stillness Sam recognized from a stint training with a martial arts expert—the kind that told you here was a person who could explode into motion, and take you down before you could blink. His spidey-senses warned him to proceed with caution. Apparently this job was not going to be as straightforward as it had appeared.

He met her cool, assessing gaze with his best bland expression, and waited for her to make the first move.

One slash of an eyebrow arched. "Mr. Ross, I presume."

She didn't offer her hand, so Sam responded with a curt nod.

The other eyebrow joined the first before returning to neutral. "If you'll follow me, Mr. Ross, I'll show you to your quarters." She turned her back on him and strode away, obviously expecting him to follow like a good little lapdog.

Sam figured he might as well start as he meant to go on. "It's Sam, not Mr. Ross," he called after her. "And getting settled in can wait. Right now I'd prefer you introduce me to Miss Smith."

She halted and pivoted, the full force of that steely gaze boring into him.

A lesser man would have backed down, stuttered an apology. But Sam was made of sterner stuff. "Please," he added, keeping his tone firm and to-the-point, while making it obvious the effort at politeness was a token afterthought.

Her lips quirked ever so briefly, and as she strode toward him she stuck out a hand. "Marguerite Danvers."

Sam noted the slightest nostril-flare accompanying that announcement, and hazarded a guess she was less than thrilled to be named after a flower—a fact he only knew because marguerite daisies had been his grandma's favorite bloom.

"You can call me Marg." Although she pronounced it with a soft "g" her tone was anything *but* soft, suggesting dire consequences if he dared call her Marguerite.

Sam managed not to wince when she gripped his hand so tightly it felt as though his bones were grinding together.

She released his hand and, when he manfully showed no inclination to flex his crushed digits, her gray eyes sparkled with amusement. She'd won the dominance challenge, and they both knew it, but he'd also earned a modicum of her respect. "You and I are going to get along just fine, Sam. Let's go check what Bea's up to."

Sam frowned, mentally scanning his employment documentation, but could only recall his patient referred to as "Miss B. Smith." Nor could he recall Mrs. Bridges mentioning the girl's first name. He took a punt. "Bea as in… Beatrice?"

"Yes." Marg's lips compressed to a grim line. "Though it might interest you to know that Bea's previous guardians referred to her as 'Beta'."

Beta. The second letter of the Greek alphabet.

Sam blanched, rocking back on his heels as the full import of Marg's explanation smacked him upside the head. They hadn't believed this girl deserved a name—only a designation, like she was some freaking subhuman lab-rat instead of a human being. "Jesus Christ," he muttered.

Marg must have had exceptional hearing, for she folded her arms over her chest, and gave him some truly superb cold hard bitch that was at odds with her conversational tone as she said, "When Sally came on board, she decided on the name Beatrice. Sally adores the English royals," she added by way of explanation. Followed by a little shake of her head and an eye-roll, as if to convey fond exasperation, but those gray eyes were still cold and hard and watchful as she observed his reactions. "Most of us think that's a bit of a mouthful, though, and shorten it to Bea."

Sam swallowed the myriad questions clamoring in his head and said quietly, "Bea, it is, then."

Marg rewarded his ready acceptance and disinclination to pry with one of her clipped nods, and beckoned him to follow.

Sam trailed her through to what turned out to be a spacious kitchen, dominated by a huge, solid wood table that could have sprung fully formed from the pages of Country Living.

None other than Sally Bridges, resplendent in be-ruffled floral apron, stood at the counter, kneading bread dough. She glanced up as Marg and Sam entered, and greeted them with a smile. "Oh good, you're here. How do you like your eggs, Samuel?"

"Please, call me Sam," he said, his gaze sweeping the room. "And I like my eggs however you care to cook 'em. Thank you for the offer of breakfast, by the way. I'm starving."

He shucked his pack and leaned it against the wall. Ignoring the glances Sally and Marg were shooting at each other, he visually assessed the girl seated in the wheelchair at head of the table.

Her head had tilted to one side until her chin almost rested on her collarbone. Her shiny mane of naturally curly hair hung over one shoulder in a loose, fat braid. Her complexion was clear and smooth, pale but healthy-looking. Good muscle-tone—no atrophied muscles that he could detect beneath the shapeless gray sweatpants and loose black long-sleeved tee she wore. Surprisingly, there were no support straps to prevent her slipping out of the wheelchair. A good sign. Likewise that neither her hands, which lay relaxed atop her thighs, nor the sneaker-clad feet resting on the footrest of the wheelchair, were twisted—

His gut swooped. He'd been told Bea was in a persistent vegetative state. PVS patients were awake but unaware of what was happening around them. Some could open their eyes, even track objects. Others could move their limbs slightly, though such movements were reflexes rather than reactions to external stimuli. Bea's eyes were closed—nothing unusual in that; PVS patients had regular sleep-wake cycles. But instinct prompted him to approach her—the same visceral instinct that insisted he drop whatever he happened to be doing to check on a patient he'd left only moments before, because he knew something was wrong.

He needed to see her eyes—gaze into them to gauge what it was about her that disturbed him.

He strode forward, peripherally aware that Marg and Sally had stilled and were watching him like hawks. He dropped to his haunches before Bea and took her hands. "Hi, Bea. My name's Sam."

Save for the slow, even rise and fall of her chest, there was no response.

In the back of his mind, Sam noted her hands were cooler than he'd expected given the sun pouring in the windows and the warmth of the room. "Bea," he said, firmly and clearly. "I need you to wake up now."

Nothing.

"Open your eyes, Bea."

He waited. Still nothing—not that he'd expected any response to his command... had he?

He mentally shook himself, trying to shrug off a sense of foreboding so powerful that the fine hairs on the back of his neck were standing at attention. He reached up, and with the pad of his forefinger, gently pushed up her left eyelid.... And was confronted by an orb of breath-stealing, far-too-intense-to-be-natural blue.

He inhaled sharply. "Whoa." That was... unexpected.

There was a muffled protest—from Sally Bridges, at a guess—that was quickly shushed.

Sam ignored his audience of two. Interesting. Bea's left eyelid had remained open after he'd removed his fingertip.

He carefully opened her right eyelid and eased his hand back. Ditto with the right eyelid.

He backed off. "Well done, Bea," he said, smiling to convey approval, even though all the approval and encouragement in the world wouldn't make an iota of difference to a PVS patient like Bea. And then, as he gazed into those inhumanly blue eyes, the smile froze on his face.

What the—?

He cupped her face in his palms, tilting her head.

No. He hadn't imagined it.

He watched the telltale moisture form in the duct of her right eye. "How long has Bea been PVS?" he asked, without taking his gaze from that glistening teardrop.

"I took over as her primary caregiver five years ago," Sam heard Marg say.

With a bent knuckle, Sam oh-so-carefully caught the plump tear tracking down that perfect cheek and held up his hand, knowing in his gut both woman would understand exactly what he was showing them.

"PVS patients can shed tears," Marg said. "It's not unheard of."

She was right, of course. But this? This was more than the spontaneous crying, moaning, laughing, and even screaming, considered within normal parameters for a PVS patient. Sam knew it absolutely. He knew it in his heart and soul and the very marrow of his bones.

And then, as if she'd read his mind, Bea's pupils dilated and those remarkable blue eyes were focusing... on *him*. And damn him to hell and back if he couldn't almost *feel* the emotion pouring from her in waves. Determination. To... to....

To make him understand that she was... she was... *trapped?* Inside in a physical shell that refused to function as it should?

Sam had to lock his muscles to prevent himself recoiling. Jesus, Mary and Joseph. There *was* awareness in those inhumanly beautiful eyes. "I understand," he blurted. "I'll help you however I can, Bea, I promise."

If he'd hoped for some miraculous physical reaction from her, some acknowledgement of his outburst, he was sorely disappointed. He knew Bea had understood him, though—believed him, too—because a breath sighed from her body, long and slow, heavy with some unnamed emotion.

He stared at her, fascinated and horrified in equal measure, as that spark of awareness was extinguished, leaving only gloriously blue, chillingly blank orbs.

God— Sam caught the thought before it could fully form, for it seemed the worst kind of travesty to importune the very deity who'd condemned a thinking, feeling human being—a girl who'd barely begun to experience life—to such a fate.

As he straightened from his crouch, he distinctly heard Marg declare, "You don't understand a damn thing, Samuel Ross. But you will."

He turned to the two woman, questions bubbling on his lips, in time to witness Sally Bridges hug Marg, and for Marg to pat the shorter woman on the shoulder before extricating herself and smoothing her tunic.

Marg glanced up, caught Sam's gaze, held it. "Sal," she said, "you were right: He's just what she needs." And although Sam was one-hundred percent certain he'd caught the glimmer of tears before Marg strode from the kitchen—because from the stricken expression on Sally's face, she'd caught them, too—well, neither he nor Sally were brave enough to broach the subject.

Sally cracked three eggs into a bowl and began to whisk them vigorously. Sam planted his butt on the chair nearest Bea and stared into her unseeing eyes, willing that spark of awareness to return.

CHAPTER TWO

A HUMAN WOULD HAVE been overwhelmed by both the number and magnitude of the tasks ahead—not to mention the necessity of prioritizing them. So it was fortunate that Jay was not human.

Locating the Beta unit she'd recently learned existed sat high on Jay's current list of priorities. Her self-proclaimed "bestie" Caro—fraternal twin of Jay's boyfriend Tyler—would doubtless insist on referring to the Beta as Jay's older sister. In truth, the term *twin* would be more accurate, because the same human genetic material used to construct Jay, a Gamma unit, had obviously been used during the creation of the Beta, and both Jay and the Beta had been created in the image of a woman named Mary Durham, their creator's deceased wife.

Discounting the nature of any supposed "relationship" between Jay and the Beta for the moment, Jay understood the workings of Caro's mind enough by now to know that Caro would consider the Beta *family*. Moreover, whether the Beta was labeled *sister* or *twin*, and proved fully functional or as defective as the wheelchair in the photo indicated, so far as Caro was concerned *family* should be at the top of any list—a fact Jay could easily prove by revealing the Beta's existence to Caro and the rest of the Davidson family.

Uncharacteristically, however, Jay remained undecided over whether to tell them. Much depended upon Tyler and Caro's mother Marissa, and her reactions to the events of the past two days. And Jay believed Marissa would hardly be in a forgiving frame of mind given their shared history, and the undoubted trauma of recent events.

Marissa would likely be even less inclined to forgive if she learned that, while she'd lain in a drug-induced slumber, her newborn infant had been kidnapped to use as leverage to get to Jay.

Jay parked the vehicle she'd hired—a hire vehicle had seemed a prudent precaution now that her SUV could be recognized by a certain party—and paused to rub her breastbone, where a too-familiar ache had lodged. Marissa had indicated that she'd liked Jay once upon a time. Before Marissa had understood what Jay truly was. Before she'd understood how deeply her son, Tyler, had fallen for the "glorified calculator" Marissa had once accused Jay of being. And to Jay, it was obvious as udders on a male bovine that, despite the lengths she had taken to keep the Davidsons safe, Marissa would prefer Jay vanished from their lives.

Logically, Jay couldn't find it in herself to blame Marissa for that preference. Strange, therefore, to again experience this unrelenting, throbbing ache—a physical symptom of how much it hurt to know that Marissa, a human Jay had admired from the moment they'd first met, would rather she didn't exist.

Jay snorted a sharp breath through her nostrils. *Bah!* as Alexander Jay Durham, the man she had called "Father", had liked to say. Emotions, those complex human states that provoked often irrational behaviors, as well as disturbing physical and psychological changes, were at best distracting and inconvenient, and at worst, dangerous. They were insidious things that snuck up on one, and impaired one's ability to make sound judgments. She would be better off without them. And yet....

And yet, even if she could somehow twist time and revert to her state of being *before* Tyler had wormed his way into her artificial heart and irrevocably altered her, Jay would not. Now she knew a little of what it meant to love, and to be loved, she would not willingly relinquish those feelings—difficult as they could be to live with.

Unfortunately, Jay didn't possess enough data to ascertain whether Alex had designed her in the expectation she would evolve in such a way, or whether it had been a spontaneous, unforeseen development. If only Alex, the one human who might have accurately predicted the far-reaching ramifications of loosing an emotion-fueled cyborg on an unsuspecting world, still lived. If only—

Jay shut down the part of her brain that had begun to replay her role in her creator's demise, and blotted the annoying moisture welling in her eyes with the heels of her hands. It would not be prudent to confront the Davidson family with watery eyes. Tyler and Caro would double-team each other to ferret out the cause of her tears. Marissa would likely believe Jay was doing what humans termed "turning on the waterworks" in an attempt to garner sympathy. And Marissa's husband Michael would be torn between the desire to assist Jay, in the hope of making amends for his past deeds, and the desire to protect his family from further harm.

Jay inhaled, drawing oxygen deep into her lungs, and exhaled slowly, steadily, refocusing her thoughts.

A suitable lab was also a high priority, however any premises would have to be selected with a great deal of care, so as not to alert certain interested parties. Too, sourcing the array of equipment necessary to repair the Beta's defects could prove problematic.

Jay was not programmed with a tendency toward paranoia but until she could personally examine Evan Caine's remains, and personally confirm the covert team experimenting with self-aware cyborgs had been disbanded, she wasn't about to take unnecessary risks. In fact, it might be more prudent to utilize the sole satellite laboratory she hadn't dismantled, cleared out, and then sold off after Father's death. It remained undiscovered to date, suggesting it was as safe an option as any—albeit a somewhat primitive one.

There was also the mystery surrounding the photo that had alerted Jay to the Beta unit's existence. Or, more specifically, the *identity* of whomever had left the envelope containing the photo at her friend Allen's studio.

The envelope had been addressed to "JAY"—the letters neatly printed by hand in blue ballpoint ink—and Allen had passed it on to McPhee, a mutual friend who'd planned on visiting Jay to drop off a painting. For now, that unknown party's motives could only be surmised—a waste of energy and resources. Jay would act when more information became available.

There was one last priority to consider. Tyler. Her boyfriend. The young human male who professed to love her.

Would he still love her after all that had transpired?

Could he still love her after what she had put him, and his family, through?

Jay raised her hand to the door buzzer. And, even as a part of her brain noted that her chest felt tight and her heart rate had escalated, another part accepted the presence of these physical symptoms and suppressed the prompt to run an internal diagnostic. Apprehension, Jay decided, was a very uncomfortable human condition indeed.

She jabbed the buzzer in three short bursts and waited.

She heard the thuds of hurried footfalls, and through the hazed glass of the door's window, spied a fuzzy silhouette. Not Tyler. His father.

Michael-who-preferred-to-be-called-Mike Davidson yanked open the door.

The expression in his eyes, the compressed lips and tight muscles of his shoulders, shrieked tension, however Jay hadn't detected any raised voices that might indicate an argument taking place.

Observing Michael with all of the enhanced senses at her disposal, Jay concluded he didn't appear overly upset, or distressed in the manner she had previously observed whenever he and his wife had a disagreement. Hmmm. If she had felt the need to pin a label on Michael Davidson—something Jay had discovered humans frequently liked to do because categorizing their peers made them feel more secure—she would have chosen *harried*.

Michael blew out a strong exhalation that puffed his cheeks. "Thank God you're here. Quick—before he escapes."

He?

Jay confined her reaction to a slow blink. At this stage of human development, Marissa's not quite three-day-old infant son should hardly be capable of the coordination required to suck his own digits let alone trying to escape out an open door.

Nor could Jay picture Tyler making a break for it. Her boyfriend wasn't the kind of attention-seeking human who felt the need to draw all eyes by "making an exit". Of course, if provoked, Tyler had been known to exit in such a way that no one would doubt his feelings—as Marissa had learned to her cost. But Jay couldn't visualize Michael taking steps to keep his oldest son in the house if Tyler desired to leave. As Tyler might say, that wasn't the way his father rolled.

Perhaps Matt, Caro's boyfriend—

No. A scan of the interior of the house detected no extra male humans.

Before Jay could request clarification, Michael grabbed her arm and yanked her inside, kicking the door shut behind him. He sagged against the doorframe, snatched another breath and, inaudibly to a human but not to a cyborg, counted to five before meeting her gaze with a tilt of his lips. "Wait for it," he said, cocking his head, obviously listening for some cue.

Jay was still analyzing Michael's interesting responses when "it" careened through the kitchen doorway and darted across the passageway into the sitting room, disappearing from view.

She analyzed the visual snapshot she'd taken of the creature, comparing it to the other data her sensory receptors had gleaned.

Ah. She turned her gaze on Michael, and raised one eyebrow. Since Tyler's father was most definitely human, and might well be too distracted to interpret the meaning behind the gesture, she added, "I presume you have an excellent reason for choosing this particular moment to fulfill the terms of our wager."

By "this particular moment", Jay alluded to what they both knew was going to be the polar opposite of a happy reunion. Jay had only to evaluate previous reactions from Davidson family members to past events to know there would be explanations demanded, less than satisfying answers offered for the sake of those directly affected, recriminations leveled.

Michael scratched his chin. His lips twitched, and the skin at the outer edges of his eye sockets crinkled as he fought to contain a smile that Jay identified as a perfect example of *wry*. "He wasn't due for another few days," he said. "The breeder screwed up the dates and arrived while I was giving Danny a bath. Marissa was napping so Caro answered the door." He shrugged. "No way could I put the woman off and ask her to keep him a few more days once Caro laid eyes on him. She swears she'll take him if you're not keen, by the way."

Jay directed a portion of her attention to the hallway. The scrabbling of claws and a sudden yelp indicated her prize had inadvertently introduced himself to a piece of furniture. Or perhaps a wall. "Hardly practical," she informed Michael, "when Caro is sharing a rented apartment, spends barely any time in it, and hasn't got a dime to spare after her myriad expenses are deducted."

"Expenses" in Caro's case meant clothes, and materials to construct clothes, followed closely by shoes and any other accessories deemed necessary to outfit a budding fashion maven.

Mike's sigh accompanied an eyes-to-the-ceiling gesture that managed to convey both pride and exasperation. "Of course Tyler pointed that out to her. And they've been bickering about it ever since."

The yelp had heralded a series of high-pitched whines that showed no sign of ceasing any time soon. Mike winced and scrubbed a hand over his face. "God. If he wakes Danny again, Riss will kill me." He brushed past Jay and strode off down the hallway.

Jay doubted Marissa would *literally* kill her husband, but a mother protecting her infant was certainly capable of inflicting serious bodily harm upon anyone she deemed a threat to the infant's wellbeing, and Jay couldn't imagine Marissa being the exception to that rule. Too, while afflicted by the post-birth hormones coursing through her body, Marissa might consider it quite logical to blame Jay for both the pup's presence in her house, and the disruption it had caused, despite Jay not being privy to Michael's plans. It would be prudent to take immediate action to prevent a ruckus that would disturb young Daniel Robert Davidson's routine. "Wait," she called to Michael. "Let me deal with this."

Michael halted and flattened himself against the wall as though trying to make himself a smaller target. "Be my guest. And for all our sakes, I sure hope you have better luck than I've had calming him down. Once he gets going—"

"I understand. Time is of the essence."

Jay accessed her databases. Perfect. Female canines nursing offspring secreted what was known in laymen's terms as "appeasing" pheromones. These pheromones soothed the puppies, and provided reassurance and comfort. She tweaked the chemical balances within her body and began to secrete an appropriate pheromone concoction through her pores. She would of course train the pup to respond solely to her commands, but for now there was no logical reason not to "cheat" via the judicious use of pheromones.

The pup's whines subsided, and then he gave an "*Arroooo*" that could easily have been interpreted as the canine equivalent of a question.

"*Komm*," Jay said.

Her command was answered by the sharp clicks of claws on wood, and then a dark-brown head crowned with floppy ears poked around the corner.

The pup's eyes were yellow rather than the more common— and desirable—brown. Right now, those "bird of prey" eyes were eyeing Jay like she was some never before encountered, wholly unpredictable creature.

"*Hier!*" Jay crouched and clicked her fingers, effectively wafting more "feel good" pheromones in the pup's direction.

He crept from behind the wall and stood there, quivering, allowing Jay to get a good look at him.

A breeder would likely describe the pup's coloring as solid liver head, ticked liver-and-white body with black saddles. Translation: Solid chocolate-brown head, and a speckled brown and white coat with black patches. And unsuitable for showing or breeding purposes due to aforementioned yellow eyes and black patches.

If the pup were capable of such emotions, he might well be grateful for his perceived shortcomings, given they had doubtless prevented the breeder from docking his tail—a common practice with this particular breed.

Jay stared at the pup, unblinking.

The pup cocked his head and stared back.

Jay slowly extended her hand. "*Komm.*"

The little canine yipped, and launched into motion, rocketing toward her and eliciting a startled grunt from Michael, who was still plastered against the wall.

The pup skidded to an ungainly halt and mashed his muzzle on Jay's knee. He licked her hand, and then crawled into her lap to sniff her thoroughly. Jay remained perfectly still, allowing the pup to do as he willed. He obviously expected reciprocal attention, and Jay would bet a considerable portion of her monetary wealth that he had been getting a whole lot of it from the Davidson family—especially Caro. But he would have to learn that Jay considered attention a *reward* for appropriate behavior, not a right.

The pup finally ceased sniffing and licking and wriggling, and lay quietly across Jay's thighs. He was a quick study—not surprising given the traits of the breed. German Shorthaired Pointers, also known as GSPs, were generally highly intelligent and bold creatures. This pup epitomized the often boisterous nature of the breed, and if care wasn't taken, that trait could easily become aggressiveness toward owners. In other words, the dog would establish its dominance over its human owner and then treat that owner accordingly. But to Jay's mind, given the ease with which GSPs could be trained, and their affectionate natures, any such tendency was the fault of inexperienced owners. GSPs were known to flourish with owners who were firm, confident, calm, and consistent. As humans liked to say, it wasn't rocket science.

She dropped a palm to the pup's head and fondled his ears. *"Braver Hund."*

"Braffer hoont?"

Michael's pronunciation was close enough that Jay didn't feel obliged to correct him. "It means 'Good dog'," she said.

"I guessed as much. Why give commands in German?"

Jay scooped the pup into the crook of one arm and pushed to her feet. "It seemed appropriate given the origins of the breed." And would reinforce to the pup that Jay was the one it must obey without hesitation.

"Ah." Michael emitted what his daughter Caro had labeled a snort-laugh. "And here I figured it was some super-duper secret canine training method known only to dog whisperers," he said.

Jay extended the range of her sensors to pinpoint Tyler's whereabouts, and headed for the staircase. Her heart rate had escalated. Her mouth had ceased to produce sufficient saliva, and her body was… was….

She sought a suitable descriptor. Vibrating. No. *Thrumming*—a sensation she had come to recognize signified eagerness and excitement. An all-too-familiar tugging sensation urged her to keep moving. And, if she had been a human fond of fanciful imagery, she would have described herself as propelled by need and want and desire for the object of her affection. *Tyler*. She craved his touch in the same way some humans craved their drug of choice.

Despite the need to give herself over to these disturbing inner drives, Jay had learned enough about parent/child relationship dynamics to comprehend that Michael would be discomfited and perhaps embarrassed by what she intended to do to his son the instant she saw him again. Michael accepted at an intellectual level that his oldest male offspring loved an inhuman machine, but seeing it in action, confronting the reality, was another matter entirely. Perhaps a distraction would be prudent. "You got me," she said.

"Come again?"

"I refer to canine training methods."

His eyebrows had furrowed and his lips had parted. His gaze focused on her, unwavering. He shifted, pushing away from the support of the wall so that his torso tilted slightly toward her.

These physical cues indicated curiosity and interest. Excellent. "I do indeed have a super-duper secret canine training method, and it is not one a dog whisperer would have access to." Hmm. That wasn't entirely true, Jay realized, recalling a past conversation with Tyler. Wall outlet plug-ins that released calming chemicals to assist in the treatment of overly nervous pets were easily obtainable.

"Any time you feel like putting me out of misery," Michael said. "That's a hint to spill your secret, by the way. Now, would be good. Especially if Caro's going to be looking after that little monster. He's barely slept five minutes since the breeder dropped him off, and now look at him. She'll be beside herself trying to figure out how you managed it."

Jay didn't bother to glance at the pup to confirm what she already knew: He was asleep. "There is no need for Caro to take him. He was intended for me. It would be rude and ungrateful not to accept him in the spirit with which he was given."

Michael opened his mouth—to voice a protest, no doubt—but Jay continued before he could speak. "If I've given you the impression that raising this pup will be an imposition and an annoyance, then I owe you an apology. If I had been given an opportunity to select a canine companion on my own, this little one is almost exactly the creature I would have chosen." She held up a hand, pre-empting the response she observed bubbling to his lips. "I say 'almost', only because I would have chosen a female. Now, having interacted with this male pup, I am no longer convinced a female would have been the best choice."

She cocked her head, observing Michael closely. "In fact, when it comes to selecting the perfect canine to suit my needs, I find myself wondering whether you are able to read my mind. Thank you, Michael. He's a delight."

He rewarded her attempt at reassurance with a crooked grin that reminded her so much of his son, Jay's pulse ratcheted up another notch. Her core temperature rose, flushing heat through her body. Yet she chose not to dampen this physiological response. It was human. And Tyler deserved more than an analytical, unfeeling, inhuman *thing* that couldn't comprehend his emotional and physical needs.

After what she'd put him through, Tyler deserved all the humanity Jay's evolution made her capable of providing. She hoped, for his sake, it would be enough.

She sensed Michael waiting for her to elaborate and perhaps answer his request to reveal her "secret". Likely he would appreciate the revelation all the more if she delayed his gratification, and so she remained mute until she reached the stairwell and had negotiated the first riser. Only then did she look back over her shoulder and say, "It's all in the way I smell, Michael. Right now, I remind this pup of its mother. It's that simple."

Michael's slow nod told her that he understood it truly wasn't simple at all. And, since explaining the process would delay her reunion with Tyler, she was grateful he didn't request further clarification. Instead, his eyes twinkled mischief at her, and he said, "I think I'll keep that to myself and go with you being a puppy whisperer. I'd recommend you do the same. It'll drive Caro crazy."

Since Jay knew Caro well enough to agree with that last statement, she saw no need to linger.

She had taken but two steps when she heard Caro entering through the backdoor leading in from the yard. Jay inhaled, separating out and analyzing the scents. Caro had been picking apples. Meaning that if everything went well, and Marissa did not demand Jay leave the house, Jay could offer to bake an apple pie for dessert. But now was not the best time to discuss such trivialities. Best make herself scarce before Caro waylaid her.

"We'll talk tonight, after everyone's in bed." Michael's softly pitched words drifted up to her. "Go on up. He's in his old room—not that you need me to tell you that."

Jay sprinted up the stairs while Michael, mind reader that he was, strode off to intercept his daughter before Caro realized that Jay had arrived, and commandeered her attention. A bloom of warmth spread in the pit of Jay's stomach. Michael, as humans liked to say, had her back.

She halted by the door to Tyler's old bedroom. This was it. Make or break time.

As though sensing his mistress's uncertainty, the sleeping pup whimpered. Jay soothed him back into slumber by smoothing the fur down his spine. Unfortunately, her own concerns could not be so easily soothed. As always, they centered on her illogical but painful yearning for the young human male currently hiding out in this room. Whether he still wanted her in his life once the pros and cons had been weighed. Whether he could forgive her for putting his family at risk simply by existing. Whether he still loved her....

Or had finally wised up to the insanity of a human loving a machine, and decided to move on.

Excitement and eagerness at the prospect of seeing her boy-friend again had been supplanted by another emotion—one that clamped Jay's chest and squeezed like some giant vise, and made the back of her throat ache as she struggled to swallow a huge lump that she knew wasn't real, but physically affected her just the same. And when she lifted her hand to the door handle, a part of her was shocked to see her hand tremble. The desire to run back downstairs and use Caro to avoid this confrontation was almost overwhelming.

Jay analyzed her physiological responses and searched her da-tabases for information, determined to put a name to this debilitating emotion that had so thoroughly ensnared her. Names were powerful labels—hence her creator's reluctance to bestow one upon her. Hence the irony that she had eventually taken his middle name for her own.

Yes. Naming this emotion would be the first step toward de-feating it.

Data from countless sources poured into her brain and in a microsecond, she had her answer. Ah. So this was what dread felt like. It was a minor miracle that humans functioned at all when-ever they fell victim to it.

Jay scrubbed the palm of her hand down her jeans, gripped the door handle, and opened the door to Tyler's bedroom.

He lay stretched out on the bed, hands behind his head. A sheaf of the manuscript paper he used to notate songs and music sat in his lap. His eyelids were closed, highlighting the blue-black smudges of sleeplessness.

Jay inhaled sharply, locked her shaky knee joints, and wedged her shoulder against the doorframe to counteract abrupt dizziness. She performed a swift diagnostic scan of her systems, which only confirmed what she already knew: There was nothing that needed attention, nothing that required recalibration. Which of course meant her reactions were solely caused by him. Tyler. The young human male who meant so much to Jay that she would willingly sacrifice herself to keep him safe.

Too, she would let him go if he demanded it of her. Or, if the rational part of her brain deemed it the only way forward for them both, she would push him away, do whatever it took to make him hate her enough to excise her from his life and his heart... even if it meant she would spend the rest of her existence mourning his loss. And if Jay had possessed a soul, and believed in an afterlife, right now she would have prayed to every deity humankind believed in for that day to never come.

"God, Caro." Tyler puffed out a breath, all the while keeping his eyelids firmly shuttered. "Can't you see I'm working? What does a guy have to do to get some alone time around here?"

"It's me."

His eyelids shot open. He rolled off the mattress, scattering manuscript leaves as he launched himself at her.

As much as Jay wanted—needed—to have his arms around her, she fended him off with the palm of her hand. "Careful."

He halted, the hurt in his expression swiftly morphing to concern. "What the fuck did Robot-Boy do to y—? Oh." His tension visibly eased as he gazed at the sleeping pup.

"He's exhausted. Do you have a box, or somewhere I can put him?"

Tyler glanced around his room. "Here." He strode to the battered dresser beside the bed and yanked open the top right-hand drawer. "There's a bunch of my old t-shirts in there—should make a pretty comfortable bed for the little guy."

Jay carefully decanted the pup into the makeshift bed. Before she could turn, Tyler's arms crept around her waist and he tucked her in close to his body, resting his chin atop her head.

He inhaled, and when he exhaled, she felt the shudder that coursed through him. He remained silent for fifty-three seconds—a span that Jay knew humans considered to be a significantly long moment.

"God. Jay. You're finally here." He murmured the words into her hair. "I should never have left you with him. If anything had happened to you, I swear I would have hunted Sixer down and—"

"Gotten yourself killed," Jay said briskly. "It would be the height of stupidity for a human to pit himself against Sixer. Never make the mistake of thinking he's anything like me, Tyler."

She felt his flinch at her blunt words, and turned in his arms to meet his deep, chocolate-brown gaze. "You made the right choice, Tyler. There wasn't anything you could have done to assist me. It was your baby brother or me. There wasn't any other choice you could have made."

Tyler swallowed, his gaze searching hers. Yet another significantly long moment passed before he nodded. "I know. Doesn't make my decision easier to bear, though. I had to trust you could save yourself but it almost killed me, Jay. He shot you multiple times with whatever the fuck that weapon was, and God, you looked real bad. I thought…."

He closed his eyes and learned his forehead against hers. His hand crept to her nape, cupping it, infusing her cool skin with his human warmth. "I believed he was gonna destroy you. I thought I'd never see you again."

There were a number of assurances Jay might have given but she doubted any of them would benefit Tyler. His emotions were too raw for platitudes.

Nor would detailing exactly what had happened between Sixer and herself alleviate Tyler's obvious anguish. Such facts would only serve to highlight how helpless she had truly been. So Jay opted for humor—a well documented distraction technique that served humans well during stressful or unhappy situations. "Apparently, Sixer was programmed to be what is commonly referred to as an 'ass man', as well as a 'chest man'."

Tyler's chin lifted and he stared at her through slitted eyelids. His fingers clamped around her nape. "What. The. Fuck?"

Apparently dark brown eyes could turn molten and fiery with repressed rage. Fascinating. "As you witnessed," she said, "he shot me in the chest."

Tyler's lips compressed. "Three times."

"That is correct. He woke me to assist him. However, when it came time to facilitate his escape, he mistakenly believed he had to incapacitate me again. So he—"

"Shot you in the ass?"

"As I was already in motion, his second shot missed and entered my thigh, but I believe he was aiming for the buttock."

She waited for him to laugh. Or at least crack a smile. But her attempt at humor had missed the mark and Tyler was counting beneath his breath. He'd only reached *three* when he hissed from between tightly compressed lips, "Show me."

Jay blinked. Even though there was no possibility she had heard wrongly, perhaps she had misunderstood some essential subtext in that terse demand. She decided it was imperative to request clarification. "Show you my buttocks?"

"Yes."

No misunderstanding then. How… unexpected. "Now?"

He released her and stepped back, dropping his hands to his sides. His hands clenched and unclenched. Clenched again. Crimson blotches mottled his neck and throat. "And your chest, too. I need to see what he did to you."

He noted the gaze she shot toward the door and swiveled on his heel. "Now, Jay," he threw back at her as he locked the bedroom door to insure their privacy.

Jay healed with inhuman speed, and her injuries had been minor. In mere days, there would be no evidence of the five wounds she'd taken during her encounter with Sixer to distress Tyler. However, perhaps seeing the evidence firsthand, knowing absolutely that she had taken no lasting harm, would help him to shed whatever misplaced guilt and anger he harbored over his inability to protect her.

"Very well." She shucked her t-shirt, kicked off her sneakers, and shimmied out of her jeans. She hadn't bothered with a bra this morning so that was one less item of clothing to remove. The leg of her underpants could easily be tugged up to reveal the healing wound on her buttock, and after a quick internal debate, she could see no harm in leaving them on. There was no reason to remove her socks—that portion of her anatomy had not been injured. And so she stood there in her underpants and socks, waiting for Tyler to do… whatever it was he needed to do.

CHAPTER THREE

TYLER APPROACHED HER as a human would approach some wild creature that might bolt at the slightest provocation. "Is something wrong?" she asked.

He waited until he stood directly before her, half an arm's length away, before responding with, "Does it hurt?"

And then, before Jay could formulate a response, he reached out, skimming his fingertips over each slightly raised disc of newly formed dermis. The first atop her left pectoral muscle… the second opposite the first… the third atop her left internal abdominal oblique. Sixer had been precise with his aim, and the projectiles had been designed to lodge in muscular tissue rather than rip through organs and splinter bone—not that Jay's skeletal structure could be damaged by such small projectiles.

Each touch of Tyler's fingertips left behind a tingling trail of heat. Jay inhaled, willing her racing pulse to calm, but as her diaphragm expanded, Tyler moved closer.

His palm flattened over her abdomen. "Tell me," he said, using the clipped tone that indicated he would accept no prevarication on her part.

"If you refer to the wounds inflicted to my torso region, then no, they don't hurt." He was already aware that she didn't experience pain as humans did, but Jay believed he wouldn't appreciate the reminder at this particular moment. "The projectiles entering my body caused negligible physical damage," she told him. "The damage caused when Sixer digitally extracted them was more severe, however it is healing well. In a few more days, the areas where the dermis has re-grown will be imperceptible to the human eye."

His eyes appeared to darken a few shades—a fascinating phenomenon that Jay would have liked to test further, but this was hardly an opportune moment to propose an experiment.

"*Sixer* dug the bullets out of you."

Jay nodded. "Three of them."

"Three?"

"He correctly estimated it would take three specifically designed projectiles to completely incapacitate me and render me insensible of my surroundings. I regained conscious awareness as the third projectile—" she covered his hand with her palm "—the one that caused this wound, was being extracted."

He didn't respond, and his silence grew heavy.

Jay had believed she knew Tyler well enough by now to accurately gauge his emotional state at any given time, but clearly she was mistaken in that assumption. Right now, the physical cues he was giving off were contradictory in the extreme. He radiated textbook symptoms of anger, frustration, concern *and* desire, and she found herself unwilling to make an educated guess as to his current state of mind for fear that she was wrong.

Best to wait until she had gathered more data.

Too, her own responses surprised Jay. Beneath Tyler's hand, her skin prickled. The fine hairs on her arms and nape had responded by rising. Her breathing had quickened, and even though she knew her heart wasn't literally fluttering in her chest, "fluttering" was an accurate description of the strange sensation.

Her salivary glands had increased production of saliva, moistening her mouth, and some instinct prompted her tongue to dart out and lick her lips—a gesture that drew Tyler's gaze. And then the heat of his gaze enveloped her, flushing her body with still more warmth.

Jay didn't have any issues regarding nudity. As she had informed Allen when he'd interviewed her for the position of nude life model, it was just a body: Every human had one. She'd concluded during her first day at Greenfield High that young human males considered her form and facial features pleasing, despite making no effort whatsoever with her grooming, nor exuding appropriate pheromones to attract such attentions. In fact, the attention her physical form had garnered back then had been most inconvenient.

Now, having interacted more freely with humans, she understood that by today's standards her physical form fell into the category of "unconventional beauty"—a quality that was sometimes considered desirable precisely because it *didn't* conform to the social norms. This knowledge pleased her—not because her evolution from unfeeling machine to one capable of an ever-increasing range of emotions gave her the capacity to embrace vanity, but because she knew that *Tyler* appreciated the unconventional beauty of her physical form.

Just as she appreciated his. The width of his shoulders, the expanse of his chest, the lean musculature of his belly, the narrow hips and powerful thighs of a young, physically fit human male.

Tyler could be described as a typical "jock" but for his hands—large and strong, yes, but with long, sensitive, talented fingers that coaxed songs from the strings of his guitar fit to make angels weep. Despite modern-day reluctance to use the word "beautiful" to describe a male, to Jay, Tyler was beautiful.

To her, he was precious, not only for his physical form and his unique talents, but for the way he made her feel alive and cherished—so much more than a cleverly crafted machine conceived and designed by one brilliant, flawed man.

She had never felt more alive, more cherished than now, when Tyler had inched close enough that each of his exhalations was an exquisite torture—a tantalizing near-kiss from phantom lips hovering above her skin. And then the phantom kiss was reality, for he bent his head and pressed his lips to the scar above her left pectoral.

Jay's inhalation sounded loud and harsh and demanding—a stark contrast to the smooth, gentle, petal-soft pressure of Tyler's lips as he kissed the second scar.

The palm resting on her abdomen moved, skimming upward, coming to rest on her ribs, below her breast and oh, how she yearned for… for… something she was at a loss to define, as though some alien part of her had burst to life, demanding more.

And then Tyler was exerting pressure with his palms, turning her, and although she could easily have resisted, Jay surrendered to his will.

Now both his hands settled on her hips, holding her slightly away from him. Facing this way, unable to observe his face to gauge his expressions, waiting and wondering what he intended to do next, only heightened the anticipation throbbing through her veins. And when he swept his palm over her buttocks, a thready moan that was so needy, so full of want, so… *human* that it seemed to come from another being altogether, escaped her lips.

His fingertips gently probed the area surrounding the scabbed wound on the back of her thigh. "And this one?"

Jay shook her head to clear the haze from her mind. "It is taking longer to heal because it lodged so deeply in my flesh. The last two projectiles resulted in some loss of function and I had difficulty digging them out."

She sensed movement behind her, and realized that Tyler had knelt. His fingers hooked the waistband of her underpants, and before she could offer to remove them, he skimmed them down her thighs.

Jay's exhalation exited her throat in a series of feline-like mewls. She didn't understand how having someone she cared for remove a piece of her clothing could affect her on so many levels.

Her capacity for logical thought was rapidly shrinking. Her ability to sense the world around her was diminishing, as more of her receptors diverted to analyze what Tyler was doing to her, and why her nerve endings seemed to be sparking beneath the slow stroking of his palms down her flanks. Right now, she would be fortunate to hear someone knocking on the bedroom door.

"If you were human," he murmured, his cheek resting against her left buttock, "this would leave a horrible scar."

"It will heal without scarring," Jay felt compelled to remind him. "My dermis is extremely resilient. And I'm sure I recall mentioning I do not feel pain the way humans do."

"I'm grateful for that," he said, coaxing her to lift first one foot, and then the other, to remove her underpants from her ankles. "God, I'm so grateful you aren't human, Jay. Because if you were, you'd have died. I'd have lost you, and I couldn't bear to lose you again."

He surged to his feet, his arms wrapping around her hips and urging her flush against him.

Jay swallowed, tried to speak, but the words caught in her throat and died unspoken. Just as well, for she suspected anything she uttered would be garbled and likely make no sense whatsoever.

The walls of the bedroom seemed to contract, cocooning them both in a haven that blocked all intrusions from the outside world. There was only the fabric of Tyler's jeans scraping the backs of her thighs, the heat of his body blanketing her spine, the pressure of his fingers as they flexed against her waist, the brush of his worn t-shirt across her shoulder blades, the warm caress of his exhalations against her bared skin.

One of his hands drifted from her waist, but before the protest that bubbled to her lips could escape, he had swept back her hair to expose her nape and pressed his lips to a highly sensitive spot below her right ear.

Jay gasped. Her diaphragm heaved as she fought to inhale sufficient oxygen, fought to contain the sensations sweeping through her—sensations that were scrambling her rational thoughts and turning her into a creature that yearned for nothing else except Tyler's heat, Tyler's caresses, Tyler's kisses.

Tyler.

At some level she comprehended the danger of letting emotions swamp reason, and struggled to regain the ability to think clearly and logically—a futile effort, for no matter how she tried to think logically she didn't know what to do—what to say, how to act.

Remain passive and let nature take its course?

State clearly to Tyler that she welcomed the next step, so there could be no misunderstandings?

Perhaps it would be more prudent to show him, rather than tell him—Jay was all too aware that at times her manner of speaking and the way she expressed herself could disconcert humans. But what was the best way to show Tyler she truly wanted to be intimate with him?

And, to complicate matters further, her brain chose that moment to replay a previous encounter with Tyler. One where she'd
been ninety-five-point-seven percent certain she'd correctly
interpreted his emotional and physical state, and had indicated
her readiness for intimacy by grasping his hand to lead him to
the bedroom… only for Tyler to turn her down, insisting she
wasn't ready.

The encounter unspooled in her mind.

*HOW TO PUT THIS so Tyler would understand? "I have extensively
researched human sexuality and I am fully aware of what's involved," she told him. "Further, if you have concerns at my
readiness, I am capable of manipulating my body functions to
insure my—"*

*She broke off as she noted him biting his lip. It appeared he was
attempting to hide a smile. Likely, this was one of those times
when detailed explanations were not appropriate. But she couldn't
help feeling… unappreciative of his capacity to be amused by her
at this current time. "Perhaps it would be best if I did not explain
my capabilities in this instance."*

*"Yeah," he said. "Awesome as it is to know you can get yourself
all fired up without any help from me, we guys kinda prefer to
think we're the ones responsible for girls 'getting ready'. If you
know what I mean."*

*"Then before I provide you with any further amusement, per-
haps you would care to explain what you meant by your previous
statement about 'readiness'."*

*The instant the words left her lips, Jay knew she should have
made an effort to moderate her tone, but it was too late. Tyler
would have to, as Caro would say, deal.*

Thankfully, he didn't take offence. In fact, if his pulse rate and relaxed muscles and even breathing were any indicator, he was now calm and unworried. Which was very confusing indeed.

She re-ran the significant portions of the encounter in her mind, analyzing them for nuances she might have misinterpreted. But there was no misinterpreting what she had seen and heard. Tyler had clearly indicated he desired intimacy. She'd made it clear she desired it, too. Yet he'd turned her down.

What was she missing?

One's first sexual encounter with a new partner was purported to be a significant act that, inevitably, complicated everything. Surely, then, there must be multitudinous things for a young human male to be worried about? Then again, perhaps Tyler's reticence stemmed from there being another person in the house— his ex-girlfriend, no less. But that was an excellent reason to retreat to the bedroom, which, after all, was not only a room with a bed, but a private area where one person could bed another.

Some of her confusion must have shown in her expression for he endeavored to explain. "I mean you're still treating this like some lab experiment—you're analyzing everything. When you're too caught up in the moment to be analytical about it, then you'll be ready."

"But if I'm too caught up in the moment to analyze it, how will I recognize my readiness? How will I know I'm... ready?"

"Believe me, you'll know."

BELIEVE ME YOU'LL KNOW.... What manner of explanation was that?

A wholly inadequate one, that's what.

Jay set that problem aside for the moment and turned her mind to other, hopefully more fruitful issues. "Ready" was an adjective meaning "Completely prepared or in condition for immediate action or use or progress. Mentally disposed. Made suitable and available for immediate use." If these definitions were to be believed, then Jay had been "ready" back then, and she was "ready" now. However it was obvious that dictionary definitions did not take into account the opinions and prejudices and life experiences of the young human male she desired to be "ready" for.

A frustrated sigh hissed from her lips. When you were a cyborg who happened to be evolving—also known as "struggling to understand and cope with the human emotions that smacked you upside the head at the most inconvenient moments"—was it too much to ask that your boyfriend clue you in to exactly what "ready" entailed when it came to matters of intimacy? She was rapidly drawing the conclusion that her vast intellectual knowledge of human sexuality was useless in this situation, and if Tyler believed she wasn't "ready" then there would be little she could do to convince him otherwise.

Well, other than ripping off his clothing, tossing him on the bed, and taking the matter in hand. Which might not be advisable considering her inexperience with the mechanics of such matters. She might scare him off. Or worse, accidentally injure certain important male parts.

No. Best leave it up to him and hope that he correctly interpreted her responses. But… what if Tyler truly didn't understand what she wanted right now? What if she had completely misinterpreted his expressions and tone of voice, his actions and body language, and his removing her clothing had merely been the most efficient way to reassure himself she was healing adequately?

She needed to tell him exactly what she wanted and—

She didn't know the right words to use in a situation like this, and her clumsy attempts to encourage him might ruin the mood.

She shook her head. Make a decision Jay!

Right. She needed to *show* him. But how best to do that?

She could kiss him, of course. But they'd kissed many times, and not progressed to intercourse. So….

So, she would obviously need to kiss him differently, in a way that would leave him in no doubt that *now* was the perfect time to take the next step.

Now, if only she could figure out how to do that.

Before she could access information about the different methods of kissing, Tyler turned her to face him. "Jay?" He cupped her chin, coaxing her to meet his gaze. "Are you okay?"

She opened her mouth to inform him exactly how she was feeling, and then shut it again with a snap. She snatched one breath. Two… and endeavored to sort her emotions into something that could be explained with mere words.

Her breath whooshed out. "Epic fail," she muttered.

"Huh?"

She reached up to smooth the crinkle between his brows with a fingertip. "Right now I am incapable of thinking logically. All I can think about is you, and what you're doing to me—what *I* want you to do to me. I don't know how else to express this Tyler, but I'm *ready*. Do you understand what I'm telling you?"

Before he could respond, she rushed on, the words tumbling from her lips. "Please say you understand. And please don't tell me I'm not ready. I don't think I could bear for you to tell me that right now."

The pupils of his eyes dilated. A flush of crimson stained his cheekbones. The muscles in his jaw clenched and then relaxed as he swallowed.

If his throat was as dry as his swallowing indicated, Jay hoped it was for the right reasons—overwhelming desire, for example—and not because he was about to tell her something she didn't want to hear. Such as she wasn't "ready".

Damn, but she was beginning to loathe that word. In fact, she was sorely tempted to make it her mission to have it excised from the English lang—

His mouth captured hers, lips punishingly hard, tongue demanding entrance.

Warmth bloomed in the pit of her belly, expanded, filling the cold spaces that had lodged in her heart since the moment Sixer had ripped her from Tyler's side. She parted her lips and kissed him back, pouring all her illogical, terrible, *wonderful* want and need and yearning into the kiss.

His fingers speared into her hair, grabbed handfuls and tightened, holding her still as he took what he wanted.

Jay's brain registered that moving her head while his fists were clamped around hanks of her hair would result in the human equivalent of pain, and possibly the unintentional removal of some hair. She ignored the warning. She laced her hands around Tyler's waist and shuffled backward, drawing him with her.

Her heart galloped in her chest as he deepened the kiss, and she instinctively responded by matching his desperation, his ferocity. Please let him not realize she was maneuvering them both toward the bed. And if he did, please let him not conclude she was still analyzing, extrapolating, planning her next move, and therefore not fully engaged in the heady thrill of this moment. Please let him only see and recognize the truth—that right now, for Jay there was only this... this... raging need and the lure of the mattress and a vision of Tyler's body sinking into hers when he claimed her.

In other words, the only planning she was doing right now centered on the fact there was a large, comfortable bed in the room, and she intended to make full use of it to—

The edge of the mattress butted her thighs and she allowed Tyler's forward momentum to topple her backward until she lay across the bed. He didn't attempt to prevent himself falling and landing atop her, though he did have the presence of mind to brace himself on his forearms so Jay didn't bear his full weight. Not that he could have hurt her, given she was far more resilient than any human girl put in a similar situation.

Concerned for his comfort, Jay widened her thighs to accommodate him. She could feel him pressed against her. And despite her practical inexperience she knew that, physically at least, he was as "ready" as she to take this significant next step.

She gazed up at him, willing him to kiss her again, willing him not to ruin this moment by thinking too hard about why this might not be such a good idea.

He gazed back at her, and she could see the question forming on his lips.

Please, no. Now was not the time for questions.

Unexpected tears burned her eyes and she blinked them back. This time the desire to cry was… was… not something she could explain. It wasn't anything like the pervading sadness and sense of loss she'd felt during the times she'd mourned Father's death, nor the misery she'd endured throughout the months she'd been separated from Tyler.

"God. Jay. What's wrong?" He voiced the question in a hoarse, anguished whisper.

"I don't know."

"If you don't want this, please tell me now and we can stop, okay? You don't have to do anything if you don't want to."

"I *do* want this."

"Then why are you crying?"

"Because you hesitated!"

She winced at the shrill tone of her voice. She sounded like a spoiled child denied a treat. Deep breath, Jay…. "And I thought you had decided not to proceed because I'm not… I'm not…." She angled her head to focus on the wooden desk, scarred and pitted with age. She couldn't look at Tyler right now, didn't want to face the truth in his eyes.

"Because you're not human?"

"Because I'm a cyborg. Because I'm not a real girl, merely a skillfully constructed facsimile of one. And why would someone like you want to be intimate with a thing like me?" The hurtful label Tyler's mother had thrown at her burst from her mouth. "What young male in his right mind would want to have intercourse with a *glorified calculator*?"

Tyler slipped his palms beneath her shoulder blades, wrapped his arms about her, and buried his face in the crook of her shoulder. "I'm still majorly pissed that Mom called you that. It was cruel. If you'd held her upside down and shaken her 'til her teeth rattled, no one would have blamed you."

"They're only words. It didn't hurt at the time."

"But it does now."

The faded wallpaper behind the desk blurred. "Yes. It does now. I don't know why."

"Because words are powerful things, Jay. That's why I'm compelled to write lyrics for the music I compose."

She absorbed this insight and nodded agreement. Tyler's lyrics were indeed powerful. And wonderful. And sometimes terrible, too.

He nuzzled her throat. And the sensation of his lips against her skin skated a delicious shiver down her spine. "Why did you stop kissing me, Tyler?"

The tantalizing nuzzling ceased, and he raised his head to meet her gaze. "There was something I wanted to ask you before we went any further. But I was too chicken-shit to come right out with it so I was plucking up the courage. No pun intended."

"You can ask me anything. You know that."

He shifted restlessly atop her. Jay braced for the worst and adjusted the angle of her head until she was staring at the ceiling.

"You don't, um, have periods," he said.

This was no time to be pedantic, so even though he'd uttered a statement rather than phrasing a question, she answered, "Correct."

"But everything, um—you know, works okay. Right?"

She cocked an eyebrow and lowered her gaze to his face. What she saw there made her rethink the question she'd been about to ask—the semi-humorous-with-the-merest-hint-of-a-challenge one. The one where she pointed out that they had effectively been living together for many months, and not only had Tyler seen her naked, she'd modeled nude for a group of male artists, and surely everything was in the right place and looked as it should or someone would have commented on it by now, so what led him to speculate that things might not "work" as they should? Instead, she said, "Yes. Everything works."

Another endearing flush painted his cheeks. "Just checking. You know—that we're, uh, fully compatible in, uh, *that way*. Not that I'd give a shit if we weren't. Because there's, uh, plenty of other stuff we can do. And even if we couldn't have sex because we weren't physically compatible and, uh, *stuff*, I'd still love you and want to be with you. You know that, right?"

Jay's body felt light, buoyant, as though she could float from the mattress. Her lips curved and she had the unsettling desire to scream with the sheer joy of having someone like Tyler love her. Because screaming might be misconstrued she whispered, "Ditto."

He grinned down at her, relief emanating from him in waves. "Good to know."

Considering the significance sexual intercourse held for young human males, Jay was surprised it had taken Tyler so long to broach this subject. "Why have you not initiated this conversation with me before?"

"I told you. I was too chicken-shit. *Bwark.*"

"I feel compelled to be very clear to prevent future misunderstandings. We are indeed physically compatible. As I informed you once before, I have all the correct female parts."

"Right. Got it. Except I'm guessing you can't get pregnant? And that we don't have to worry about condoms."

"Those are excellent assumptions, which both happen to be true. Although I have a uterus, it—"

He lowered his head and kissed her, long and slow and so thoroughly, that Jay didn't think about anything else but kissing him back for a very long time.

When she could think again, all she could focus on was the most efficient way to divest Tyler of his clothes so they were skin to skin, everywhere, with no more barriers to keep them apart. And then he stroked her flesh and Jay felt as though she'd caught fire.

What he did to her, what he taught her and how he made her feel—loved and cherished and unique and precious—was so much more than she'd imagined it could be.

And afterward, she lay loose-limbed and dazed and happy, finally comprehending at every level what all the fuss was about. And thankful, too, that her creator had seen fit to include all the necessary female parts to fully experience the act of intercourse. She hoped that, had he been alive today, Alexander Jay Durham would have wholeheartedly approved of the way those female parts had recently been put to use.

Tyler pressed a kiss to her forehead, smoothed the tangles from her face.

Jay gazed into his eyes, noted his smug expression, and blurted, "I must thank Nessa the next time I see her."

Tyler stiffened, and his expression blanked in the careful way of a young male trying not to reveal his emotions—a *tell* that informed Jay he was struggling with some inner turmoil.

Oh dear. Apparently, bringing up your partner's ex immediately after engaging in intercourse was a surefire way to ruin the mood. It was at times like this it became abundantly clear to Jay that, when it came to relationships, she still had a great deal to learn.

She smacked Tyler lightly on the arm. "Stop over-thinking it. From what I know—" she tapped her head to indicate knowledge based solely on books and texts and online data "—if both participants are virgins, sex can be very awkward. It was my first time, Tyler, but obviously not yours. I made an educated guess based on my own observations, known facts and rumor, that your first time was with Nessa, and that she was not a virgin when you began dating her. I merely wished to express my gratitude for your expertise."

He opened his mouth, clamped it shut again, shook his head. And to Jay's relief, his lips finally curved into a wry grin.

"For the record," he drawled, "it's better form to compliment the guy directly to show your appreciation for his, ah, *expertise*, rather than give all the credit to his ex-girlfriend. And FYI, now that Nessa's in a stable relationship, it might not be the best idea to bring up her past. Sure, she got around at high school and had a bad rep, but Chandler might not know that, okay? I know you 'n Nessa are friends now, but it could be kinda awkward to bring up that stuff."

Jay processed this information and made another educated guess. "You still have reservations about her. And you do not feel comfortable with her knowing intimate details of our relationship."

He nodded and flopped onto the mattress beside her, flinging an arm over his eyes. "People always used to underestimate Nessa because of the way she dressed."

Jay recalled her first encounter with Tyler's ex-girlfriend, and had to agree. Nessa had appeared to crave the kind of attention she'd received from hormone-fueled young males who couldn't see beyond her brief, too-tight clothing, bottle-blond hair, and liberal application of cosmetics.

"It was one of the things that used to frustrate the hell out of me when we were dating," Tyler was saying. "You know, that she coasted by on her looks and used them to get what she wanted. I always knew she was smart, though. She just used to hide it really well."

"Yes, she is quite intelligent." Jay wasn't merely being kind. Among other indications, Nessa had been smart enough to finally trust Jay and reveal that Sixer was blackmailing her for information.

As though reading Jay's mind, Tyler said, "I'd bet my guitar she knows there's something off about Sixer. And right now, she thinks you're a little bit, um—"

"Eccentric?"

He snorted. "Eccentric's as good a word as any for your awesome cyborg skills, I guess. Look, Nessa respects you and trusts you, Jay. You helped her when it would have been easier to leave her hang. God knows she would have deserved it after what she pulled. But if she ever starts comparing you with Sixer—"

"She might guess we're not human."

"Yeah." He pulled Jay close and spooned her, his arms tightening around her protectively. "And even though you and Nessa are friends and all, the way I see it, the fewer people who know what you are, the safer you'll be."

And the safer Tyler and his family, and Nessa, and everyone Jay had interacted with, would be.

"I understand. I'll be careful around her." She alligator-rolled within the circle of Tyler's arms until she faced him.

"What are you thinking?" he asked.

"I'm thinking that I am forced to conclude it would be prudent to ignore Nessa's role in your sexual education, and allow you to be entirely smug about your sexual prowess."

He kissed the tip of her nose. "My *prowess*. Mmm. That has a nice ring to it."

"A great deal of prowess," Jay informed him, simply for the pleasure of watching him smile. She loved it when he smiled. She loved it when he did other things, too.

Hoping he'd get the hint, she moistened her lips with the tip of her tongue, inviting his kiss.

His gazed focused on her mouth, and he did kiss her, softly and sweetly, and then not so sweetly at all. Jay pressed close and wrapped herself around him, delighting in his groan, loving that she could affect him this way... and wishing that time would stand still so she could savor this moment. Unfortunately, wishes were generally useless and never came to fruition. Like now.

Because her auditory receptors informed her that Tyler's sister had learned of her arrival, and was now bounding up the stairs.

The door handle rattled and Caro hissed, "Tell my brother to quit doing whatever he's doing to you behind that locked door—which is totally, like, ewwww to even think about, by the way."

"Shit." Tyler leaped from the bed and grabbed for his clothes.

"Her timing is appalling," Jay murmured.

"I'll say."

Jay climbed from the bed, peripherally aware the first item of "clothing" Tyler donned was the wristwatch she'd presented to him when he'd completed his first semester of college. He only removed the watch to bathe. Or, as recent events had proven, during periods of intimacy—he'd been concerned about the strap scraping her skin as he'd explored her body. Pleasure coursed through her at this evidence of how he valued her gift.

"Get your butt out here, Jay!" Caro's hiss was louder this time. "And you, too, Tyler! And where's that puppy? He'd better not be in there with you, coz if he's been watching you two getting it on he'll be scarred for life, and no way am I paying for a puppy psychologist!"

Of course, the pup chose that moment to wake and attempt to clamber from the drawer.

Jay rushed to save him from a fall. And just as she reached the pup and lifted him from the nest of t-shirts, he peed all over both her *and* the contents of the drawer.

"Ah, Tyler?"

He zipped the fly of his jeans and glanced up. "What's wr—? Ah, crap."

"It wasn't crap, it was urine," Jay retorted. "And a considerable amount of it for such a diminutive creature. You'll need to launder all the clothes in your top drawer."

"What's going on in there?" Caro rattled the door handle again.

"Go away!" Tyler's shout was muffled as he pulled his t-shirt over his head. "We'll be down in a minute."

Jay strode to the door, unlocked it, and opened it enough to thrust the pup at Tyler's sister. "Please take him outside and introduce him to a convenient bush. Now."

Caro wrinkled her nose and gingerly took possession of the pup. "Oh dear. Did he—?" Her eyes rounded, and she bit her lips against a grin as she registered Jay's lack of clothing. "Wow. Um, take as long as you need, okay. And feel free to borrow a change of clothes."

"Thank you." Jay shut the door against Caro's laughter, and analyzed what might have been meant by that muttered, "About freaking time!" that she had clearly heard amid more squeals of mirth.

She replayed Caro's reaction but without more data, attempting to ascertain whether Caro's "Wow" had referred to Jay's state of undress, the fact that the pup's bladder had contained so much urine, or what Caro believed Jay and Tyler had gotten up to, was futile. Besides, knowing Caro as Jay did, working through the many possible implications of that muttered "About freaking time!" would likely have given Jay a headache had she been human.

She found herself staring at the closed bedroom door, and shook her head, wondering at her lack of focus. Sex was reputed to scramble one's brains, and she now had more than mere anecdotal evidence to support the claim. "The sooner we take that puppy home so I can train him properly, the better," she announced, simply from the need to have something sensible to say.

Tyler snatched a t-shirt from a pile of clothing he'd tossed beside his bed and used it to wipe her down. "Uck. I think you might need a shower." He dumped the contents of the drawer and the t-shirt atop a used towel, and bundled them up.

Jay inhaled through her nose. The odor of canine urine wafted to her. "I believe you are correct."

Tyler stuck his head out the doorway and then gave her an All Clear signal. And as she exited the bedroom to make a dash for the bathroom, he smacked her lightly on the buttocks. "Maybe I'll join you," he said.

"Maybe I'll even let you." Jay tossed the comment over her shoulder. And, when she was duly rewarded with a sharp inhalation and the patter of footsteps racing after her, her lips curved in what humans might consider a very wicked smile indeed.

CHAPTER FOUR

J AY POKED HER HEAD out of the shower cubicle and pressed a finger to her lips to indicate Tyler should remain silent.

What the—? He shot her a quizzical glance and then the mental light bulb went on. "Caro's eavesdropping isn't she?" he hissed. Brat. His sister was gonna be very sorry for a very long time.

She shook her head. "It's your father."

Tyler gulped, scrambled back into his pants, and shot a glance at the bathroom door. A few minutes later and…. He shuddered. What his father would have heard didn't bear thinking about. Bad enough getting caught in the bathroom fully dressed, while Jay was naked as the day she was born— Uh, make that *created.*

"Do I have time to get out of here without being spotted?" he asked.

"No. But if you're looking for an excuse to be in here while I am unclothed, simply tell the truth—that the pup urinated all over me and you were bringing me fresh clothing."

Tyler nodded enthusiastically. Yeah that'd work.

"It'll be more convincing if you zip the fly of your jeans," Jay murmured, and then she ducked beneath the shower spray, shutting the cubicle door behind her.

Jee-zus. Tyler fumbled with his zipper, and nearly jumped out of his skin when his dad asked, "Jay, you in there?" The question was followed by a soft knock that was a token politeness at best, because his dad didn't wait for an answer before trying the handle of the bathroom door. "I need to speak to you. It's urgent."

Tyler flipped the lock and opened his mouth to present his excuse, but before he could speak, Mike said, "You're here, too? Good. Saves me coming looking for you." He strode up to the cubicle to tap on the door. "Keep the water running, Jay," he ordered. "Less chance of being overheard that way."

The cubicle door cracked a couple of inches, and Jay stuck out a hand. "Pass me a towel, please? I can hear easily enough over the running water if you lower your voices, but it will be difficult for you to reciprocate."

Tyler's dad passed her a towel, and she emerged a few seconds later with it wrapped around her torso.

The steam had turned her hair to ringlets. Droplets of water clung to her eyelashes and glossed her skin.

Tyler knew Jay's looks were primarily the result of her creator's vision and skill rather than solely a happy genetic accident, but despite all that, despite everything he knew about her, at times like this Jay's beauty was like a sucker punch to the gut that left him breathless. It had been this way ever since he'd glimpsed her on her first day at Greenfield High, waiting for her class schedule. And the fact she'd chosen *him*, Tyler Davidson, ex-jock-god fallen from grace relegated to the bottom of the pecking order, when she could have crooked her little finger and had any guy she'd wanted? Yeah. It still amazed him. As did the fact she'd chosen to stay.

Tyler wasn't the only one affected. Mike's eyes had a glazed look about them. And was that—?

Yep, his jaw was agape.

He blinked, and shot a glance at Tyler that seemed to say, "Sorry, my bad. But hell, you're one lucky sonuvagun."

Tyler had to agree. And he couldn't fault his dad for being gob-smacked. Each time Tyler spotted Jay wandering around partially clad, he nearly swallowed his tongue. Or walked into a wall. Or spilled a drink down himself. God only knew how Allen and McPhee and the rest of the all-male painting group managed to put brush to canvas when Jay modeled for them.

Jay scooped up the necklace she'd left on the vanity unit and fastened it about her throat, before flicking the extractor fan switch up a gear to dispel the steam that had accumulated. "I've turned off the hot water," she said. "There's no point wasting further resources. What's so imperative that it can't wait until I've showered and gotten rid of all the puppy pee, Michael?"

Tyler couldn't help grinning as he watched his dad scramble to kick-start his brain... and cover the fact he'd been caught staring at his son's girlfriend by loudly clearing his throat.

"Are you incubating a virus?" Jay asked. "You appear very pale."

Mike waved away her comment. "Either the puppy has Houdini tendencies and should henceforth be named Digger, or we have a big problem. I've a horrible suspicion it's the latter."

Jay's brow wrinkled and her killer-blue eyes narrowed. "I'm afraid I'm not following you, Michael. If my puppy managed to escape the house and dig a hole in the backyard, I can rectify any damage caused. I fail to see how any hole a pup of its age could possibly dig would constitute an insurmountable problem."

"It's not the hole," Mike said. "It's what used to be buried in the hole."

A chill of presentiment licked Tyler's spine. Shit. Please don't let me be right about this. "Could, ah, *Digger*, have buried it somewhere else?" he asked. "Have you checked?"

"For the record, I am not naming the puppy Digger," Jay interjected. "And if this missing object that has you both so concerned has been reburied elsewhere in the yard, I'm sure I will be able to locate it for you. All I require is a description—"

"You don't think the puppy dug it up," Tyler said to his dad. "You think it was taken by someone who knew exactly what they were looking for."

"Yep. That's what I think."

Tyler rubbed the bridge of his nose, his mind whirling with worst-case scenarios. Nausea churned in his gut. This was bad—real bad. "Fuck."

"My thoughts exactly." Mike pressed a fist to his stomach, as though his gut pained him. His face looked pinched with worry. And Tyler figured that right now, his own expression would be a perfect mirror of his dad's.

Jay uttered a noise that successfully conveyed frustration. "Will one of you please tell me about this missing object that has you both so spooked? Or will I have to pick you both up by the scruffs of your necks and shake it out of you? Which will necessitate dropping this towel, thereby causing you both extreme embarrassment."

Her attempt at humor again missed the mark. Tyler couldn't look her in the eye. After everything she'd done to keep them safe, the past was again coming back to bite them all in the ass. "Dad found the hand you planted at the explosion site to make everyone think you'd been blown to bits. He brought it back and gave it to me—to prove you were gone. We had a ceremony in the backyard to bury your remains."

"And that hand is now missing."

"Yes."

"Ah." Jay nodded. "Now I understand your concerns."

Tyler wanted to punch his stupid-ass former self in the face. "We thought you were dead. There was no body to bury and I…. Hell, I just needed some closure. And when you came back into my life, I had other things on my mind. Shit, Jay, I can't believe I didn't think to tell you—so you could dig it up and destroy it, or something. This is my fault."

"We are equally to blame, Tyler. I knew exactly what had been done with the decoy hand I constructed. I watched you bury it."

He lifted his chin, a part of him refusing to believe what he was hearing. "You were *watching*?"

"Yes." She folded her arms across her chest.

Wow. Tyler didn't know what to say—or think for that matter. This was heavy stuff. He would need some time to—

"Let it go," his dad said. "You know why Jay couldn't risk revealing herself at that time."

Tyler's throat was too tight to speak but he managed a terse nod of acknowledgement. Of course he understood Jay's reasons. But, as the memories of that dark time in his life hovered, waiting to pounce and drag him under again, it was damn hard to fight the remembered anguish—hard not to feel…. Betrayed. She'd watched him bury what they'd all believed were her sole remains. She'd witnessed how gutted he'd been to lose her, witnessed his pain. And yet she'd remained hidden, silent.

As though reading his mind she said quietly, "I did as much as I dared to give you hope, Tyler."

His gaze strayed to the thumb drive nestled in Jay's cleavage. She'd threaded it on a heavy silver chain, and now wore it as a necklace. The only time she removed it was to bathe. That thumb drive stored only one file—a song he'd written and recorded for her. He'd hidden the drive alongside the spare house key before he and his family had fled Snapperton because he hadn't been able to bring himself to believe she was gone. He'd hoped for a miracle. And when his family dared return home, and Tyler discovered the thumb drive missing, it *had* given him hope. Even if it had begun to die in the months that had followed before Jay'd shown up to rock his world all over again, that hope had been a precious thing. He'd been a mess, but it would have been so much worse without that small hope to cling to.

Jay was right: She'd done what she could to let him know she'd survived. Anything more would have endangered them all. He had no right to be pissed at her.

"I could have refused to let you bury the damned thing." Tyler's dad raked a hand through his hair and sighed. He exuded a deep-seated weariness that had Tyler secretly worried.

"I should never have brought it home," Mike continued. "But I figured it was safer than leaving it lying around for just anyone to find. And it seemed wrong to leave even a part of you behind after everything you'd done for us, Jay."

"Thank you, Michael." Jay's slow nod seemed to both acknowledge and dismiss a fraught past that had transformed Mike Davidson into Michael White, a man ripped from his family because of his unique skills, and blackmailed into hunting Cyborg Unit Gamma-Dash-One, AKA Jay Smith and more recently, Jaime Smythson.

"You must be aware that I could have dug up the hand and disposed of it at any time, with none of you the wiser," Jay said. "I chose to leave it buried there because it...." She appeared to be searching for the right words. "It *comforted* me to know that you mourned me—a machine. It gave me hope. It gave me a reason to fight for a dream, when it would have been far more logical to inter myself somewhere until the danger to you all had passed."

Tyler gulped. She seemed calm enough on the surface but her eyes shone with unshed tears. He knew how hard it had been for *him*, believing that Jay had sacrificed herself to save them and been destroyed in the bomb blast.

Burying her remains. Discovering a sign she might have survived. Hoping, praying that she would come back to him. And then, when she hadn't, trying to accept her loss and move on. For his then seventeen-year-old self, those months without her had seemed like a lifetime. But he'd never considered how hard it might have been for *Jay*. He had presumed she'd simply gotten on with covering her tracks, deleting her previous identity from public record, tidying up loose ends. He hadn't considered that she, too, might have suffered emotionally.

God, he'd been a fool—and a selfish one at that, thinking only of himself. At least he'd had his family to help ground him. Jay'd had no one.

She placed her hand on his arm, yanking him from a mire of self-recriminations. "None of you are to blame for my illogical decisions," she said. "But there is now more to be considered than merely a missing cybernetic hand." She rubbed an eyebrow—the gesture so intrinsically human that Tyler's heart flip-flopped. "I need to get dressed and we need to talk. All of us. No exceptions."

Tyler's dad shifted uneasily. "But—"

She made a slicing motion with her hand to silence his protest. "No buts, Michael. It's not right to keep the full truth from Marissa any longer. We need to tell her everything—just as I need to tell all of you what happened after Sixer left. I want everyone to have all the facts before any decisions are made."

"You're right." Mike nodded slowly, and Tyler thought he seemed relieved.

No surprises there. Tyler both understood and agreed with the reasoning behind keeping the full truth from his mother and his sister, but it hadn't sat well with him. He didn't like secrets. He'd kept a few big ones himself. He knew firsthand how secrets destroyed trust and ruined lives. Keeping this one must have been doubly hard for his dad. But even though Jay happened to be right, didn't mean it was gonna be easy coming clean. Jay's actions might have made it possible for Tyler's dad to return to his family, but Tyler's mom had taken a long time to trust her husband again. His parents' relationship was still fragile. And Jay's relationship with Marissa Davidson was still pretty damned rocky, too, which made things real awkward.

On his mom's part, Tyler got the impression fear was the main reason Marissa was playing nice, rather than any real desire to have Jay be a permanent part of their lives. Tyler had made it crystal clear that if his mom badmouthed Jay again, or tried to force a choice between her and Jay, the shit was gonna hit the fan big-time. He hoped it wouldn't come to that, but right now, observing Jay's carefully expressionless face, he was afraid it might.

And he was afraid, too, of something he was barely able to acknowledge: that Jay might take the choice from him. If she concluded that her presence threatened their safety, she would leave… and there would be nothing Tyler could do to stop her.

"I'll be down in five minutes," Jay said, her crisp no-nonsense tone a clear dismissal.

Mike left without a word but Tyler lingered, half-expecting Jay to at least hint what she planned to discuss.

"You, too, Tyler," she told him. "Go put the clothes through the washer before you forget and they're irredeemable. I'll be down shortly."

He frowned at her, unease churning in his belly. "Are you okay, Jay?"

When she finally answered, her voice was small and thin and wholly unlike the capable Jay she usually presented to the world. "No, Tyler, I'm not okay. I believe… I might be scared?"

He opened his arms and moved, meeting her halfway as she stumbled into his embrace and wound her arms about his back to hold him tight against her. She buried her face in the crook of his shoulder and he could feel her shaking. He wasn't sure he wanted to ask but he had to know, so he forced the question from his tight, aching throat. "What are you scared of?"

"That when I tell you everything you'll want me to leave."

"Funny," he whispered into her hair, "because *I'm* scared you'll decide it's better for everyone if you vanish again." He cupped her face, raised her tear-drowned gaze to his. "I don't want you to leave me, Jay. And just so's you know, if you *do* leave, I'll spend the rest of my life tracking you down so I can kick your ass before I kiss you senseless. We're in this together, okay?"

She managed a smile. "Okay."

He kissed her hard and quick, and then left her clutching her towel and wrestling with her demons. It wasn't the most difficult thing he'd ever had to do but it came damn high on the list. Ditto with steeling himself to keep walking rather than lurk by the bathroom door in case she tried to do a runner. He didn't think she would—not after what he'd just told her—but she was a cyborg, and although he loved her, he didn't always understand her thought processes. It boiled down to trust. He had to trust her. And so he collected the puppy-pee-doused clothes and headed downstairs to chuck them in the washer.

When he ventured into the yard, he found his mom and sister

sitting on the park bench-style seating near the outdoor grill. His sister had propped baby Danny over her shoulder, and was patting his diapered bottom and cooing nonsense at him. Jay's puppy lay on its back in Tyler's mom's lap, all four paws in the air, while Marissa absently stroked its belly. His dad was standing beneath the apple tree, hands shoved deep in his pants' pockets, staring down at the patch of disturbed earth.

Tyler's mom spotted him heading for the tree, and the gentle smile she'd sported while observing Caro with Danny melted into something thin and brittle. "What's all this about, Tyler?" she asked. "Mike's being mysterious." Her gaze darted to her husband, and by the time she turned back to Tyler, her expression had morphed into a full-on frown.

Tyler wasn't going to be drawn. Nor was he going to spout platitudes to keep his mother happy. "Jay needs to talk to us. There's some stuff we need to know."

His mother's expression blanked. "Jay's *here.*"

"She arrived—" Tyler glanced at his watch "—about an hour ago. We had some catching up to do."

He rolled his shoulders, waiting for some smartass innuendo from his twin. But apparently Caro had decided to cut him a break. She'd pressed her lips tightly together, though, and her expression seemed a little... *pained.* He'd bet some substantial "alone time" with Jay that Caro was biting her tongue in an effort not to say whatever was currently skating through her brain. He appreciated her efforts. Last thing he needed was his mom going off about what he and Jay had gotten up to in his old room.

"You all knew she was here," his mom said, glancing at her husband, the hurt etching her face so obvious Tyler would've had to be blind not to spot it. And then she ducked her head, belatedly hiding her expression as she petted the puppy lying in her lap.

Tyler inwardly cringed. This was gonna be a freaking nightmare. This was what happened when people kept secrets from family. "Caro only found out a short time ago," he felt compelled to say—more so his mom had the comfort of knowing she wasn't the only one kept out of the loop, than to keep Caro out of the firing line. His sister was way more than capable of standing up for herself.

Marissa nodded, grasping at the pathetic excuse for an olive branch. "Where—?"

Jay had exited the back door on silent cat-feet. If not for the fragrance of the soap she'd used wafting to his nostrils, Tyler wouldn't have known she was there until she slipped her hand in his and gave it a firm squeeze. "Hello, Marissa," she said.

"Looking good, Jay!" Caro's gaze raked the black yoga pants and royal blue tunic top Jay had borrowed from her suitcase, and gave an approving nod. She eased to her feet with one hand cupping the back of Danny's head, careful not to disturb her baby brother, and made a beeline for Jay. When she'd gotten close enough, she halted and leaned in, obviously expecting Jay to hug her.

Tyler hoped Jay would understand the cue and respond appropriately. Now was not a good time for her "differences" to be on display. Now more than ever, if his mother was going to accept what had happened, and forgive Jay's part in it, Jay needed to appear human.

His breath whooshed silently out as Jay embraced his sister. "I miss you, Caro," Jay said.

"We *so* need to organize a girls' day out," Caro said. "So I can take you shopping and nag you into upgrading your wardrobe. And don't give me that face. I know what you're like. I bet your current stash of jeans, t-shirts and hoodies have been washed so often they're almost threadbare."

Tyler grinned at Jay's borderline horrified expression. She was definitely more your buy the basics online and get them delivered kinda chick, than a shop 'til you drop and max out your credit cards mallrat. Not that Jay had to worry about mundane things like credit card limits, but the almost unlimited funds at her disposal didn't stop her from wearing her clothes into the ground. In fact, other than the silky blue robe he'd saved up to buy her, the last time he remembered Jay wearing anything new was the dress Nessa had talked her into buying.

Tyler fought to contain what would doubtless have been a goofy grin. Man. He had fond memories of that dress. Short, and revealing in all the right places. Even Caro might approve— although his fashionista sister would have kittens at the street sneakers Jay had paired with it.

"Afterward, we can put our feet up at home and order takeout," Caro was saying in a wheedling tone. And then she upped the wheedle-factor with what she probably imagined was the frosting on the cake by adding, "I'll even paint your toenails."

Jay crinkled her nose.

"It'll be fun." Caro adroitly changed the subject before Jay could mount a protest. "Can you believe how much weight Danny has put on already?"

Jay opened her mouth and Tyler's hand inadvertently convulsed around hers as he visualized her spouting a bunch of dry data about average growth rates for infants and suchlike.

She squeezed back, and he felt instantly ashamed. And pissed off, too, that Jay should have to censor herself around his family. Bad enough she had to hide her true nature from everyone else she encountered, but the people here already knew what Jay was. She should feel comfortable enough to be herself around them.

Jay gave his fingers another squeeze. Realizing she'd sensed his anger, Tyler made an effort to relax and let it go. For now.

"He's very sweet," she said, reaching out to stroke Danny's cheek with a forefinger.

"Except when he poops." Caro wrinkled her nose. "Then he's the total opposite of sweet."

Tyler snorted, wholeheartedly endorsing that statement. The last diaper he'd changed had been vile. He would never understand how such a tiny baby could contain that much godawful stinky poop.

"I was looking through some old photos, and he's the spitting image of Tyler as a baby." Caro eased Danny from her shoulder and, without a by-your-leave, plunked him in the crook of Jay's arm. "'Bout time you got some one-on-one time with your Auntie Jay, little man," she cooed.

Jay freed her hand from Tyler's to cradle Danny more securely. She seemed a little startled but aside from that, she was holding the baby like a pro—doing a far better job of it than the first few times Tyler had held his baby brother. He'd been clumsy as, inwardly freaking out that he was doing it all wrong, and praying Danny wouldn't start to cry. Or mess his diaper. Or upchuck all over Tyler's favorite t-shirt.

From the corner of his eye, Tyler spotted his dad heading for the bench seat—probably to restrain his wife from leaping up to snatch poor baby Danny from the clutches of the inhuman cyborg girl and—

His brain mind chose that precise moment to replay a memory he'd done his utmost to suppress. Jay's lifeless body sprawled on the concrete. The emotionless cyborg assassin Evan Caine had sent after Jay holding Danny in the crook of one arm. That cold, flat voice telling Tyler to choose between his newborn brother and the girl he loved....

A chill clawed Tyler's heart as he shook off the memory. His little brother and his family were safe. Jay was—

Fuck. He couldn't deny the truth: Jay would never truly be safe because of what she was, and what she represented to men like Caine. That was the one thing Tyler could be grateful to Sixer for, because the cyborg's first action after Jay had freed him from Caine's control had been to take out his former master, and raze his lair to the ground so there could be no more cyborgs created and enslaved like Sixer had been.

Tyler carefully hid his turmoil before switching his attention to Jay, who was gazing at the baby in her arms. Her expression was blank—scarily blank—and if not for the tears streaking her smooth, flawless cheeks, he'd have thought she'd zoned out to perform a system recalibration or something.

His gut twisted into a knot. Something was up. Something big. And as much as he wanted to get to the bottom of it, he was über-conscious of his mother's eagle-eyed, judgmental gaze. Now would be a real good time to enlist Jay's help to make coffee.

"Jay—"

Damn. Too late. Caro had moved closer and now she slung an arm about Jay's shoulders. "Jay? Are you all right, sweetie?"

"I'll be fine, Caro." Jay's voice sounded normal but the lie was obvious from the tears she couldn't seem to control. "Let me return Daniel to Marissa so we can get this over with." And before Tyler could react, Jay had ducked beneath Caro's arm and was striding toward the bench.

He made a move to follow her and do... *something*, he didn't know what, except that every instinct screamed he needed to act as a buffer between Jay and his mom.

Caro's hand snagged his upper arm, hauling him to a halt as

she hissed, "Don't. I have a good feeling about this."

He glanced over his shoulder at his sister, incredulous. "A *good feeling*?" he whispered for her ears alone. "Are you nuts?"

Caro threw him a sympathetic smile. "It'll be okay, I promise. Just let this play out, Tyler. Trust me, okay?"

He shook his head. "You'd better be right, sis."

"Aren't I always?"

Despite his concerns, a laugh escaped. "Hardly." But he was grateful as all heck when Caro grabbed his hand and, with no attempt whatsoever at subterfuge, dragged him closer to eavesdrop on the little drama. Well, here's hoping it would only be a *little* drama this time, because honestly? Tyler didn't know how much more drama he could take.

Tyler's dad glanced up as Jay approached. Mike had obviously noticed the tears for his face creased in concern, but thankfully he didn't say anything to draw attention to them. Marissa was making a point of fussing over the puppy, and Tyler figured she was delaying the moment when she'd be forced to interact with the "robot".

Jay halted in front of bench and stood there, silently waiting to be acknowledged.

But when Tyler's mom finally got the balls to glance up and meet Jay's gaze, Jay didn't say a word. She pressed a kiss to Danny's forehead and held him out to his mother… who made no move whatsoever to take him.

"What's wrong, Jay?" Marissa demanded.

"Everything. Will you take him, Marissa? Please."

Tyler's mom narrowed her eyes but continued petting Jay's puppy. "Why?" Short and sharp and accusatory, a verbal slap in the face. "Does he make you uncomfortable? He's only a baby."

Tyler bristled, wanting to jump to Jay's defense, but Caro's whispered, "Here it comes," held him back.

"It hurts," Jay said, the tears still trickling down her face as she cuddled Danny to her again.

Tyler's mom blinked at this unexpected response and her hands stilled. "What do you mean?"

"I will never have a baby of my own, Marissa. And I believed I had accepted that as a consequence of existing in the form that I do. But I was wrong. I love Daniel the same way I love all of you—like you're my family. But right now, holding Daniel hurts so much it's hard to bear. I feel... broken."

Christ. Tyler squeezed his eyes shut. His head hurt, and his heart, too. Not for himself, but for Jay. If it hadn't been for those telltale tears, no one would have known about the anguish she was suffering deep inside.

He opened his eyes in time to see his mother scoop Jay's puppy from her lap and hand him off to Tyler's dad. Then Marissa stood, smoothing the skirt of her dress, and all Tyler could think was, *Well, that was a bust....* Except, abruptly it was the complete opposite, because his mom threw her arms around Jay and hugged her... and rubbed her back while Jay cried awful, noiseless tears that were somehow worse than normal tears, because even though Jay was hurting, she obviously felt she couldn't let go completely for fear of disturbing the sleeping baby in her arms.

"Whoa." Tyler heaved a shuddering breath. "I so didn't see that coming."

Caro sniffed and blotted moisture from her eyes with the heels of her hands. "Told ya."

"Think everything's gonna be all right with Mom now?" he asked.

"Depends."

"On?"

"Whatever you'n Dad haven't told us."

Tyler's sigh gusted out, ripe with defeat and a big heaping of guilt. "Um, yeah. About that—"

"Save it. You'll only have to repeat yourself when we do the family conference thing." Caro threw him a mock-glare. Tyler knew it was a mock-glare because his twin's real glares were scary-ass things that made a guy's balls shrivel and his hair stand on end.

"We need coffee," she said. "And chocolate cake. Lots of chocolate cake."

Tyler left his dad to supervise, trusting Mike would intervene if anything went pear-shaped, and followed his sister into the kitchen. Because if Caro believed that coffee and chocolate would help them all get through the shit-storm that was about to be unleashed, then Tyler was totally on board with that.

HE SHOULD HAVE brought the whole damn cake out first time around and saved himself another trip to the kitchen. Caro had been right: Copious coffee and large wedges of the chocolate cake she'd baked that morning had helped. In fact, all the pieces had vanished in mere minutes, save for a few chocolaty smears and crumbs.

Tyler divvied up the last of the cake, transferred the wedges to a serving platter, and carried it back into the yard in time to hear his dad ask, "So, what's the verdict?"

Tyler dumped the plate on the outside table as Jay straightened from her crouch and brushed the dirt from her hands. She strode over to the outdoor faucet to wash up, and then shook her hands dry while Tyler waited, pulse ratcheting into overdrive, for her to share her findings.

"There's nothing to report."

"Huh?" Tyler stared at Jay, wondering if he'd heard right. She had walked the entire backyard, and thoroughly investigated the surrounding area where they'd buried the decoy hand. She had to have discovered *something*. "What do you mean?" he demanded.

"I should rephrase: There's nothing to report that will assist us in identifying and locating the person who dug up and removed the decoy hand, and did such a shoddy job of replacing the soil it was glaringly obvious the earth had been disturbed. I can only assume this was deliberate—to alert us that the decoy had been removed. A generic tool, such as a trowel, was used for the purposes of digging. I discovered some partial boot imprints that suggest the person was likely male, medium build, average weight, and wears the same sized boot as a large percentage of males in this town—including your father. And I found some dark-washed denim fibers that suggest the man caught his pants on a protruding nail when he brushed up against the fence."

"Or his jacket," Caro said. "He might have been wearing a denim jacket and caught his sleeve. You know, when he bent down or something."

"That, too, is a possibility. I would need a lab to confirm absolutely. However, knowing absolutely is not going to assist us at this time."

"So we've got diddly." Tyler's dad grabbed a generous slice of cake and devoured half in one bite.

"When I get home," Jay said, "I'll do some further investigations—identify any newcomers to the area and decide who to begin questioning and how best to go about it."

Tyler's dad paused, the remaining portion of his piece of cake halfway to his mouth. With undue care, he replaced it on his plate. "I could do that," he offered.

Tyler released his sharply indrawn breath and exchanged a troubled glance with his sister. Sure, their dad was good with computers—better than good. But Mike's unique skill set was what had brought him to Caine's notice in the first place, and started the mess that had kicked off this whole chain of events. It was so *not* a good idea for him to start snooping around electronically and risk getting flagged.

Tyler caught the panicked expression on his mother's face, and was racking his brains for the best way to shut down his dad's offer when Jay did it for him. "We both know you have unique skills, Michael," she said. "And we both know I can perform this task with less effort and far less personal risk."

Tyler held his breath until his father nodded. And the relief on his mother's face was painful to witness.

Thank God Jay had no qualms about asserting her own superiority when it came to covert computer stuff. And thank God she'd called this family meeting, because even though the future was up in the air, Tyler figured he wasn't the only one feeling like a huge weight had been lifted from his shoulders. Keeping secrets from your family sucked, but now, thanks to Jay, they were secrets no longer.

Jay had asked permission to start from the very beginning, insisting it was the most efficient way to insure everyone had all the facts. Mike had backed her up, and she'd made it clear she expected him to jump in whenever his role in past events melded with her own timeline. It'd been a smart move on Jay's part because, sure enough, Tyler's mom had proven deeply curious about a bunch of stuff that her husband had kept from her, which had taken the focus off Jay. So, happily, confession time had turned out not as bad as Tyler had imagined.

At least, it hadn't been so bad once his mom had gotten over her initial freak-out that, a) there was a rogue cyborg on the loose, and b) immediately after giving birth she'd been *drugged* by aforementioned cyborg... who'd then snatched Danny.

Of course, it helped Jay's case immensely that everyone now understood she hadn't hesitated to sacrifice herself for Danny. And that Tyler's dad had been concerned enough for Jay's welfare to demand to see her injuries—"Right here, right now, no excuses, Jay!"—to confirm for himself they were healing properly. Tyler wasn't ashamed to admit he'd been just the slightest bit pleased by his mom and sister's horror at the still healing wounds. He got the feeling that what could have befallen Jay had Sixer not exploited a command loophole to further his own agenda, had been driven home.

Bottom line? His mother might come across like a hardass, but she was a fair person at heart. And now she couldn't overlook that her husband had been through hell, that Jay had done her utmost to protect the Davidson family at huge cost to herself, and that both had good reasons for keeping secrets.

In the end, Tyler's dad got off with a mini-lecture about how destructive secrets could be. Tyler got a watered down version that still made him cringe. Jay got another hug for being smart enough to insist those secrets finally be revealed. And it seemed like the uneasy truce between his mom and Jay had morphed into a true peace.

Tyler was simply relieved as all hell his mom didn't blame Jay for being the catalyst that had brought Sixer into their lives. She seemed to finally accept that Jay was as much a victim of circumstance as her own husband had once been—and Sixer, for that matter. Though that last was much harder to swallow. Tyler wouldn't want to be Sixer if he was unlucky enough to come face-to-face with Marissa Caroline Davidson any time soon.

Knowing his mom, she would take him apart with her bare hands and stomp all his cybernetic parts to itty bitty pieces.

Tyler watched Jay lean forward to fondle the pup's ears and then shoo him away when he tried to gnaw on the laces of her sneakers. How could she be so calm about the implications of that photo? In hindsight, Tyler had to admit the chances of Jay having a cybernetic twin somewhere out there had been pretty high. Jay was a Gamma unit. It was only commonsense to presume that Alpha and Beta units would have come before her—and that they would have been defective in some significant way that had necessitated the creation of subsequent units. But this irrefutable evidence of another cyborg that looked like Jay blew Tyler's mind.

Apparently he wasn't the only one.

"Are you sure it's not you, Jay?" Caro asked, squinting at the photo. "I mean, you before you were, uh, *perfected*."

"I'm sure."

"What about fingerprints?"

"No fingerprints on the photo or the envelope. Handwriting on the back of the photo matches that of the envelope. Generic blue ballpoint used both times."

"Besides, fingerprints only help if they're on file somewhere, right?"

"Correct."

Caro passed the photo back to her dad, who stared at it through narrowed eyes as though willing it to reveal its secrets. "Any ideas where this photo could have been taken?" he finally asked. "Or, more importantly for now, who left it for you?"

"What if it was Sixer? What if he's baiting you again?" Marissa had gone sheet-white, but Tyler suspected it was a symptom born of fury rather than fear.

"It wasn't Sixer," Jay said.

"How do you know for sure?" his mother asked.

Tyler knew from his mom's tone that no way was she letting Jay get away with what, to her mind, was an unsubstantiated statement of fact.

Jay must have come to the same conclusion. "Sixer exudes a particular odor, which is what alerted me to his presence in the first place," she explained. "I detected it on the note he left for me when he drugged you and took Daniel. There is no such odor detectable on this photo, nor on the envelope. Too, based on Sixer's previous actions, there is a high probability he would use knowledge of the Beta unit's whereabouts as leverage to extract something he believed he needed from me. It is my belief that he would not be bothered with such cat and mouse games: He would simply contact me and be done with it."

The bottom dropped out of Tyler's stomach. "You really think he'll contact you again?"

Jay opened her mouth, paused to reconsider what she'd been about to say, and then answered, "Yes," with such calm surety that Tyler had to struggle to beat back the wave of panic that weakened his knees and threatened to tip him on his ass. "Jesus," he whispered, realizing how stupid he'd been to assume Sixer would leave Jay be.

"It's to be expected." Tyler's dad scratched the stubble on his chin. "Jay's the only one Sixer knows who's like him. Of course he's going to contact her sooner or later—if only in the hope she can give him a purpose and help him find his place in the world."

Wow. That was deep.

Caro caught Tyler's eye, and in the strange way of twins who shared a deep connection, he knew his sister was thinking the same thing. Intellectually, they both knew their dad's five-year absence had changed him. But at times—like now—it was a little shocking to be directly confronted by evidence of those changes.

"Now I know what to expect, I can handle Sixer," Jay said. "He caught me unawares—hence the reason he could so easily exploit my vulnerabilities. Next time I will be better prepared."

"If he lays a hand on Danny again, I don't care what he is, I'll take him apart." His mom sounded so fierce and implacably determined that Tyler shivered.

"If he touches that child again I will render him immobile, and give you step-by-step instructions on how to dismember him," Jay said. "And then I will crush his components to dust, and obliterate every particle that remains of him from this earth."

"Sounds good to me," Caro interjected. "Guy's a loose unit."

Tyler attempted to hide how freaked out he was at the prospect of confronting Evan Caine's cyborg again by snorting. "Loose unit. Yeah, that's one way of describing him."

"I have not given up on Sixer entirely," Jay said. "However, what he will ultimately become, and whether he proves too dangerous to allow complete autonomy, still remains to be seen."

"You have a containment plan," Tyler's dad said, clicking his fingers at the inquisitive pup to draw his attention from Jay's shoelaces.

"I have been experimenting with various projectiles along a similar vein to those used to disable me. Before long I will have developed projectiles that are far more efficient than those Sixer used on me."

Tyler's dad nodded tersely. "Any weapon that takes two shots to disable, and three to fully immobilize the target, should be considered a last resort. Relying on it, or having it as the only weapon in your arsenal, is a ticket to your own funeral."

"Agreed."

Tyler darted a gaze at his mom and inwardly winced. Mike Davidson had slotted seamlessly into his old life, and was back teaching computer science. He'd, frankly, always been a bit of a nerd. Now he sounded like a total badass: harder, more capable, ruthless—someone you wouldn't want to mess with. Talk about smack you upside the head with a total world-view shift.

Tyler's mother shifted Danny from the crook of her left arm to the right, and flexed her shoulder joint.

"I can hold him for you if you're getting tired," Jay offered.

"If you're sure?"

Jay's smile was the merest bit lopsided but it was only really noticeable if you knew her intimately, like Tyler did. "I'm sure," she said, and held out her arms for the sleepy infant.

It was a start. A real good one considering his mom had shot down Caro's earlier offer to put Danny in his cot. Not that any-one could blame Marissa for not wanting to let Danny out of her sight even for a moment.

Tyler watched the soft smile curve Jay's lips as Danny yawned, snuffled, and settled back to sleep in her arms. And felt a glimmer of hope that the pain of never having a child of her own would be lessened somewhat by access to his baby brother.

"So, let's recap." Tyler's dad scrubbed his face and blinked twice, scrunching and relaxing his facial muscles as though shedding fatigue and stress by strength of will alone. "There's a Beta unit somewhere out there, but we have no idea where. We don't know whether she's compos mentis or the cybernetic equivalent of comatose. Nor do we know who's caring for her. Some unidentified party with a hidden agenda has seen fit to make Jay aware of the Beta unit's existence via the photo. The same, or possibly a different unidentified party, also with a hidden agenda, is now in possession of Jay's decoy cybernetic hand. And at some stage, Jay expects a visit from a rogue cyborg whose agenda we can't even begin to fathom. I'd say we're pretty much screwed until someone clues us in."

"Gosh, that sums it up very nicely, Michael," Jay said, her tone oozing so much fake admiration that Tyler's dad barked a laugh.

The pup took that as his cue to yip back, provoking reluctant smiles all round.

"So, where the hell do we go from here?" Tyler asked.

"Language," Jay chided, patting Danny's back for emphasis.

"Sorry."

Tyler's mom surprised them all—well, the humans anyway—with her input. "I think Jay's first port of call should be to talk with Allen, and then visit the café out front of his studio to quiz the regulars. One of them might have spotted the person who left the envelope at Allen's studio. It's somewhere to start," she said defensively, noting Caro's gaping mouth. "Unless you have a better idea?"

"It's an excellent suggestion," Jay said. "And I promise to keep you informed if any further information comes to light. However, my first priority is to negate any potential threat that Sixer might present. His thought processes are too dissimilar to mine for me to be confident of predicting his actions. I need to make it clear that he is to stay away from you all or there will be dire consequences."

"I presume you're gonna do a disappearing act, then." Caro's snippy tone made it obvious she wasn't happy about the prospect. "When?"

"Soon. I have to do this, Caro. Sixer is too unpredictable."

"I don't like it," Caro announced, and her sentiment was echoed by her parents. Tyler remained silent but only because Jay hadn't yet indicated he wouldn't be accompanying her.

As though sensing his thoughts, Jay looked him straight in the eye and said, "You need to go about your usual routine to allay the suspicions of anyone monitoring you. Once they realize I've gone, they'll likely focus their attention on finding me. I can't risk you being used against me, Tyler. I need to do this alone."

He opened his mouth to protest, but the words died in his throat. Shit. She was right. He was a weakness that Sixer wouldn't hesitate to exploit. "I know," he finally said. "I don't have to be thrilled about it though."

"Smart decision, son."

Tyler thought his dad sounded as relieved as his mom looked right now. And Caro, too. All the tension had drained from their faces. And yeah, it gave him warm fuzzies to know they were worried about him, but the person they needed to be worried for was Jay.

No one said anything for a long moment. And then the puppy broke the awkward silence by scrambling from the bench seat onto the table, and burying his nose in the last piece of chocolate cake.

"Hey, that was mine!" Caro grabbed the pup and held him up to her face to scold him. "Chocolate's supposed to be real bad for dogs," she cooed to the pup. "Oh yes it is!'

"He'll be fine," Jay assured her, soothing Danny, who'd startled at Caro's shout and was now whimpering fretfully.

"Hey, I know what you can call him," Caro said.

Jay gently jiggled the baby and arched one eyebrow. "Oh?"

"Choccie. You know, short for 'Chocolate'."

"Over my lifeless body," Jay told her, taking the pup and tucking him beneath her other arm.

Caro's answering grin was pure evil. "Then you'd better come up with a name real quick. Like, before something you don't approve of sticks."

"I'll take that under advisement."

"So?"

Tyler snickered. Jay should know by now Caro wasn't gonna let this go.

"So, what?" Jay asked, feigning confusion.

"What are you gonna name him?"

Jay smiled serenely at her best friend. "When I think of a suitable name, you'll be the third to know."

Tyler compressed his lips so he didn't ruin the moment by laughing. Wait for it....

Caro's pout was right on cue. "Seriously? The third?"

"The third," Jay said, firmly. "After the pup and Tyler."

"I guess I can live with that."

"I'm glad to hear it," Jay said. "And if you're very lucky, I'll even pick a name you can pronounce."

Caro stuck out her tongue—her default response whenever she couldn't come up with a witty rejoinder—and it was all so *normal* that Tyler forced himself to fully relax and enjoy the moment.

He was in the backyard with his family and his girlfriend. Everyone was together, everyone was getting along, and for now, everyone was safe. He counted his blessings, because one thing he'd learned since meeting Jay, was to count 'em while you could. You never knew when some megalomaniac with delusions of grandeur would set you in his crosshairs. Or when some rogue cyborg was gonna try messing with your girlfriend.

CHAPTER FIVE

THE THREE-DAY INTERLUDE at the Davidson family home had turned out a great deal more pleasant than Jay had anticipated. Tensions had briefly escalated again the first evening, when the subject of sleeping arrangements had been broached, however Tyler had quickly smoothed over the awkwardness, announcing he would sleep downstairs on one of the couches rather than share his old room with Jay. He'd claimed he didn't like disturbing her when he couldn't sleep. And, rather than consider the reality that a cyborg didn't require sleep, and would hardly be disturbed by a human pacing the floors—as Tyler tended to do when in the throes of composing a new piece of music—Marissa had simply lamented that her son's insomniac ways hadn't improved any.

Jay admitted to taking what she'd later identified as mild offence at Tyler's clumsy signals for her to remain silent and let him do the talking, and at the time had countered with a firm statement that she would be quite comfortable "sleeping" on the couch. That wasn't to say she hadn't been *tempted* to explain that although she did not *require* sleep, if she felt any requirement to mimic the state at least *she* wouldn't suffer any discomfort lying on one of the Davidson family's well-used, somewhat saggy couches, that were hardly optimal sleeping surfaces. But she hadn't given in to the temptation because she saw no reason to exacerbate a potentially fraught situation.

Tyler shouldn't have felt compelled to prompt her not to tromp all over Marissa's desire to continue treating her like any other human purporting to be her son's girlfriend. Jay again considered discussing the matter with him, but ultimately deemed it prudent to let it go. It was her problem, not Tyler's, that it was becoming increasingly more challenging to suppress her human side and be the cyborg that was immune to hurt feelings.

Detecting potential social minefields, however, was becoming a little easier. As was navigating them without attracting too much unwanted attention—although Jay could still find herself floundering, despite blink-of-an-eye access to extensive information on any subject. Parent/child dynamics was one such constant source of both confusion and fascination. Take, for example, a son sleeping in the same room as his girlfriend. To a parent, "sleeping" in the same room appeared to be synonymous with their son and his girlfriend having sex under their roof. And to a parent, it frequently appeared perfectly reasonable to insist on separate rooms in an effort to prevent such an act from taking place—surely an illogical reaction if the parent already knew that their son and his girlfriend were sharing an abode and presumably having intercourse.

So far as Jay could determine, the reasoning was along the lines of "my house, my rules"—even if such rules wouldn't prevent one party from sneaking into the other's bed if either the son or girlfriend felt the risks of being caught worth the reward.

In the end, no one had slept on the couch because Caro had insisted on what she'd called "a mini sleepover" in her old room. Jay wiggled her sparkly-purple-painted toenails—one of the

many rituals Caro had forced her to undergo. Others had included the application of mudpacks, manicures and pedicures,
makeup sessions, gorging on Caro's chocolate stash, raiding the
freezer for ice cream, and whispering long into the night until
Caro couldn't keep her eyes open any longer and fell asleep. Jay
would even go so far as to admit she'd enjoyed these rituals. And
yes, she had felt pride in Caro's envy of the steady hands that
allowed Jay to achieve a perfect "cat's-eye" with liquid eyeliner
first time, every time.

She adjusted the parameters of the current search, her fingers
keying in the new data too fast for the human eye to follow.
Simultaneously, she replayed a particularly satisfying interlude
between herself and Tyler at 2:15 am on the second night, com-
piled a list of items she needed to order for her puppy, and
planned a week's worth of frozen meals to cover her impending
absence. Tyler was a competent cook, but often neglected to eat
properly when she wasn't around.

Hmmm. Perhaps scheduling regular reminders on his mobile
phone would assist his memory?

Perfect. That was exactly the kind of action a human girlfriend might take—the kind of thing that a young male might
complain about to his friends, while being secretly pleased his
girlfriend cared whether or not he ate regularly.

Then again…. Perhaps such reminders would simply irritate
him.

The shower in the ensuite started up—Tyler was taking a
break from the song he was currently working on. Disappointment stabbed her. He wouldn't perform the song until he was
satisfied with it and she had hoped to hear it tonight, before she
had to leave.

She abandoned that thought-thread for now and resumed a

previous one revolving around her continued fascination with sibling dynamics. Her visit with the Davidsons had not disappointed in this respect. There had been the usual bickering and banter to analyze, plus the rivalry over who got to do what, and when, with the newest member of the family. Jay'd had no idea that walking a slumbering infant in an overly complex piece of machinery called a "stroller" was considered such a desirable activity. Add an untrained, spoiled puppy to the mix, and she had plenty of data about sibling interactions to replay and analyze.

On the subject of the newest addition to Jay's household: When she had announced to Tyler that she had chosen a suitable name for the pup, he had asked her not to reveal it to anyone, including himself. He'd claimed it would be "amusing as hell to watch Caro turn herself inside out" to extract the pup's name from Jay.

Jay had agreed, and been duly treated to lengthy bouts of Caro pleading, pouting, wheedling, threatening, and finally resorting to increasingly outrageous attempts at bribery. Inevitably, Caro had given up on Jay and turned her efforts to extracting the information from her brother, who'd predictably taken great delight in informing Caro he hadn't a clue what name Jay had chosen.

Marissa had not been at all fazed by the carryings on, but Michael hadn't been so sanguine. He'd taken Jay aside and begged her to come clean for the sake of his sanity.

Jay, taking pity on both Mike and Caro, had announced that "Brum", a diminutive form of *Brummer*, was a good strong name for the adult dog the pup would eventually become. However, after enduring seventeen minutes of the pup's yipping, and its attempts to crawl into her lap and chew the steering wheel during the car trip home, Jay had informed Tyler that she might yet change the pup's name to *Bello*, which meant "barker". Brum must have preferred his original name, for he had subsequently settled down in the backseat and behaved himself the rest of the trip.

Jay glanced toward the second doggie bed she'd bought to encourage Brum to nap somewhere other than her lap while she worked.

Excellent. The pup was still sprawled in his bed, tired out from their walk. Her lips curved at the memory of him careening around the park, startling at anything at everything, until he'd flopped down atop Jay's feet and crashed into sleep.

Another memory imposed, this one carrying with it the sheer wash of pleasure she'd felt upon unlocking the front door of number sixty-four Parkway. It was illogical to have become so attached to an arrangement of walls, furniture and belongings, but she couldn't deny the physiological and mental shifts that had resulted in the brownstone coming to represent an elusive human concept labeled "home." Along with pleasure, ushering Tyler and the pup inside and shutting the door behind them, had provoked the release of tension in smaller muscles, deepened breathing, a slowed pulse rate, and a number of other subtle physiological changes.

Or perhaps it was not the building. Perhaps it was the knowledge that only when she was alone with Tyler, could she truly be herself. Perhaps home was not a place but a *person*, and for Jay, Tyler had become synonymous with "home".

A series of soft beeps called her full focus to the program currently running on her laptop. She analyzed the results... and quickly concluded there was no pleasure whatsoever to be extracted from her current lack of progress in locating Sixer.

A similarly thwarted human might have indulged in some filthy swearwords, glared at the laptop monitor like it was to blame, pounded her fists on the desk, or thrown something at the wall. Perhaps all four if the situation had warranted such a tantrum. Because it was not in Jay's nature to allow frustration over lack of success the upper hand, she adjusted another search parameter... and refused to give credence to a tiny part of her that insisted indulging in a small tantrum might turn out to be somewhat satisfying.

She had other leads to pursue. Tantrums were a waste of energy.

"Any luck?" Tyler padded into the room off the lounge that Jay had turned into a library-cum-office. He rested his palms on her shoulders to lean in and kiss her cheek, and the impulse to turn her head and demand a real kiss buzzed through Jay's veins. That impulse wasn't helped by the fact Tyler wore nothing but sweatpants that hung low enough on his hips to hint at the waistband of his boxer shorts.

He looked—

What had been the phrase Caro had once used to describe her boyfriend Matt? Ah, yes. *Eminently lickable.* And Tyler smelled wonderful, too—of soap and vanilla shampoo and healthy human male.

A shaft of heat swirled low in Jay's belly and muscles lower down involuntarily clenched. She analyzed these physical reactions, and identified the sensations as desire... which she would not be acting upon at this moment, tempting though the thought might be.

She cleared her throat. "No luck yet."

"Bummer."

Jay decided this was as good a time as any to practice one of those shrugs humans used to convey that they weren't particularly bothered by something. "I would have been surprised if Sixer had made it easy for me to trace his whereabouts."

"Yeah, I'd have been suspicious as hell if you'd tracked him down quickly. Sixer's too smart to slip up. He'll make you work for it." Tyler perched on the edge of the desk and swung his bare foot. "So, reckon you'll have better luck with that guy my dad recognized?"

"I believe so. It won't be too much longer before I have something concrete."

Jay had obtained a list of Goodkind Electronics employees reported to have sustained fatal injuries during the bombing of the bunker housing Caine's clandestine cybernetics project. And yesterday, while Tyler had been at classes, Jay had driven back to Snapperton to show the list to Tyler's father. She trusted her own security precautions one hundred percent, but although Michael Davidson's skills in that regard were superior to most, transferring the file electronically wasn't worth the risk—not when Jay could easily drive down and give it to him in person. It wasn't like driving for hours without a break fatigued or taxed her in any way.

Michael had scanned the list and pointed out a young technician who'd been brought to his attention on two occasions. The first had occurred when Evan Caine had personally requested an in-depth background check on the man before he was shifted to another section—an R and D department Michael's personal security access insured he could obtain little more than rudimentary information about. The second occasion had been when Michael was obliged to write the man up for a security breach.

Evan Caine hadn't made a habit of offering people second chances once they'd screwed up. Apparently, the skills one Seth

Kyle Williams brought to the table had been deemed too valuable to lose, and he'd escaped termination. Given the way Michael's expression had blanked as he uttered the word "termination", Jay understood the more sinister use of the word could well have applied in this instance.

It would be far more efficient to gather data directly from the scene of the bombing but for now, the risks of doing so in person remained unacceptably high, forcing Jay to rely on other sources of information. One such source was the preliminary autopsy report on Frank Sloane, the tech rostered on with Williams.

The report indicated Sloane had been in the main lab and had died instantly, his injuries consistent with being caught in an explosion. What were presumed to be Williams' remains had also been recovered. Eventually it might be possible to identify the remains, but as Jay well knew, anyone with the right skill set could fake a person's death.

After illegally accessing all manner of private personal information, and taking stringent measures to thoroughly cover her tracks, Jay had ascertained that an unidentified John Doe matching Williams' physical description had been dropped off at a small, understaffed medical facility two townships over from the bomb site. The John Doe had been unconscious, concussed from a blow to the head. Also noted were a dislocated shoulder, a cracked rib, contusions on his face, back and torso, and a number of other minor, non-life-threatening injuries.

A staff member had recorded the incident as a probable mugging—a logical conclusion given the neighborhood crime statistics. This assumption had not been verified, however, because shortly after the patient had regained consciousness, and before he could be questioned, he'd vanished from his hospital room. Since the costs of his treatment had mysteriously been settled, neither hospital staff nor authorities had been inclined to pursue the matter further, presuming the man had discharged himself and shortly afterward arranged for his bill to be paid.

Jay had confided to Tyler that she believed Sixer had chosen to spare Williams, and had extracted him from the lab prior to the explosion. Too, it appeared highly likely Williams' injuries had been inflicted by Sixer during the process of convincing the young tech to accompany him.

In Tyler's opinion, among other things, Sixer needed to work on his powers of persuasion.

If Sixer *had* been involved in the young man's disappearance from the hospital, there wouldn't be much of a trail to trace— Sixer was too careful and methodical for that. But if Williams had walked out on his own, Jay was confident she could locate him. The majority of modern-day humans—even those who had reason to be paranoid about surveillance—were too reliant on technology to completely eschew it. Thanks to data mining algorithms like the one she'd written, one careless act could leave a digital footprint that Jay could trace back to the source.

She checked the second of the two laptops sitting on her desk for new results on Goodkind Electronics employee ID 102212. "Gotcha," she said, for Tyler's benefit. "Proof that Seth Williams is indeed alive and well."

He blinked. "That was quick."

"Yes."

Jay analyzed Tyler's responses—head cocked, brows slightly arched, eyes a little wider than usual, torso angled toward her— and surmised he wished her to elaborate on her methods. And then he confirmed it absolutely by saying, "So? Don't keep me hanging—I want to know how you did it. Spill."

Satisfaction curved her lips. She'd correctly interpreted his body language and it felt... *good.* "Would you like the long explanation or the short one?" she asked.

He gave her what she now recognized as his "Are you freaking kidding me?" eyes.

"The short one, then. Fantasy, food chemical intolerances, whole food stores, inhalers and facial recognition software."

Tyler blinked slowly and snapped his sagging jaw shut. "Okay, if you don't want to tell me—"

"That *was* the short version, Tyler."

"Then either I'm not fully caffeinated and my brain's gone to sleep, or my brain cells eked out my ear last night and are currently residing on my pillow. Or—"

"Or I'm being deliberately obtuse."

He waggled his brows at her. "You said it, not me."

Jay allowed herself a full-blown smile, liking the way he bantered with her.

Pause current thought-thread.

It was something his twin, Caro, also did. Their father Michael, not so much. There was, Jay believed, too much history between them for Michael to tease her in such a casual fashion. He had shown with words and actions that he cared for her wellbeing, but he was far too aware of the harm she was capable of inflicting to let his guard down completely. And Marissa.... Caro had recently admitted her current relationship with Nessa, her former best friend and Tyler's ex, was a "work in progress" and Jay believed that an excellent summation of her own relationship with Marissa.

Jay did not possess enough data to make an educated guess how the Davidson's newest addition would react to her when he was old enough to form opinions. Hopefully the child's increasing awareness of the world around him would not include the

ability to sense her "otherness", forcing her to resort to pheromones in order to successfully interact with him. Using such
methods to soothe a domesticated animal, or as a distraction to
deflect a strange human's suspicions was one thing, but it would
be morally reprehensible to manipulate a child in such a way.

Resume.

"Very well," she said, "the long explanation it is. Seth's position within Goodkind Electronics required him to delete all
social media accounts, save for a professional page overseen and
maintained by GE's media department. That was standard for all
employees of a certain level—as was the requirement to use
company-issued cell phones, laptops and tablets. Of course, Seth
hasn't used a company cell phone since he went to ground."

Tyler snorted. "Dude would have to be brain-dead to do that
if he's trying to keep a low profile."

"Agreed. Consequently, my algorithm could not solely rely on
mining data from common sources such as vehicle hire, motel
and hotel registrations, and rental properties—although the
chances of successfully securing a rental property given his current circumstances are remote. However, I was fortunate that
medical records I obtained state one Seth Kyle Williams is an
asthmatic, who is highly intolerant of sulfites."

Tyler's brow crinkled. "Sulfites?"

"Sulfur-based compounds that occur naturally, but are commonly used as preservatives and enhancers in both food and
drugs. His medical practitioner recommended he avoid a common sulfite preservative known to be potentially harmful to
asthmatics, and which is frequently found in drugs used for the
treatment of asthma. My algorithm tracked pharmaceutical
companies that had developed preservative-free asthma treat-
ments, and providers and outlets that have made these

medications available to the public. It also tracked stores providing sulfite-free foodstuffs and offering a home delivery service."

Tyler scratched his chin. "Clever. But Seth Williams can't be the only guy out there who's allergic to sulfites. And I'm guessing he's not using his real name, right?"

"Correct. Although Seth obediently deleted his social media accounts, the data posted is still available if you know where to look. He belonged to a number of science fiction and fantasy reader forums, and had contributed frequently to posts advising readers where to source various out of print books in those genres. He is on record as stating so long as he has a good book to read, he can endure anything the world throws at him—a common attitude amongst devout readers. His username on these forums was NewbornDragon."

"This is getting real interesting." Tyler made a rolling gesture with his hand to indicate she should continue.

"The algorithm cross-matched the names of all characters in the science fiction and fantasy novels NewbornDragon had listed in his 'favorites' lists, with recent online purchases of sulfite-free foodstuffs and sulfite-free aerosol bronchodilators. The name that flagged on all counts was *Randall Thor*—an unsubtle play on the name of the main protagonist in one of NewbornDragon's favorite fantasy series. From there, it was a simple matter of ascertaining the delivery address—which happened to be a motel room—and using facial recognition software to verify that Randall Thor is indeed Seth Kyle Williams."

Tyler frowned. "If I'd gone to ground and was hiding from a rogue cyborg, I doubt I'd be careless enough to get caught on camera."

"He's more careful than your average person—he paid online using a generic preloaded debit card—the kind purchased by those who don't have access to a credit card. In addition, he paid cash to purchase the card. But you might be surprised at how easy it is to be accidentally photographed or videoed. In this case, Randall Thor answered his motel door to sign for a delivery, and unknowingly ended up in the background of a selfie snapped by a couple staying at the same motel complex. The female member of the couple uploaded the photo her social media account. My facial recognition software did the rest."

"Impressive."

"Yes." Jay wasn't a fan of the human habit of being falsely modest.

"So I guess you're leaving sometime tonight to pay Seth Williams, AKA Randall Thor, a visit."

"Correct."

"And you don't want me to know where you're going. Or for me to come with."

"Also correct. I anticipate an absence of three days, and you have already missed too many classes."

Unsaid was something they both knew: He would only slow her down.

His lips thinned. "I get why," he said. "Don't much like it, though."

"Would it help if I got down on my knees and apologized profusely?"

"Nope. I'll get over it." He glanced at the area beneath the window, where Brum's doggie bed had taken up residence, and chewed his lower lip. "Who's gonna look after Brum while I'm at classes? He'll wreck the place if he's locked up during the day."

"I entertained the thought of taking him with me."

Tyler puffed out a sharp breath. "You gotta be kidding me. You're seriously considering taking along an untrained puppy?"

"I said I *entertained* the thought, Tyler. I didn't say I was prepared to act on it. The attention Brum would require far
outweighs any benefits of having him accompany me. I have
requested a favor from Allen, and he has agreed to watch Brum
during the day." Jay cocked her head, closely observing Tyler's
reactions. "Will it inconvenience you to drop Brum at the studio
on your way to classes? I would expect you to take the SUV, of
course. If you drive to the campus rather than using public
transport, the time saved will mean you won't have to get up
earlier than usual to stop by the studio."

"You seem to have thought of everything," he muttered.

"Yes."

When Tyler didn't say anything more she added, "And it
would be very helpful if you questioned Allen about the letter,
and any strangers he might have noticed in the area lately."

His posture altered, chin lifting, shoulders rolling back, spine
straightening. "You trust me to do that?"

"Yes."

"Wow."

That "wow" was uttered so softly on an exhalation that Jay
didn't believe he had intended her to hear it. Of course, she trusted him. And understood the instincts that drove him to show
that he could protect her, too. She possessed those same instincts
magnified tenfold. Which was precisely why she had allocated
him this "safe" task that she hoped would satisfy him for now.

"I may have to relocate Seth, hence why I could be gone a few
days," she said. "I'll get a message to you as soon as the opportunity presents itself."

He nodded, veiling his expression into something resembling
neutral that of course she saw through immediately. "I'll be back
as soon as humanly possible," she told him, knowing he would

fret until she returned, and knowing there was little she could do about that.

"Make that as soon as *inhumanly* as possible," he told her. "It'll be a damn sight quicker that way."

She smiled at his poor attempt at humor, and did the only thing she could think of to make her departure a little easier on him: took his hand and led him upstairs to their bedroom, where she employed a mutually satisfying, age-old distraction technique designed to wear him out.

It worked exactly as she'd hoped.

Jay kissed Tyler's brow and eased from beneath the covers, leaving him to the oblivion of sleep. She grabbed her boots from the foot of the bed, and the items of clothing she'd previously laid out on the dresser, and headed into the ensuite to change. Once dressed, she tucked a small wad of large denomination bills, a credit card and driver's license in one of her many fake identities into one pocket of her exercise pants, zipped it securely, and quietly exited the ensuite.

So far, so good. Now she had only to retrieve one more item from her office, and exit the house without disturbing Brum. With luck, both pup and boyfriend would sleep through the night.

As she reached for the bedroom door handle, she allowed herself one final glance over her shoulder at Tyler's sleeping form. Her heart seemed to twist in her chest, wringing a painful gasp from her throat. And it took all the willpower with which she'd been programmed to strangle the impulse to wake him, and allow him to come with her.

CHAPTER SIX

J AY PARKED THE UNASSUMING vehicle she'd hired in a parking lot that serviced a number of stores, including an open all hours fast food restaurant. Once inside the restaurant, for the sake of appearances she purchased a burger, ate a few bites, and then discarded the remains on the nearest table as she headed to the Ladies.

She entered the first of a half dozen cubicles, and wedged the plastic-wrapped package inside the toilet cistern. So far as hiding places went it was imperfect, but less risky than leaving it in the car. Or carrying it on her person. It would be, as Caro liked to say, a disaster of monumental proportions if it fell into the wrong hands during this coming encounter.

Exiting the restaurant, she scanned the vicinity for unwelcome observers. And once satisfied she had attracted no undue attention, she jogged the six blocks to the motel.

The schematics for the motel complex had confirmed that her options for entering the motel room undetected were severely limited. Digging a tunnel wasn't logistically sound. Climbing onto the roof and removing a section to allow entry, carried with it an unacceptably high probability that her actions would be noted and reported to authorities. Ditto with smashing through a rear wall. Her best option was the usual method of gaining admittance to a motel room: entering via the front door.

Her internal timepiece informed her it was 05:41. The motel complex was partially shielded from the main roadway by a stand of trees, and only the rare dedicated jogger or walker was up and about so early. Jay dialed back her speed to a relaxed yet purposeful walk, projecting "I've been for an early morning run and I have every right to be here". She had already taken the precaution of tying back her hair, and as she passed the motel reception area, she twitched the hood of her sleeveless hoodie to partially conceal her face.

Nearing Seth Williams' motel room, she refocused her sensors.

One inhabitant. Good.

At the door she paused, narrowing the range of her sensors still more.

The blackout curtains were closed, and the sole inhabitant's breathing and pulse rate indicated sleep. Even better.

She rapped softly on the door and continued rapping, aware the muted noise would take a few moments to filter through to the man inside.

It took less time than she'd anticipated before she detected the groan of a human woken from a deep sleep. The groan was followed by the hissing slide of bed linen, the thump of feet hitting the floor, and finally, footfalls indicating the motel room's inhabitant was approaching the door.

The footfalls abruptly ceased approximately an arm's length from the exit.

Jay could hear the man inside fidgeting, and surmised he was debating whether to answer the door. Or perhaps venture close enough to peer through the peephole. She angled her body so her face couldn't be seen. If Seth Williams wasn't fooled by her precautions, as a last resort she would force her way in. With luck it wouldn't come to that. The less she scared him now, the more chance he would cooperate in the future.

A hoarse voice called, "Who is it?"

Jay confirmed the male occupant's identity by analyzing his vocal patterns. The distortions were within acceptable parameters—doubtless caused by a combination of the mild dehydration expected after a night's sleep, and still healing facial injuries. "It's Gabi," she whispered, modulating her own voice to mimic that of Seth's younger sibling.

"Who?"

Jay increased the volume of her voice a little and injected a hint of panic into her tone. "It's *me*, Seth. Gabi."

A pause—as might be expected when you'd been abruptly woken, and then forced to confront the likelihood that the lengths you'd taken to conceal yourself had failed dismally.

It wouldn't be prudent to give Seth time to think logically, and realize how unlikely it was that, of all people, his teenage sister had been the one who'd tracked his whereabouts. "I'm in trouble," Jay said, playing on the protective instincts an older sibling might harbor for a younger. "Let me in before someone sees me!"

Jay heard Seth lunge for the doorway, and the unmistakable sounds of him fumbling with the privacy lock. The hinges of the door squealed as it opened and a thin-faced man sporting an impressive case of bed-head peered out from the gloomy room. "Gabi! How'n the hell did you figure out—?"

"That Randall Thor is Seth Williams?" Jay shouldered through the door, forcing Seth to take a step back. She shut the door behind her and flipped the latch. "And that you didn't end up smeared all over the lab in the bomb blast like your colleague

Frank Sloane? It wasn't difficult."

Seth backed up until his calves smacked the edge of the sagging double bed. "You're not Gabi."

"Excellent deduction."

His face drained of color save for the mottled smudges of fading bruises. "You sound exactly like Gabi."

"Yes. All thanks to a 'Happy Birthday Seth' video Gabrielle uploaded to one of your social media accounts prior to you deleting them."

Seth's legs folded and he sat down on the mattress in such a hurry that he bounced. His complexion turned an interesting shade of pale green. "Shit. You're her—Gamma."

"Another excellent deduction," she told him in the voice she preferred—the one she'd come to think of as her own. "And might I add that I appreciate very much you referred to me as 'her' rather than 'it'?"

"You're here to... to... terminate me."

Tremors wracked his too-thin body. The man was terrified. Time to play up her human tendencies.

Jay retrieved the asthma inhaler from the nightstand and handed it to him.

When he'd used it, and his wheezing had subsided, she told him, "You couldn't be more wrong. I'm here to discover why Sixer chose to spare you the fate of your colleague, and why he let you walk out of that hospital room."

Now that death wasn't imminent Seth had rallied somewhat, though to Jay he still nailed that human saying comparing someone to a deer caught in vehicle headlights. "I got the hell out of there the minute I came to," he said, a touch of indignation threading through his tone. "That... that... *thing* didn't have anything to do with it."

Jay snort-laughed.

Seth startled, doubtless reacting to what he would consider a wholly incongruous sound issuing from the vocal cords of a cyborg.

Jay marveled again at how perfectly one utterance could convey a combination of scorn and disbelief. "Oh puhlease," she said, treating him to a Caro-worthy eye-roll that made his jaw sag. "You seriously believe a cyborg like Sixer couldn't have snatched you from the hospital room and made you vanish without a trace? Think about it, Seth. You sure as hell didn't get there on your own, so the chances are ludicrously high that Sixer dropped you at the ER. And I'd bet my left hand that he *let* you walk out of that hospital room, *and* paid your medical bill. What I'd like to figure out is why."

She hadn't believed that Seth's eyes could get any rounder but she had been mistaken in that assumption. In fact, she now completely understood the origin of that anatomically unlikely description, "His eyes looked like they were about to pop out of his head."

"Shit!" Seth scrubbed a hand through his matted mop of hair. "You think Sixer knows where I am? Like, right now?"

"If he doesn't at present, it's only a matter of time. Even though you were reportedly deceased, *I* found you without much trouble."

Seth had regressed to trembling like a leaf about to fall from a tree and his teeth were visibly chattering. He wrapped his arms around his middle, wincing as he did so—evidence that the injuries he'd suffered at Sixer's hands were still healing. His current attire of baggy gray boxers and a once-white singlet only highlighted his air of vulnerability. "What are you going to do to me?" he asked.

Jay yanked the hood from her head, shook out her ponytail, and crossed her arms over her chest. "I'm not Sixer, Seth. The sooner you realize that, the better. So here's my proposal: You help me and I'll help you. For instance, this motel room might be cheap but that sulfite-free food delivery, and the special delivery from the pharmacy, must have eaten into a chunk of your available cash. I can help you with your cash flow issues."

His answer was too quick. "I'll do whatever you want."

And say whatever he believed she wanted to hear, Jay thought, noting the perspiration beading his forehead and upper lip. If he feared *her* as much as he obviously feared Sixer, she wouldn't be able to trust him. If she stashed him somewhere, he would require constant supervision or he'd bolt given the slightest opportunity. She needed to convince him that cooperating could be mutually beneficial for them both.

She crossed one foot over the other and folded herself into a cross-legged position on the threadbare carpet. Seth's current perch on the edge of the bed meant she had to look up to meet his gaze—a calculated attempt to give the impression he was the more dominant person in the room.

Seth might have been scared but he wasn't stupid. A wry twist of his lips told her he wasn't buying her ruse. "You're much better than Sixer at passing for human," he said.

Jay resisted the impulse to raise one eyebrow and give some excellent sarcastic face. Hah. He had no idea. "Yes, I am," she said. "However, I'm hopeful that, given time, Sixer will embrace more humanlike attributes."

Seth managed to summon a bark of what Jay presumed was supposed to simulate laughter. "If by 'humanlike' you mean getting a kick out of blowing shit up and hurting people, then he's already there," he said.

A heavy weight seemed to press down upon Jay's shoulders. Since she knew absolutely that there was no such physical weight currently resting anywhere on her person, she instinctively began to run a system diagnostic. And then the truth struck her. This sensation was a physical manifestation of guilt. Guilt for what she had potentially unleashed by freeing Sixer from the core commands that had constrained him. "What Sixer did—the people he killed, those injured in the explosion—that's on me."

Seth's brows pleated as he chewed over her statement. "You seriously want me to believe *you* feel responsible for what that amped up, robotic Ken-doll did?"

"Yes. I seriously do. Because I seriously am responsible." Her attempt at humor didn't provoke a response so she continued, "Once Sixer removed the projectiles that had incapacitated me I could have fought him. Instead, I gave him what he wanted: his freedom. I knew the risks and I did it anyway because I pitied him. Discounting all logic, I chose to trust him. When he blew up that bunker and killed innocent people, he betrayed that trust."

This time Seth's reaction was an almost textbook example of a snort-laugh. Some of the tension had drained from his muscles. Good. He was starting to trust her a little.

"None of us were innocent," he said. "Look, Sixer scares me shitless. I knew I was sticking my neck out proposing we scale back trials until we'd implemented more efficient controls, but I risked it because I *knew* the command protocols were too open to interpretation and too easily exploited. Case in point: *You're* only walking around right now because Caine screwed up the command and Sixer wasn't compelled to terminate you on sight."

The jury was still out as to whether Sixer would have succeeded had he pitted himself directly against Jay in a physical battle—

one without the advantage gained by using EMP projectiles—but she nodded, motioning for Seth to continue.

"You aren't the only one repelled by the idea of a self-aware creature being compelled to do whatever it's told," he said. "The whole thing made me sick to my stomach. I don't blame you for giving Sixer an out so he couldn't be controlled." His gaze sharpened. "And how did you do that, exactly?"

Jay channeled Tyler's "you gotta be freaking kidding me" expression.

Seth rewarded her efforts with a lopsided grin. "Worth a shot. Look, if anyone's to blame for Sixer turning out to be a freaking psycho, blame the guys who programmed him—" he jerked his thumb at his chest for emphasis "—and couldn't do half as good a job as your creator did with you."

Jay nibbled her lower lip, but ceased when she noted Seth's expression. Apparently he found her "human-ness" increasingly fascinating. "That's an interesting way of viewing recent events," she said. "And if what you say is true, why do you not appear to suffer any guilt over what happened?"

"Wasn't like I knew that nut-job Caine planned on using his pet cyborg as an assassin." He shrugged. "Once I was promoted to the inner circle and working directly on Sixer, I was screwed. Only way I was leaving Caine's employment was in a body bag. I gathered as much information as I could without getting pinged by security, and did whatever I had to do to get through the day. But if *I'd* been in Sixer's shoes, I'd have gone after Caine and the labs, too. Best way to make sure the bastards couldn't build another fucking machine and send it after me."

"I can't fault your logic—nor Sixer's instinct to protect himself. However, I find the collateral damage unacceptable. I don't regret freeing Sixer. In fact, I would have done so without any attempts on his part to compel my assistance. But I deeply regret the ramifications of the choices I made."

Seth leaned forward, his eyes narrowing to slits. "He compelled you? How?"

Jay cocked her head and allowed a slight smile to play across her lips. "Do you wish to know because you fear Sixer may compel me again?" She paused, gauging his reactions minutely. "Or because deep down, you would not be averse to commanding a cyborg to do your bidding."

There it was. The raised heart rate, the fleeting gleam in his eyes—quickly masked but not quickly enough for a cyborg of Jay's abilities. It was not wholly unexpected given Seth's background. Better men than he had been tempted by power.

"I'd only use you if Sixer made a grab for me again," he muttered as he lowered his gaze to stare at his bare feet.

"And the road to the hell that humans profess to believe in is purportedly paved with good intentions," Jay told him. Before he could mount an argument he couldn't win, she continued, "My command codes died with my creator. But perhaps you, too, could coerce me to do your bidding—provided you had the stomach to drug a woman who'd recently given birth so you could snatch her newborn baby and use the child for leverage. Would you have the stomach for that, Seth?"

His chin whipped up and the face he presented appeared so horrified, that even though he couldn't yet force words from his throat she knew the answer was a resounding "No". Finally, he managed to choke out, "Sixer snatched a *baby*?"

"Not just any baby." Jay toyed with the end of her ponytail, drawing out the moment for maximum impact. "The infant in question was my boyfriend's baby brother."

Seth mouthed the word *boyfriend* before the impact of her

statement overrode his wonder that a cyborg had claimed such a close relationship with a human. "Jesus, Joseph and Mary. Did he—?" His Adam's apple bobbed as he swallowed convulsively. "Did Sixer hurt the kid?"

"No."

Seth leaned his elbows on his bent knees, the tension draining from his body in a long, slow sigh. His murmured "Thank God" indicated his moral compass was more or less functional—at least where the wellbeing of infants were concerned. Even so, Jay didn't resist the impulse to make him squirm a little more. "Although there's still Sixer's threat to snatch the baby and sell him to some childless couple to consider," she said, choosing to leave out some pertinent facts.

It wasn't exactly lying by omission. After all, she could not confirm with one hundred percent certainty that if Tyler *was* foolhardy enough to attempt to track Sixer down at some later date, and somehow managed to succeed in that endeavor, Sixer wouldn't make good his threat.

Seth met this latest evidence of Sixer's ruthlessness with a flinch and another muttered imprecation. Jay waited for him to regain his composure, and mentally debated the most efficient way to enlist both his assistance and continued cooperation.

"Will you help me take Sixer down?" Seth asked.

"You are concerned that Sixer will use your sister against you."

He nodded.

"And you think the best way to insure her safety is for me to eliminate him."

More enthusiastic nodding.

"What leads you to believe that Sixer is more of a threat to you than Evan Caine?"

Seth's response came quick and sharp, ringing with certainty. "Caine's dead."

Jay merely arched a brow and waited.

"You think that insane bastard could still be alive?" Seth's voice had risen until the final word was little more than a high-pitched squeak.

"Until such time as I personally view Evan Caine's remains, and personally verify they *are* in fact his remains…." She let the rest of her statement trail off, leaving Seth to form his own conclusions.

"Fuuuuuck." A despairing sigh spilled from his lips, and Jay didn't think she would be remiss in concluding he was now inclined to embrace her offer.

A buzz vibrated the rear pocket of her jeans. She stood, extracted the mobile phone, and tapped her forefinger on her pursed lips, cautioning Seth to silence. Once he'd nodded assent, she swiped the screen to answer the call. "Nessa."

"Jay! Thank God you weren't asleep or something, and you picked up."

Nessa's voice sounded strained and tight. "You're afraid," Jay said. "What happened?"

"I saw him. At least, I think it was him—didn't get a good look at his face coz I just freaked out and turned right around and ran back to the motel but— Oh, shit. I really think it was him. What if he tries to make me do something awful again? Oh my freaking God, Jay. What should I do?"

Nessa's panting breaths indicated she was on the verge of hyperventilating. Jay couldn't risk that happening: It would not only cause Nessa distress, but also cause an intolerable delay before Jay could resume her interrogation of Seth. She would have to talk Nessa down. "Take a deep breath in through your nose. Hold it. Hold it a bit more. Now exhale slowly through your nose. Good. Again." She waited for Nessa to comply. "Better?"

Silence. Jay visualized Nessa nodding, and then realizing Jay wouldn't be able to see the gesture. Wait for it....

"Sorry," Nessa whispered. "Yes, much better. Thanks."

"Now, who do you think you saw?" Jay asked the question even though there was only one person who could be responsible for Nessa's panicked, desperate tone and the fear that practically zinged down the phone line... and he wasn't strictly a *person* at all.

"Sixer."

"Where are you now, Nessa?"

"Snapperton Motel," uttered on an exhalation that was a borderline sob. "In the bathroom, so I don't wake Chandler."

"Snapperton." That was... unexpected.

An unhappy laugh burst from the phone's speaker. "Chandler insisted I try'n make amends with my folks again, so he drove me down last night."

It couldn't be easy revisiting the past—trying yet again to prove to the parents who had tossed you out, and turned their backs on you, that you'd changed for the better and were worthy of their trust. Full marks to Nessa for having the courage to try. And to Chandler, who cared so much for Nessa that he would do his utmost to make this reconciliation happen. Jay believed the majority of his peers would have bailed on someone who carried as much baggage as Nessa did, long before now.

Nessa was still caught up in her explanation, the words tripping over themselves in her eagerness to get it all out. "Except I chickened out, coz, you know, the last time I visited them didn't go so well." A gross understatement if what Jay knew of the encounter was any indication. "But Chandler was really great about it, and he got us a room so I could go later this morning, but I couldn't sleep so I got up to go for a walk and I'd gotten as far as the parking lot and that's when I saw him, Jay. The guy who looked like Sixer. He... he was unlocking the door a few rooms down from ours. I-I think he's staying here! God. He's here, Jay. What do I do?"

Jay had no doubts that Nessa had correctly identified Cyborg Six-Point-0, AKA "Sixer". She may not have gotten a good enough look at Sixer's face to verify his identity beyond a doubt, but her subconscious had filled in the blanks and triggered an instinctive flight reaction. Nessa's one and only face-to-face encounter with Sixer had been both prolonged and terrifying. One did not easily forget such an encounter.

Well, that neatly solved the problem of tracking Sixer down... and caused a number of other problems—the most pressing being how to extract Nessa from Snapperton, because Jay didn't believe for a second that Sixer hadn't sensed Nessa's presence. The fact that he'd ignored her was a sign that she did not feature in his plans—for now, at least. But Jay wanted Nessa and Chandler safely out of the way. Humans had a habit of becoming collateral damage when Sixer was around and, despite a rocky start, Jay had become... *fond* of both Tyler's ex and the unlikely young man who'd captured Nessa's heart.

Three sharp raps echoed down the line, closely followed by Nessa's gasp as Chandler called, "You okay, babe? You're not sick from that burger last night or something?"

"Put Chandler on the phone, Nessa."

"Wh-what are you gonna tell him? That I'm p-paranoid?"

Nessa's voice sounded thick and miserable—as though she was on the verge of tears. But more worrisome than that was the underlying resignation in her tone. Jay felt a sharp twinge in her chest region. Nessa's path hadn't been an easy one, and her self-esteem had taken a massive hit. Rather than stand up for herself, she tended to accept—and even expect—poor treatment and put-downs.

Jay moderated and softened her tone. "I believe you, Nessa. I'm going to ask Chandler to drive you back home right now, okay? In fact, why don't you put your cell phone on speaker so you can listen to what I tell him?"

"It's okay. I trust you, Jay. You're good people."

"Thank you, Nessa. I appreciate that more than you could know. If Chandler asks for details, I'm going to cast our problem child in the role of a blackmailer I paid off on your behalf. In this case, I'm subscribing to the adage that the best lie contains ele-ments of the truth. It's up to you what else you choose to reveal to Chandler."

There was a prolonged pause while Nessa absorbed this, and then she whispered, "Thanks, Jay."

Jay cast a glance at Seth, who'd leaned back on his elbows, legs dangling off the end of the mattress. Curiosity burned in his eyes, turning them from an unexceptional mild gray to incisive silver.

She held up her hand, fingers and thumb outstretched, and mouthed, *Give me five.* He nodded, but didn't shift his focus from her face, as though intent on guessing the nature of the drama playing out down the phone line, and Jay's role in it.

"Jay needs to talk to you," Jay heard Nessa announce, and then Chandler's voice came on the line. "Hey, Jay. What's up?"

Jay didn't try to sugarcoat the situation, and stuck to as much of the truth as she was willing to reveal. Sometimes she thought it would be easier to simply tell Nessa and Chandler exactly what she was, and then deal with the fallout. But so much worse than the possibility of losing their friendship, was the prospect the revelation would endanger them. The fewer humans who knew what Jay was, the better for everyone.

Suppressing a sigh, and wondering how it had all gotten so very complicated, she said, "When Nessa last visited her parents, she encountered a young man who turned out to be a very unpleasant individual. He didn't physically harm her but he scared her, and tried to blackmail her."

Chandler's indrawn breath and continued silence indicated Nessa hadn't revealed anything about her encounter with Sixer. Since the truth of the incident didn't portray Nessa in a particularly good light, Jay couldn't blame her for keeping it quiet.

"Nessa came to me for help, and I paid him off," Jay continued, careful not to mention Sixer's name aloud. All she needed right now was for Seth to panic and do a runner. "I believed I'd made it worth his while to leave Nessa alone. Apparently I was mistaken."

Chandler was aware that Jay was financially very well off. He should therefore conclude the pay-off had been in cash, and that the figure had been substantial.

"Yeah, I get what you're saying," he said. "So I'm guessing this asshole's turned up again, right?"

His tone was belligerent, spiked with undercurrents of fear and worry. Chandler had never struck Jay as the kind of male who would lead with his fists without considering the pros and cons, however love did strange things to humans. She would have to quash any plans to hunt Sixer down and tear him limb from limb before they got off the ground. "Right," she said. "Since he didn't heed my message the first time around, he obviously needs further convincing."

"Tell me his name and I'll—"

"Put yourself at risk, thereby scaring the hell out of your girl-friend, who just so happens to be crazy in love with you. Leave this to me, Chandler. I have... resources."

He was silent for so long that Jay ventured to say, "Please, Chandler."

"Those 'resources' you mentioned better include paying someone to put some major hurt on this dude this time. I want him to suffer for what he's doing to Ness, you hear what I'm saying?"

"I hear you. Consider it done."

"Good."

That had definitely been a snarl. Aware of Seth's continued regard, Jay confined her reaction to a blink. Caro had labeled Chandler a "sweet guy with nerdish tendencies" and Jay had never before heard him sound so... so... *feral*, so prepared to inflict grievous bodily harm. Caro would doubtless have been shocked, whereas Jay approved wholeheartedly of Chandler's transformation since becoming Nessa's very significant other.

"One last thing, Chandler."

"I'm listening."

"Don't grill Nessa about this. She doesn't need to rehash the past—she's been through enough with this creep. Can you please take her home right now? Just pack your stuff, get in the car and go. I need to know she's left Snapperton and is safe with you."

"He's here, isn't he? That's why she's so freaked."

Chandler was too smart for his own good. Jay watched Seth minutely observing her and kept her expression neutral. "Something like that," she said, holding her breath and hoping Chandler wouldn't choose to be difficult.

"We're outta here in five. I'll get Nessa to text you when we're home."

"Have her phone me," Jay told him. "Texts are too easy to fake."

"Got it."

"I have to go."

"Jay? Be careful."

"I always am."

The instant she disconnected her cell phone rang again. It was not a number she recognized but she had a very good idea who it would be. "Hello, Adam."

"I remain undecided about taking on that label," Sixer said. "As I'm sure you are aware of that, I can only presume you are reluctant for whomever you are with to know you are speaking with me."

It was a statement of fact and required no response so Jay merely asked, "Why are you ringing me?"

"Vanessa Ward saw me entering my room at the Snapperton Motel. Correct?"

"Correct."

"I feel compelled to assure you that my purpose for being in Snapperton is not to harm or intimidate either Vanessa Ward or the Davidson family."

Jay remained silent, goading him to speak.

"Do you not believe I am speaking the truth?" he asked.

"Actions speak louder than words, Adam. In this case, the actions I refer to are the continued wellbeing of Miss Ward, her current boyfriend, and the Davidson family. Have I made myself clear?"

And Cyborg Six-Point-0 surprised her by responding, "Crystal," before disconnecting the call.

Not so long ago, Sixer's programming would have made such a flip response inconceivable. The possibility that Sixer, too, was evolving beyond the parameters of his core programming was high. But that possibility wouldn't stop Jay carrying out her plan. Sixer was still too much of an unknown quantity—too... *inhuman* and lacking in empathy. Ergo, he couldn't be trusted to put the welfare of humans Jay cared about above his own.

The only thing that Jay could be sure Sixer respected was superiority. And he had bested her—albeit by unfair means—therefore, in Sixer's eyes, she was inferior, and unworthy of his respect. For now, it suited Sixer to play along with her demands, but if his agenda changed, Jay had no doubts whatsoever that Tyler, his family, and Nessa, would simply become pawns in Sixer's endgame.

Jay needed to earn Sixer's respect by proving herself superior to him. Only then could she be sure that he would heed her demands.

She slipped the phone back into her pocket before pinning Seth to the spot with what Tyler called her "badass cyborg-chick" look. "I'd suggest you find some clothes."

He scuttled off the mattress and rummaged on the floor beside the bed until he'd unearthed a pair of wrinkled khakis and a grubby, white button-down shirt. As he dressed, he shot glances at her that were doubtless meant to be surreptitious but completely failed in that regard.

She pointed to the loafers he'd tossed beside the wardrobe. When he'd stamped his sockless feet into them she said, "Spit it out."

"Spit what out?"

He met her gaze but his attempt at faking confusion was laughable. She gazed back at him, unblinking. "You've been staring at me like I'm some lab-rat that's just verbally informed a bunch of scientists it doesn't appreciate being poked and prodded. Frankly, Seth, it's getting old. I'm blessed—or cursed, depending on your point of view—with the ability to feel and emote. I have even been known to cry on occasion. However, in my current mood I'm more likely to kick someone's ass than shed a tear, so you'll simply have to take my word for it. Now, can we please move on?"

Seth shook his head in a way that indicated disbelief. "You're pretty fucking incredible, you know that, Gamma?"

"You mean my *creator* was pretty fucking incredible. And my name is Jay."

Planting his butt on the mattress, Seth waved a dismissive hand. "I'm not disputing Alexander Durham was a genius—your very existence is evidence of that. He might have built you, and made you look human—even programmed your brain to act like one when it was logical to do so—but not even a mad genius like Durham could give a cyborg a soul. You developed *that* all on your own."

Jay rocked back on her heels. It felt like... like....

Like her stomach had plummeted to her toes, and her heart had performed a flip in her chest cavity. "You believe I have a soul?"

Seth gave her "Well, duh!" eyes. "Technically, Sixer's built to the same specs as you—different genetic material of course, because yeah, Caine was that much of a narcissist—but that's merely cosmetics."

A buzz hijacked Jay's brain, momentarily paralyzing her as the implications of Seth's last statement seeped into her consciousness. If she'd been human, she would have presumed she was entering a state of mild shock.

"But the two of you might as well be different species," he was saying, unaware of her inner turmoil. "Sixer's a thinking, reasoning *machine* with all the empathy of an amoeba. You, on the other hand, have evolved into what's essentially a human being that just happens to reside in a cyborg shell. You, my dear Gamma—"

"Jay," she corrected automatically. "My name is Jay. Please use it."

The still functioning part of her brain noted the triumphant "See? What did I tell you?" glint in his eyes. "You, my dear, *Jay*," he said, speaking slowly, as though relishing each word, "are a fucking amazing gift from God—an artificial construct with a soul."

Jay forced back the numbness of shock—or whatever it was that currently inhibited her ability to function. She sniffed in an affected manner, and injected a casual tone into her voice, pushing away intruding doubts that she could pull it off. "Hah. I don't believe for a second that *Sixer* was built to the same specs as me. My creator worked alone. He never revealed the secrets of my construction to anyone."

Something shifted in Seth's eyes. "You don't know?" He levered himself from the mattress and stood. Slowly, carefully, as though he feared she would slap him away, he cupped her chin in his hands and tilted her face, staring intently into her eyes. He blinked. "Shit-oh-dear, you really don't know."

Jay narrowed her eyes at him and he quickly backed up, hands raised in an unmistakable "Don't shoot" gesture. And then he said, "Evan Caine was Alexander Durham's illegitimate son."

CHAPTER SEVEN

I NTERESTING. AND POTENTIALLY very useful information indeed—provided there was any truth to Seth's claim. Until now, Jay had failed to unearth any significant connection between the two men that would explain Caine's obsession with Jay's creator, and his subsequent attempts to duplicate Alex Durham's life's work. Unfortunately, extracting more information from Caine's former employee and verifying the truth was going to have to wait. "Cadillac Escalade," she announced.

Seth's jaw sagged. "Huh?"

"Less memorable than Hummers, at least." She vividly recalled peering through the upper story window of Father's home at a convoy of the vehicles… and the devastating event that had heralded their arrival at the house.

Pivoting on her heel, she strode to the window that looked out onto the scraggly strip of garden bordering the driveway leading to the reception area. A simple matter of adjusting her visual sensors to allow for the drapes and…. There it was. 2014 model. Black with tinted windows. One driver and two passengers—all human. All armed.

Turning back to Seth she said, "We have to go."

He goggled at her. "Now?"

"Now. Please don't forget your asthma medication."

"Who?—"

"Feds. A posse of Caine's surviving cronies. Members of some as yet unidentified interested party." She shrugged. "Whoever they are, they're here and, as the saying goes, loaded for bear. Call me presumptuous, but I'm guessing you'd rather not stick around to determine who they are, and what they want."

Seth blanched. "No, but—"

"Better to discover those very pertinent facts from a distance, on your own terms, correct?"

"Yes, but—"

"They've pulled in out front of Reception. I don't make a habit of hazarding guesses but I believe they'll take the softly, softly approach."

Seth shook his head, then pinched the bridge of his nose, obviously trying to focus his thoughts. "Which is?"

"Browbeat the motel proprietor into unlocking the door to your room, rather than heading straight here and busting it down. That gives us a few minutes at least."

He steadied himself by gripping the edge of the small dining table. "To do what?"

"To escape, of course. It's not like we can stroll out the front door without being seen and pursued." She wrinkled her nose. "Although it'd be interesting to discover if I am capable of outrunning an Escalade while you're slung over my shoulder."

Seth's face took on that unflattering, sickly greenish cast again. "There's no back door," he said.

"I know. Luckily there *is* a bathroom and a convenient wall that leads straight out to the rear of this complex."

She grabbed his upper arm and towed him into the bathroom, shutting and locking the door behind them. "Please stand back a bit. I haven't got time to be neat about this."

Seth crouched against the freestanding side of the shower cubicle, and stuck both arms over his head. Reassured by his
unquestioning compliance—in this matter at least—Jay examined the bathroom layout. Toilet, pedestal washbasin with two
shelves above it for toiletries. Shower cubicle tucked into the rear
corner of the motel unit, and facing the flimsy internal wall that
backed onto the tiny kitchenette. Three-foot gap between that
shared internal wall and the shower unit's opening—barely large
enough to comfortably accommodate a decent sized bathmat and
a person exiting the shower....

Punching through that three-foot span of blank wall to the
right side of the shower unit would lead directly outside, behind
the motel complex, giving them a chance to escape unseen. It was
the best option—and the one that would cause the minimum of
damage to the room. It was, after all, hardly the motel owner's
fault that he had unknowingly registered Randall Thor, AKA
Seth Williams, as a guest.

Jay reached into the shower cubicle to turn the water on full.
If the intruders believed Seth was bathing it might buy her a little
more time—time that could significantly decrease the chances of
being spotted and immediately pursued. She danced her fingertips over the blank piece of wall, listening for variances that
indicated wall studs and framing. Satisfied, she karate side-
kicked the dry wall a half-dozen times in quick succession, each
time targeting a different section of the wall with the sole of her
sneaker-clad right foot.

Predictably, her footwear didn't survive such harsh treatment
intact, and rather than deal with shredded canvas and a flapping
sole, she ripped the sneaker from her foot and stowed it in her
hoodie's front pocket. Best not to leave evidence of her presence
behind. If Seth's pursuers believed he was acting on his own, they

might delay diverting more resources to their pursuit of him.

Moving so quickly her hands were blurs, Jay ripped off the smashed sections of drywall and reached into the wall cavity to yank out the insulation, until only the skeleton of wooden framing and the outer shell of clapboard cladding remained. She glanced over her shoulder and beckoned to Seth. Seeing him still cowering, hands shielding his eyes, she strode toward him, bracketed his wrist with her hand, and dragged him behind her. "Watch your step," she advised as she negotiated a piece of framing. "Shelter behind me as much as possible."

Seth managed not to trip on anything, and plastered himself against Jay as she put her shoulder, hip and thigh to the outer cladding. One concerted push detached a large section from the framing with a series of creaks and groans, its landing muted by a cushion of the neglected, weed-riddled grass behind the row of motel rooms.

Jay's enhanced hearing detected footsteps and a muted metallic jangle—keys to the rooms at an educated guess. Time to go.

She stepped through the gap, pivoted, and plucked a startled Seth from the cavity. "Hush," she murmured in his ear. "They're here."

He gulped, compressed his lips and nodded.

Taking that nod as permission to do whatever it took to get them both the hell out of there, Jay bent, slung Seth over her shoulder, straightened, and took off at a run, rocketing past the rickety swing set so quickly she set the swings in motion.

She anchored him more firmly, splaying her right hand across the back of his thighs. This next part was going to be a little disorienting for someone hanging head down. "Wrap your arms around my waist and hold on," she said, pitching her voice just loud enough to carry to his ears.

Seth took instruction well. His breathing might have been labored but to his credit, he didn't so much as squeak despite what must have been an uncomfortable position. Nor was she forced to slow while he complied with her instructions, which made the process of launching herself from the ground to negotiate the six-foot corrugated metal fence bordering the rear of the motel complex far more efficient.

Jay had cleared the fence and planted her feet on the grass verge when she detected the raised voices. For now she was safely hidden from view. She took a moment to filter out ambient sounds, and confirmed "they" had gotten into the bathroom and discovered Seth's escape route. If she'd been solo, she would have lingered to glean whatever information she could about this trio of men. But she had a vulnerable human to protect—a potentially valuable one, too. Seth's skill set could prove useful once Jay had located the Beta unit.

Priorities decided, she jogged up the street to locate a suitable vehicle to "acquire". It was either that or drag Seth, at a run, the six blocks to her car. Of course, she could carry him the whole way, but that feat of strength would hardly go unnoticed. She'd been fortunate no one had spotted her jumping the fence and she wasn't about to push her luck further.

JAY TERMINATED THE CALL as she swerved into the oncoming lane and zipped past a slower vehicle. Nessa and Chandler had arrived safely, and Jay had promised she would call them as soon as the situation with Nessa's "stalker" was resolved. Everything was in hand. Kind of. It was a pity her twin wasn't fully operational, because right now, torn in multiple directions, Jay would appreciate a clone to watch over Nessa. Instead, she was forced to rely on Chandler, a human... with no idea what he was truly up against.

As she slotted neatly back into her own lane, Seth reacted to her maneuver by stomping his foot on the passenger-side floor mat. The gesture was accompanied by a high-pitched whimper that brought to mind Brum's antics when the pup was reprimanded for bad behavior.

How strange. Why was Seth—?

Ah. She noted his white-knuckled grip on the edges of his seat and added that reaction to her current repository of observations about Evan Caine's former employee.

Time to reassure her passenger. "Given my enhanced sensory perception and physical abilities, you must realize it's highly unlikely I will wreck this vehicle," she told him. "And if a crash *was* imminent, I would either toss you to safety before impact or shield you with my own body—which, you must know, is far more resilient than a human's. Likely you would suffer only minor injuries."

"And that's supposed to make me feel better about being stuck in the passenger seat of a car driven by a freaking teenager who thinks she's a freaking racecar driver?" she heard him mutter.

Apparently, the explanation that had previously reassured Tyler as to Jay's driving abilities had little effect on her current passenger. "You, of all people," she said, "must know I'm the farthest thing from an inexperienced teenage driver it's possible to be."

His head flopped against the headrest and he loosed a heartfelt groan. "Damn. You heard that, huh?"

"Of course. Should I apologize for desiring to put some distance between us and the motel to minimize chances of a further encounter with your uninvited guests?"

He lolled his head to shoot her a sideways gaze. "If it's a tossup between the Feds—or whoever the fuck they were—and enduring your driving, then I guess I can put up with your driving."

"I'm very glad to hear it."

"But I'd be real grateful if you'd keep eyes on the highway instead of on me—you know, just for appearances sake? So I'm not a sniveling mess by the time we get to wherever it is we're headed?"

"I can do that."

"Thanks." He waited for Jay to turn her gaze back to the road before asking, "Where are we headed, anyway?"

"My creator owned a number of residential properties—each one with a concealed satellite laboratory. After his death, I cleared out all but one of the labs. I deemed it prudent to convert them into rooms that would not occasion comment if discovered. That sole remaining facility is equipped with what Alex considered 'the bare basics'. It's proven sufficient for my needs."

It had been a risk to keep this one lab intact, but Jay had deemed the risks worth the benefits of access to fully equipped premises in the event she developed some manner of defect. Too, this property had once served as a bolt hole. It had been the place where she'd retreated to lick her wounds in the aftermath of faking her death to keep Tyler safe.

"That's where we're headed?"

"Correct." She shot an assessing glance at Seth to gauge his reaction.

Surprise skated across his features. Then delight. Followed by a healthy measure of wariness. He sucked the insides of his cheeks and then ventured, "You're giving me access to one of Alexander freaking Durham's labs? Why'n the hell would you do that?"

"Because I require your assistance testing this." She reached into the sedan's center storage console and tossed him the wrapped package she had liberated from the Ladies room of the fast food restaurant. He'd said nothing about the package, nor the fact she'd left him in the car but taken the keys with her when she'd recovered it. His restraint was about to be rewarded.

She kept her gaze on the road, listening to the rip of packing tape and the rustle of plastic as Seth unwrapped the package.

"Whoa, baby." He whistled. "You made this weapon?"

"Yes."

"Does it have a metal strip to make it, you know, sorta legal?"

"I saw no logical reason to include unnecessary components."

His sharply indrawn breath, and the intonation he'd used when asking the question, suggested awe. Apparently, the ability to construct a weapon that was essentially undetectable when passing through a metal detector was something laudable in Seth's eyes.

It would have been easy to accept his praise, but some inner compulsion prodded Jay to play down her achievement. "I am not the first person to construct such a weapon," she said. "And I doubt I will be the last—unfortunately."

"You don't like them—guns, I mean."

"No. I do not believe guns are in any way, shape, or form, praiseworthy." She would even go so far as to say she disliked them—

No. *Dislike* was too weak a word. *Dislike* was the label Jay now applied to things that she felt a mild aversion for—such as pickles in a burger. And once she'd come to terms with the realization that a cyborg, who could extract nourishment from even spoiled foodstuffs, could actually dislike the taste of an inoffensive pickle, it had opened the gateway to further illogical dislikes. Her feelings about guns were not at all illogical, however, but wouldn't prevent her from using one if necessary.

Of course, she would prefer to pit herself against Sixer with only her own strength, abilities and wiles. Unfortunately, Caine's creation possessed a proven weapon that he'd already used against her on two occasions. He could not be relied on to "play fair".

"Oookay, then," Seth said. "Duly noted."

When the silence lengthened Jay offered, "It's not the weapon I require tested—it will perform the task for which it was constructed. The projectiles I intend to load it with, however, may require tweaking."

"Ummm, am I allowed to ask *who* you intend to test these projectiles on?"

"I've improved a previous design. If these projectiles work as they should, it will require only one to completely disable Sixer."

With luck, telling Seth exactly what he most wanted to hear would distract him from drawing the obvious conclusion—that *Jay* would be the test subject. Not to mention all the potential ramifications of trusting that the weapon-wielder—Seth—would immediately *remove* the projectile if it affected her as expected, rather than leaving her disabled and helpless… and a potential lab-rat for him to experiment on.

"Ho-*ly* crap on a cracker. You improved 'em? You little beauty!" Seth bounced in his seat, exuding a childlike glee. "Is this thing loaded? Can I examine the projectiles?"

"No. And not right now. I will give you access to them once we reach the lab."

To Jay's surprise, Seth didn't protest. Nor did he take the opportunity to examine the gun. He immediately rewrapped it, securing the package with the used tape as best he could before leaning over to stow it beneath his seat. At her quizzical glance he offered, "Don't want anyone to spot me playing with it. And it might be best to, ah, keep to the speed limit, too—wouldn't want to get pulled over with this baby in the vehicle. We'd be toast."

"An excellent point." And one that Jay should have considered earlier when she'd been weaving in and out of traffic. She eased off the accelerator. Confidence that she could extract *herself* from an encounter with the average highway patrol officer was one thing, but she had Seth to consider.

If she'd been human, she might have added blushing at her own recklessness to the silent lecture she gave herself. She would not have been so cavalier about taking such risks had it been Tyler in the car with her. It was laughable to compare her feelings for Seth to what she felt for Tyler, of course, but for now Caine's former employee was her responsibility.

A loud gurgle came from Seth's side of the car.

"Sorry," he said, pressing a fist against his belly. "I missed breakfast. Don't suppose there's anything edible in this car?"

Jay inhaled and analyzed the scents. "I believe someone left a Twinkie in the glove compartment. Whether it is edible depends on the expiry date." At least the preservative in the ingredients list was sorbic acid rather than sulfites.

"Twinkies? Seems there is a God after all."

Indeed. Especially since this rental vehicle should have been thoroughly cleaned by depot staff before being rented out again.

Seth rummaged in the compartment and unearthed the double pack of the snack cakes. He squinted at the expiry date. "Near enough." He ripped open the cellophane and inhaled, releasing his breath on a long, slow sigh. "Ahhh. I'm telling you, Jay, you haven't lived until you've eaten them deep-fried. I read somewhere that something truly magical happens when you freeze a Twinkie, dip it in batter, and then deep-fry it. I was skeptical until I tasted one at a state fair but they're not wrong. *Magical* is the only way to describe 'em."

Jay accessed her databases and found what seemed like an informative description of the process. By all reports, immersion in hot oil caused the Twinkie's filling to liquefy, and the vanilla flavor to impregnate the sponge of the cake. Aficionados went on to extol the virtues of the contrast between the softened, nearly melting cake, and the crispness of the deep-fried crust. Deep-fried Twinkies didn't sound at all *magical* to Jay, but they did sound interesting enough that she resolved to sample one at some stage in the near future.

Seth generously offered her one of the snack cakes but Jay shook her head. "Your requirement for sustenance is more pressing than mine." She could forgo sustenance for another thirteen hours without compromising her body's optimum physical condition, although she'd become accustomed to eating more frequently since Tyler had moved in. Speaking of food—

She made a mental note to order in a regular supply of sulfite-free foodstuffs for Seth. And to hire him a housekeeper.

"Tell me more about Evan Caine's supposed relationship with my creator," she said once Seth had demolished his snack.

He reclined the seatback and slumped, hands on stomach, legs outstretched as far as the sedan's cramped interior allowed. "Nothing *supposed* about it. You know your creator was married, right?"

"Mary Patricia Durham, nee Highton, married Alexander Jay Durham in 1961. There was no issue from their union before she passed. Alex never remarried."

"Correct. But prior to Durham meeting his future wife, he

dated a chick named Nina Berry. He met her when he was over-seas studying medicine at Cambridge—you do know he went to Cambridge, right?"

Jay gave him what she trusted were excellent, "Duh, what do you think?" eyes.

"Right. Anyway, Nina's family didn't approve of Durham—not entirely sure of the full story but her parents sent her away. And not long after, they announced to all and sundry she'd married a far more suitable, substantially older American, who just happened to be rolling in money, name of Neil Caine."

Jay risked Seth having another conniption over her driving habits to throw a long, assessing glance his way. "Following this information to its logical conclusion," she said, "Nina, pregnant with Alex's child, married Neil Caine and passed off the child as his. Alternately, Neil was aware of her circumstances when he married her, and raised the child as his own. Was Alex aware Nina was pregnant when she was sent away?" She couldn't conceive of the man she'd called Father abandoning his child, but stranger things occurred when matters of the human heart were involved.

"Don't know," Seth said. "But if he did, he never made a fuss about it—not that people did in those days. Anyway, Alex met and married Mary Highton, and once he got his degree, they upped stakes and moved to the good old U-S-of-A. Meantime, Nina and Neil doted on their only child, and young Evan didn't have a clue he wasn't Neil Caine's legitimate son until Neil did the whole deathbed confession thing before he died."

Seth sat up straighter, which Jay took to mean he was getting to what Tyler would call "the good stuff". "Evan eventually tracked his real daddy down," he said. "And somewhere along the way, decided it'd be a fine idea to pay Durham a visit. Seems

Caine-the-younger was just as disagreeable as the modern day version, because he robbed Durham blind. See, Durham was pretty stoked to learn he had an heir apparent, so he treated his son to a tour of his private lab, and did a bit of a crow about his cutting edge research. Far as I can tell, Caine decided he had to have whatever Durham was working on. So he waited 'til Durham left to attend some function, broke into the lab and cleaned it out. Notes. DNA samples. A prototype cyborg that never lived up to his expectations.

"Caine didn't have a scientific bent, but he did have a talent for using other people. He put together a team who worked on the prototype for donkeys' years but never got it functioning to Caine's high standards. They didn't have much luck replicating it, either—the female version they built went through five incarnations before they gave up and scrapped it." Seth yawned and scratched his chin. "Caine eventually decided to have another unit built from scratch. Only this time, he 'improved' it by making it male, and using his own DNA for the creation of the physiological shell. And the rest is narcissistic history, AKA Caine's pseudo 'son' created in his own image, Cyborg-Six-Point-0."

Seth had emphasized the word "improved" by raising his hands and curling the first two fingers of each hand into air-quotes. Jay gathered he didn't believe that, a) changing a cyborg's sex from female to male, and b) using Evan Caine's genetic material over Mary Durham's, had been an improvement. Or perhaps Seth was merely indicating his deep-seated aversion to Caine's creation—unsurprising given Seth's recent encounter with Sixer. But Jay didn't succumb to the lure of analyzing Seth's thought processes, and how his revelation about Evan Caine being Alex Durham's illegitimate son illuminated the motivations of the key players. She was focused on the bigger picture: the fate of the cyborg Evan Caine had stolen.

"How did you discover this information?" she asked.

Seth answered promptly. "I started getting antsy about Caine's motives, so I did me some digging. But I must've triggered some kind of internal alarm system because next thing I know, I'm up on report and some computer-whizz dude's chewing my ass and calling me all kinds of idiot. I didn't realize how much shit I was in until he admitted I was damn lucky he'd been able to convince Caine that terminating me would've been a waste of talent. And I got the distinct feeling he meant termination of the permanent, non-breathing kind. I took his advice from then on—kept my head down and did what I was told."

"Was this man's name Michael White by any chance?"

"Yeah. How'd you know?"

So Seth owed his life to Tyler's father, who'd used the pseudonym "Michael White" after being blackmailed into working for Evan Caine. "Put it down to a lucky guess," she said.

"Meaning you'll tell me once you're sure I'm trustworthy?"

"Meaning, it's not my story to tell."

He didn't press her further.

Jay didn't yet have enough data to confirm her suspicions but it wasn't a stretch to assume the "prototype" Caine had stolen had been Jay's forerunner—a *Beta* unit. Specifically *the* Beta unit featured in the photo that had mysteriously made its way into Jay's possession.

"How long 'til we get wherever it is we're going?" Seth rearranged his limbs to extract maximum comfort from the cramped confines of the sedan.

"At our current speed we'll be there in a little short of two hours."

He barked a soft laugh. "Sixer would have given me the exact time down to the last second."

Jay, too, had been programmed to be precise, but she'd learned precision was not always advisable. More often than not, it drew attention from those who didn't know what she was, and only emphasized her differences to the few who did. Seth, however, seemed far more startled when Jay displayed her human attributes. "I can be precise if it makes you more comfortable," she said.

"No thanks. I like you just the way you are."

Now it was Jay's turn to be startled. She scanned his expression for clues. "You *like* me?"

His face creased into a smile. "Yeah," he said. "I do."

Jay considered various responses. Would it be ill mannered to say she didn't know him well enough yet to have formed an opinion?

His smile widened. "Don't worry. I won't be offended if you say it."

"Say what?"

"That you've only known me a couple of hours so you haven't formed an opinion either way. And how did I know that was what you were thinking?" he added, before she could voice the question that had bubbled to her lips. "It's written all over your face."

Jay couldn't help herself: Her gaze flicked to the passenger side windshield visor Seth had lowered.

"Wanna see, huh?" He obligingly angled the visor so Jay could lean over and check her reflection in the small inset mirror.

She peered at her face and then turned her gaze back to the traffic. "I don't detect anything in my expression that would allow you to guess my thoughts so accurately."

"Is that a pout?" Seth asked. "Oh, my God. It is. You're pouting!"

He sounded delighted by the discovery. "I am not pouting," she said.

"Have it your way." He folded his arms across his chest and closed his eyes.

One minute and fifteen-point-seven seconds passed, and then he whispered, "Were, too."

She opened her mouth to refute his statement but instead of some pithy rejoinder, a wry laugh escaped. "Yes," she agreed. "I totally was pouting."

Seth's laughter spilled over, and this time Jay joined in. And decided that she might like Seth, too. Just a little. Not that she would admit it to him. At least, not until he'd proven himself trustworthy by extracting the projectile once he'd shot her.

CHAPTER EIGHT

IS HEART POUNDED like it would burst from his chest and his breath came in sharp, painful gasps. He was running. From something bad—something that was gaining on him. He dug deep and somehow managed an extra spurt of speed. It howled, and his heart seized as all the hair on his body stood to attention. He chanced a glance over his shoulder and—

Abruptly he lay sprawled on the ground. It loomed over him, licking its chops. And then it opened its tooth-filled maw and—

Licked his face.

Tyler's eyelids flew open and he found himself gazing into a pair of mournful yellow eyes. He swiped puppy-slobber from his cheek with the back of his wrist, and screwed up his nose as the canine version of morning breath hit him. Not a werewolf, then. Thank God for that. Not that he believed in werewolves or anything crazy like that but hey, it'd been a pretty realistic nightmare—no doubt caused by Brum's furry presence in his bed.

"Arrooo."

Tyler fondled the pup's ears. "You miss her, huh?"

The pup whimpered and rested his muzzle on his front paws.

"Me, too." Tyler scrubbed his face with his hands, blinked a couple of times, and glanced at his wristwatch. He loosed a heart-felt groan. Brum sure was an early riser. Maybe if he closed his eyes and feigned sleep, the pup would get the hint and—

"Rrrroooff!"

Apparently not. Grumbling beneath his breath, Tyler rolled out of bed, yanked on some clothes, and headed downstairs in search of Brum's leash.

The morning "walk" turned out to be a pell-mell sprint all over the freaking park until Brum's energy finally flagged and the pup flopped on the grass, refusing to budge another inch. Meaning Tyler had to pick him up and carry him home... and endure some of the most blatant pickup lines he'd ever encountered.

He unlocked the front door, kicked it shut behind him, and headed for Jay's study. Brum woke the instant Tyler decanted the pup into his doggie bed, and with an earsplitting *yip!* of protest, rocketed from the study.

Tyler blotted his face with the hem of his t-shirt. The heat in his face wasn't only from running 'round after Brum. Who knew so many single women were out exercising at this time of the morning? And who knew sporting a sleepy puppy draped over one shoulder was the trick to attracting their attention? Put it this way: He often took his shirt off to cool down after a run and because he was in pretty good shape, he'd gotten the odd appreciative glance. But having Brum along had taken "appreciative" to a whole new level. Not even toting a baggie of puppy poop along with aforementioned cute-as puppy had put them off.

In future, if he had Brum with him, there would be no more going shirtless after a run.... Unless he wanted to see if Jay was capable of jealousy—

Nah. Dumb idea. Jay had already proven that she could suffer jealousy when she'd dealt to Nessa, who'd been dumb enough to come on to Tyler in a disastrous effort win him back.

He snorted. As if.

His lips quirked in a wry grin. Pity he hadn't known about the puppy angle back in high school, though. Like, when he'd fervently believed that attracting female attention was the key to life, the universe and *everything*. Then again, truth be told, he would probably have chosen an extra hour's sleep over trolling for chicks at such an ungodly hour of the morning. He'd never been much of a morning person.

He registered Brum's distressed yips—the pup's kibble bowl was probably empty again—and headed for the kitchen to rectify that potentially world-ending situation before Brum's barking woke the neighbors.

The pup tucked into the kibble, leaving Tyler free to rectify his own personal world-ending situation—namely, a lack of caffeine. And, would you look at that? Jay had programmed the coffeemaker to switch on at precisely the right time.

He inhaled the mouthwatering fragrance of freshly made coffee. Damn but he had the best girlfriend ever.

He poured a mug of strong black coffee—just the way he liked it—and had just taken his first brain-cell-activating gulp when he noticed the note on the counter.

Jay had made him coffee *and* left him a note—a note that left him in no doubt that she was concerned for his wellbeing in her absence:

> *Don't forget to eat breakfast.*
> *There are toaster waffles in the freezer.*

She'd signed it with a small hand-drawn heart, and a *J*.

Tyler took another gulp of coffee, his lips tilting upward in what was almost certainly a goofy smile. Not that he gave a crap how goofy his smile was right now.

The *crunch crunch crunch!* of Brum scarfing kibble reminded him that he'd better grab a waffle or three. Jay was sure to check the packet. Or flat-out stare him in the eye and demand to know if he'd eaten breakfast while she'd been away. And he sucked at lying to her—she was too observant and knew him too darned well... as he'd discovered to his cost when he'd claimed he was no longer POed that she'd paid his first semester's fees at Wasserman College of Fine Arts. Not to mention arranged that any subsequent bills from Wasserman be sent directly to her private postbox.

He was on his third waffle when his cell phone blared, and even though it wasn't the ringtone he'd assigned to Jay's cell, his heart flip-flopped in his chest. It wasn't a stretch to assume Jay might be ringing him on a burner phone, but when he started considering the myriad reasons she might find it necessary to use said burner phone, pleasurable flip-flops turned to unpleasant pangs, and chills goosed his spine. He'd been trying to convince himself he was okay with Jay going off on her own. But he wasn't okay with it—not in the least.

Tyler wanted to have Jay's back in case anything went pear-shaped.

He wanted to eyeball this Seth Williams dude—clue him in on the heap of hurt coming his way if anything happened to Jay.

He wanted her safely back home. With him.

He grabbed his cell from the counter... and wasn't sure whether to be relieved or concerned to recognize his old roommate's number. He swiped the screen to accept the call. "Yo, Chandler."

"You got a sec?"

"Sure. 'Zup?"

"Tell me 'bout this asshole stalking Nessa."

Ah, shit. How much did Chandler know? Could be he was fishing for info, which meant Tyler couldn't risk inadvertently revealing too much. "Better ask Nessa," he said.

"Already have. And between her'n Jay, I'm not exactly happy 'bout what I'm hearing."

Jay had called *Chandler* instead of him…. If betrayal felt like a sharp pointy object lodging in his chest cavity then Tyler was experiencing a textbook case of it right now. "You spoke to Jay? When? And why the hell did she call you?"

"Yep. Coupl'a hours ago. Nessa phoned her but Jay insisted on having a word with me."

A cool wave of relief diluted the anger that had come hard on the heels of that illogical sense of betrayal.

Before Tyler could think of something halfway intelligent to say, Chandler added, "We're on our way back from Snapperton—were staying at the motel. And Nessa starts freaking out because she thinks she spotted this stalker, right? So rather than wake me and clue me in so I can rip the asshole a new one, she rings *your* girlfriend—who tells me to get Ness the hell out of there, and leave *her* to deal with it. Wanna tell me what the fuck is going on, Tyler?"

The super-pricey coffee tuned to acid in Tyler's gut. Man, Chandler was totally gone on Nessa—Tyler had never heard his old roommate sound so amped and ready to kick ass. And if Chandler got it in his head to drop Nessa off and head back down to Snapperton on his own to look for Sixer, it wasn't going to end well for Chandler. Sixer was not someone you took on face-to-face without six different kinds of backup, and even then you were playing with fire. Hell, it was all Tyler could do to stay on the line rather than hang up on his friend and immediately call home to warn his dad that Sixer had been spotted at Snapperton Motel.... And then hightail it down there in Jay's SUV to help his dad insure their family's safety.

Not that there was a helluva lot either of them could do if the rogue cyborg decided to pay a visit but Tyler wasn't gonna think about that right now.

The logical part of his brain insisted his best option was to sit tight and let Jay deal to Sixer. Without some kind of enhanced weapon—which neither Tyler nor his dad possessed—she was the only one with the slightest chance of taking Sixer out. Tyler had to trust that she would prevail and come back to him in one piece.

Now all he had to do was convince Chandler of that fact, too—without letting on that both Tyler's girlfriend and Nessa's supposed stalker were not exactly human.

Shit. What a cluster-fuck. He racked his brains for the right words and finally settled for, "Look, this guy is bad news, okay? Real bad news. So if Jay says she'll handle him, for fuck's sake stay out of it and let her do what she's gotta do. Jay's got... *resources* she can call on, okay? Best thing you can do is keep an eye on Nessa—who, by the way, will never forgive herself if you do something stupid and wind up dead."

There. Couldn't be much more blunt than that without revealing that Jay and Sixer were cyborgs.

Chandler huffed a POed-sounding breath while Tyler held his, hoping he'd convinced his friend to drop it. And finally, after what seemed like a fricking lifetime, Chandler said, "Duly noted. Gotta go. Nessa's on her way back to the car with the coffees. Talk to you when we get home."

And won't that be fun, Tyler thought as he disconnected the call.

He crammed the last bit of waffle into his mouth and rang his dad's cell.

Mike Davidson picked up on the second ring. "You'd better have a damn good reason for calling this early, Tyler."

Tyler choked down his mouthful of waffle. There was no easy way to say this so he opted for factual and blunt. "Nessa spotted Sixer at Snapperton Motel around two hours ago."

A pause and then a heartfelt, "Shit. Is Vanessa okay? Do you need me to go get her?"

"Yeah, she's okay. Chandler's with her. They're already on the road, heading for home—Jay's orders, apparently."

"Apparently?"

"Nessa rang Jay—I haven't spoken to either of them, so this is coming secondhand from Chandler. He thinks Sixer is a stalker, by the way. Jay told him she'd deal with Sixer but…. Shit, Dad, this is freaking me out. Want me to drive down so I can back you up if he shows?"

"If Jay wanted you here, she'd have rung you herself. Stay put, Tyler. Caro's at Matt's, so she's safely out of the way. I'm on leave for another week, so I guarantee your mom and Danny won't be left alone in the house."

Tyler bit the inside of his cheek until he tasted blood. It was Jay's house, and he shouldn't be making offers like this without running it by her first, but…. Hell. It was an emergency. "There's plenty of space here. We have two guestrooms."

"Your mom's trying to settle Danny into a routine—you know how stubborn she can be. But I'll see if I can talk her into taking a holiday."

A brush-off if ever Tyler had heard one. But no way was he leaving his dad to face Sixer alone. Tyler had faced off against Sixer once, and he wouldn't wish that experience on anyone—

not even a bona fide badass like his dad.

"Are *you* gonna tell Mom that Sixer's currently in Snapperton, or shall I?" Tyler figured his dad would be pissed by the threat, but right now, he didn't give a shit. Hadn't they just dealt with fallout from the last bunch of secrets?

"I'll tell her," his dad said, and it took three discordant beeps down the line before Tyler realized he'd hung up.

He slumped against the counter, ignoring the granite edge grating against his spine. That had gone well. Not. He had a sinking feeling that Jay wasn't gonna be at all happy with him either, because if she'd wanted Tyler's dad to have the latest intel on Sixer's whereabouts, she'd have rung him herself. Right?

Right, dammit. Jay was sure to have it covered, and his interference might have stuck one big-ass spoke in her carefully laid plans.

He pinched the bridge of his nose until his eyes watered. Just as well he planned on writing songs and hopefully selling the odd piece of artwork to earn a dime because he royally sucked at all this covert BS. Hopefully he'd do better at interrogating Jay's part-time boss Allen without appearing to, like, *interrogate* him.

Tyler dumped his plate and mug in the sink and headed upstairs to take a shower. A cold one. Because damn, he needed to get his head in the game or he'd screw up the one task Jay had trusted him with.

TYLER LUCKED OUT and found a park right outside number fifteen Honeysuckle Street—a property that housed Beanz Café in front, and Allen's private studio and rooms out back. Despite its location in a primarily residential area, Beanz was such a popular hangout parking spaces were often scarce. No surprises there. Any place that offered consistently excellent coffee at halfway reasonable prices tended to be a popular haunt for coffee aficionados.

He grabbed Brum's leash before the excited puppy escaped out the open car door. He tucked the pup under his arm, wincing as Brum reacted to the *blip blip!* of the remote engaging the door locks with a series of high-pitched yips… that startled an exiting café patron into slopping some of the contents of her takeaway cup over her wrist.

The beverage must have been hot because she'd removed the lid to blow on it—hence the amount of liquid she was currently flicking from her wrist and the POed expression on her face.

Ah, crap. "I'm real sorry 'bout that." Tyler tightened his grip on the squirming bundle of puppy. "He's a bit excitable after the car trip."

The woman glanced up from her wrist, her cold narrow-eyed gaze indicating he was in for a blistering public set-down. Instead, her features softened and her lips pursed. "Oh my," she said, "what a beautiful little GSP."

At Tyler's frown of incomprehension she said, "German Shorthaired Pointer. I used to know someone who bred them."

"Oh, yeah. Now I remember my girlfriend mentioning they're called GSPs."

Brum's legs wheeled, and Tyler secured him more firmly beneath his armpit. "He's her dog," he felt compelled to add. "My girlfriend's."

The woman—tall and lean with über-short white hair—moved closer. She held out her fingers for Brum to sniff before stroking his head and scratching behind his ears. When she stopped scratching, Brum butted his head against her hand, demanding more attention. "You're such a charmer—oh yes you are!" she cooed, the sweetness of her tone at odds with her spare, no-nonsense appearance and her clothing: black pants, white t-shirt and black canvas slip-ons.

Abruptly she cast her piercing gray gaze over Tyler, giving him a thorough head-to-toer that had him squirming.

Uh oh. She had to be at least a couple of decades older than him. Why was this happening? Did he have "My girlfriend's out of town, hit on me!" tattooed on his forehead or something?

He was mentally reviewing his woefully inadequate stock of polite conversation-stoppers when she asked, "What's his name?"

Tyler's shoulders sagged with relief. Not that he was arrogant enough to believe he was irresistible or anything, but this morning's close encounters of the female persuasion had made him a little antsy. "His name's Brum—short for *Brummer*."

"Great name. It's German, right?"

"Yeah." He'd opened his mouth, intending to mention Jay was training Brum to respond to German commands, when instinct prodded him to err on the side of caution. He swallowed the comment. He didn't know this woman, didn't recall seeing her around, couldn't be sure of her motives. She seemed genuine enough but for all he knew, she might be a plant sent by the same people who'd left the photo of Beta with Allen.

The woman seemed to be waging some internal debate because her brow pleated and she nibbled her lower lip. Finally, just when the silence was getting awkward, she said, "Your girlfriend's not planning to show him, is she? I hate to say it, but this little guy wouldn't get anywhere because of his yellow eyes and the black saddles on his coat."

By "saddles" Tyler figured she meant the patches of black among the speckle-y bits on Brum's coat.

"I'm almost positive she has no intention of showing him," he told her. "My dad got him for her—purely for companionship." Though that wasn't the whole truth, because Brum was the result of a dumbass bet his dad had made that Jay couldn't crack his laptop password in under ten minutes or something. "I'm sure he'd have given her a choice of puppies if she'd mentioned wanting to breed them or do shows and stuff."

"That's good then." The woman fondled Brum's ears. "There are some less than honest breeders out there, and I'd hate to hear your dad got taken for a ride."

"Me, too." It wasn't like his folks were rolling in money.

"Please don't take what I said the wrong way—this little guy's gorgeous, and he'll make a wonderful companion if he's properly trained." She wrinkled her nose. "But if he's not being shown or bred, there's no reason to dock his tail."

"Huh?" Tyler blinked, wondering if he'd heard right.

The woman hitched the strap of her knapsack more firmly over her shoulder, and took a swig of her beverage. The corners of her mouth turned down. Either whatever she was drinking tasted real bad, or she wasn't too happy about something.

"Unfortunately these guys often have their tails docked," she said. "Pointers are working dogs. Docking's supposed to decrease instances of tail injuries when they're hunting. And there are those who think it's more aesthetically pleasing."

She must have interpreted the disgust Tyler was feeling right now from his expression because she nodded sharply, and when she spoke again her tone was scathing. "I'm not one of those idiots who think it looks 'prettier', either." She bent to bring her face level with Brum as she tickled the pup under the chin. "So I'm guessing no docking for you, huh, Brum?"

Brum enthusiastically licked her cheek.

"Absolutely no docking," Tyler agreed. And he was one hundred percent sure Jay would be with him on *that*.

"Better check your girlfriend's on the same page, though," the woman said, eerily tapping in to Tyler's thoughts. "Wouldn't want Brum to go through a procedure like that for no reason."

"I will. Thanks." He stuck out his hand. "I'm Tyler, by the way."

"Marg. Nice to meet you, Tyler. And you, too, Brum." She drained the last of her coffee, and tossed the disposable cup in the trashcan. "Might see you 'round, Tyler," she said, and strode off down the street.

Tyler watched until she rounded the corner and disappeared from view. There was something fluid about the way Marg moved, some indefinable quality that made him think she would totally kick ass in a karate dojo—or any dojo for that matter.

He closed his eyes for a moment, committing her features to memory so he could sketch her when he got the chance. And then he opened the catch of the wrought iron gate, and carefully shut it behind him before setting Brum on the ground.

"Heel, Brum," he said, figuring it was worth a try. Of course Brum took no notice whatsoever, and took off down the cobbled pathway leading to the rear of the property, forcing Tyler into a run for fear the pup would hurt himself when he reached the end of the lead.

Allen hailed them from the bench seat beneath what Tyler thought might be a cherry tree. "Hey, Brummer."

Jay's occasional employer looked disreputable as ever in one of his many paint-stained shirts over baggy gray sweatpants. His bushy red mane was somewhat tamed for a change, having been scraped into a ponytail and secured with a frayed piece of twine.

Brum made a beeline for Allen and tried to leap into his lap... only to fail dismally, his hindquarters scrabbling for purchase on

Allen's outstretched legs. Allen, juggling a large pottery mug as well as a takeaway cup emblazoned with the Beanz logo, simply lifted both legs, allowing Brum to slither down into his lap.

"Nice moves." Tyler flopped onto the bench beside Allen. A glance at his watch told him he had plenty of time before his first class. Sheesh. The day had barely started and he felt worn out already.

"Rough night, eh?"

Allen's blue eyes twinkled as he handed Tyler the takeaway cup, and Tyler's brain chose that inconvenient moment to replay a rather graphic memory from the night before. He hid his flush by removing the lid and inhaling the aroma of hot, freshly brewed coffee. "Try early start—no thanks to this little guy. And you, Allen, are a god. I swear the coffee I had before heading out this morning didn't even touch the sides on its way down."

"So happened I was next in queue to get my morning poison when you rang, so consider it your reward for letting me know you were on your way." Allen drained his mug—he didn't see the point of wasting disposable cups when he was only zipping next door for coffee—and set it on the grass before turning his full attention to Brum. "So, Brum, since we can't paint your delightful mistress, how d'you feel about being our model for the next couple of days?"

Tyler choked down his mouthful of coffee before he spewed it all over himself from laughing. "Good luck with that. The only time this little guy ever sits still is when he's chowing down or sleeping. I took him for a walk this morning so he'd be tuckered out most of the day, but no such luck. It's cat-naps only, I'm afraid."

"Nothing like setting the guys a bit of a challenge." Allen dangled the drawstring of his sweatpants in front of Brum and let the pup gnaw on it. "McPhee's offered to take him for a walk if he gets too rambunctious. McPhee claims he needs the exercise, though between you and me, I think the old man can't paint dogs to save himself."

A pack-a-day voice retorted, "Happens I can paint dogs and other animals just fine, Allen. I'm simply far more inspired if the subject matter happens to be a pretty young *human* thing."

Tyler glanced around and spotted a man of around seventy, with a shock of thick white hair and a neat goatee. He lay on the grass, partially hidden in the shadow of another tree.

Tyler recognized McPhee, the artist who'd painted the nude of Jay that made Tyler's whole being thrum with awe… and more than a little envy. He would give his eyeteeth to possess half that much talent with brush and canvas.

McPhee's eyes were closed, hands clasped over his belly, bare feet neatly crossed at the ankle. And he was dressed in pajamas and a robe. Putting two and two together, Tyler's eyes rounded. Jay hadn't mentioned anything about Allen and McPhee being a *couple*. Perhaps this was a new development?

Before he could school his features again, Allen said, "Does it bother you?"

"That you and McPhee are a couple? Nope. Doesn't bother me at all." Since that was the God's honest truth, Tyler prayed he sounded sincere.

One of the guys in his high school basketball team had been outed but having a gay teammate had never bothered Tyler in the slightest. The same couldn't be said of the team captain, who'd made it his personal mission to make the guy's life hell until he voluntarily dropped out of the team. And eventually changed schools. But then, Shawn had always been a first-class douche, so no one had been surprised by his shitty behavior toward a teammate. And a part of Tyler wondered how McPhee and Allen would judge *him* if they learned what Jay was... and that Tyler was sleeping with her.

Allen slapped him lightly on the arm. "I meant that McPhee is a lascivious old bastard who adores painting beautiful girls—like your Jay."

Heat seared Tyler's face. Ah, crap. He'd gotten it all wrong and—

"Quit teasing the youngster, Allen." McPhee climbed to his feet and brushed himself down. "You know Miss Jay wouldn't approve."

"Are you threatening to tell tales on me?" Allen's gasp and the way his hand flew to his heart were Oscar-worthy.

"Absolutely."

"Humph. Go get some clothes on before I—"

"Embarrass our guest by jumping my old bones?"

"Oooh! You think you're irresistible, don't you?"

"Absolutely, darling," McPhee said, straight-faced. And then added, "Consider that endearment a public display of affection, and you'll henceforth refrain from accusing me of being embarrassed to be seen with you."

Tyler bit his lips to keep from snickering at Allen's scandalized expression. The man had certainly met his match in McPhee.

McPhee whistled and clicked his fingers at Brum, who promptly discarded the now soggy drawstring he'd been chewing and leaped from Allen's lap.

It would have been an impressive leap, too, if the pup hadn't gotten tangled up in his lead and done a face-plant on the grass. Allen, muttering to himself, set Brum to rights and unclipped the pup's leash, leaving Brum to hare off after McPhee.

"Are you sure you're okay with dog-sitting?" Tyler asked. "Brum can be a real handful."

Allen coiled the leash and then slumped against the seatback. "The puppy can't be any harder to handle than McPhee. That man…. I swear he has me running in circles."

"I know the feeling."

It was now or never. Aiming for light and casual, Tyler said, "Jay wanted me to ask if you could shed any light on whoever left that envelope for her—the one McPhee dropped off a few days back. Jay'd really like to get in touch to, uh, thank them."

Allen squinted into the distance, giving off classic "trying my best to remember" vibes. "Whoever delivered the envelope slipped it under the door—" a wave of his hand indicated the side doors leading into the studio "—and I found it when I came to open up for class. Figured it'd been dropped off by one of the Beanz staff, but then I thought about it some more and realized that was unlikely. The staff might have spotted our Jay coming and going, but none of them would know her by name, so they would surely have quizzed me about it first. *I* certainly haven't mentioned Jay's name to the staff—it's none of their business who she is, or what her name happens to be. I'm very particular about that sort of thing where my life models are concerned."

Noting Tyler's frown he added, "Stalkers. Jealous partners. People out to stir up trouble, or just plain old nosey busybodies. You name it, we've encountered 'em at some stage. Even had one so-called artist so enamored with one of the models, he tried taking sneaky photos of her on his cell phone. Needless to say, after said cell phone had a bit of an accident beneath McPhee's boot heel, our would-be photographer was escorted from the premises. Blacklisted the sleazy bastard, too—banned him signing up for further classes and put the word out around the artsy community."

"Good job," Tyler said, conveniently failing to mention that he'd spied on Jay when she'd first begun life modeling at the studio. At the time, he hadn't believed he was good enough for her—had convinced himself she was seeing someone else. He rubbed his chin, a wry smile tugging his lips at the memory. Yeah, he'd been a first degree dumbass.

"I wouldn't want anyone taking nude photos of Jay and posting them online," Allen said. "Not without her express permission."

A chill snaked down Tyler's spine. The consequences Jay being videoed while tossing Shawn into a dumpster a couple of years back had been dire enough. But now, after everything that had gone down? Chances were, Jay wouldn't even need to be performing some extraordinary feat for online pics of her to spark a nightmare scenario. In fact....

Tyler rubbed his arms as the chill turned to frost. *In fact*, it probably wasn't the best idea for Jay to life model for a bunch of artist-types, either. Life modeling nude could hardly be considered keeping a low profile. "Allen, have any of your life models been harassed? I mean, after being recognized from a sketch or painting or whatever—like, if the artworks are sold or exhibited."

Allen seemed to understand what Tyler was getting at. "I insist the model sign a release if artworks they've posed for have the slightest chance of being exhibited or sold in the future. But even if Jay *had* signed a release—which she hasn't, I might add— it's very unlikely any pieces that featured her would be put up for sale. They're practice pieces, nothing more."

It was on the tip of Tyler's tongue to ask why, if Allen's artist friends sucked so bad at painting nudes they never had a hope of selling any of their completed artworks, they bothered turning up week after week. But then he recalled a trip to a local gallery with his classmates. The paintings on display hadn't been to his taste, except for one—an abstract that had affected him so viscerally, he'd bitten his tongue for fear he'd offer to sell everything he owned to possess it. The gallery owner, seeing his interest, had told him the artist's name was Allen Miller. And the price? High enough to make Tyler break out in a sweat. Consequently, he'd been gob-smacked to learn *Jay's* Allen was in fact the illustrious Allen Miller.

Tyler clamped his lips tightly shut. Allen didn't suck. Neither did McPhee. Chances were, neither did any of the other artists who made use of Allen's studio space. And if there was the slightest chance *Tyler* had that degree of talent hidden inside him, it sure would make his dilemma about whether to concentrate fully on music versus art, a heap more simple.

"I always go for a wander during classes," Allen was saying. "I like to check out how everyone's faring—call me nosey, but it's my damn studio space so I can do what I like. And here's the thing: Jay's ability to sit still for hours on end meant we could experiment to our hearts' content with various techniques for hair and skin, and all manner of different mediums. We all sketched her in various poses. But she's flawless, your Jay, and that makes her a difficult subject to capture. A couple of the more established artists—me, included—gave it a try, but none of us were happy with the end result." Allen made a moue. "Lifeless and flat—like we'd painted an exquisite, flawless robot rather than a living, breathing girl."

Shee-it. Was that a hint that Allen had figured out what Jay was? Tyler's heart pounded so loudly it seemed to thunder in his ears. He quickly dropped his gaze to his feet and fiddled with a shoelace in an effort to hide his expression from Allen's too perceptive artist's gaze. When he thought he had his reactions under control, he straightened and dared dart a glance at the older man.

Allen's gaze was distant, his features lax and peaceful—so completely the opposite of a man closely observing his target to confirm some suspicion, that Tyler allowed himself to relax.

"McPhee's the only one who had the balls to complete a full piece," Allen finally said. "But he had no intention of selling the painting—he always intended it for Jay. And, if I accurately recall her expression when he promised it to her, she has no desire to sell it."

"Definitely not," Tyler said. "It's far too precious."

Allen's expression turned smug. "A very talented man, that McPhee."

"You're a gifted artist, too, Allen. I saw one of your works in a local gallery a few months back. It was...." He struggled to find the right words and gave up the battle. He'd speak from the heart and hope Allen didn't take offense. "It was fucking incredible."

"Why thank you, Tyler."

Noting the suppressed laughter, Tyler felt heat crawl up his neck. "Sorry. Guess I'll never make an art critic, huh?"

This time, Allen laughed outright. "Probably not, lovey. But I'll take 'fucking incredible' any day over the overwrought, adjective-ridden bullshit that's often attributed to my paintings." He scratched his chin with one paint-grimed fingernail. "To return to our original subject, I can save you some sleuthing. I've already quizzed the café staff and can confirm none of them dropped off the envelope. Meaning someone knew Jay had an association with me. And that someone strolled right through my gate, bold as brass, and stuffed the envelope under my studio door."

Tyler unsuccessfully hid a wince. "It kinda looks bad, doesn't it?"

Allen's brows arched. "Perhaps. Or it could all be very innocent. Even so, the thought of some stranger snooping around my private property when they could have simply stuck the envelope in my mailbox makes me a little edgy. May I ask what was in it?"

"A photo. Of a... relative."

Tyler didn't see any real harm in revealing that. Ditto with revealing as much of the truth as possible. "One Jay didn't know she had," he added. "But there's only a name on the back of the photo—no contact details." Fingers crossed Allen wasn't on Jay's level when it came to detecting deliberate ambiguities meant to shield the truth.

"Ah. A bona fide mystery, indeed. Sorry I can't shed more light on it."

A hunch prodded—too insistent to ignore, so Tyler went with it. "Can I borrow some sketch paper and a pencil? I want to see if you recognize someone."

Curiosity lit Allen's eyes but if he had questions, he kept them to himself. "Of course," he said, unfolding his lanky form from the bench and ambling toward the studio doors.

Tyler hesitated, debating whether that had been an invitation to follow. Allen didn't allow just anyone into the inner sanctum of the studio: He was leery of letting strangers view the various incomplete artworks scattered around. Tyler had been invited inside once, when he'd swung by after class to pick up Jay but she'd committed to staying on a bit longer. He'd give everything he owned to spend an afternoon with Allen and McPhee and the rest of the class, observing their techniques—maybe even working on one of his own projects... if he could work up the courage.

"You coming or not?" Allen threw over his shoulder. "Morning's not getting any younger."

Tyler didn't need to be asked twice. He catapulted from his seat and sprinted up the stairs into the studio.

Inside, Allen handed over a sketchbook and a charcoal pencil. "This do you?"

Tyler flipped open the sketchbook and took his first broad sweep with the charcoal. The quality of both paper and pencil made his mouth water. They were, for want of a better description, *beautiful* to use.

As he sketched and smudged and shaded, bringing the face fixed in his brain to life on the page, part of his mind wandered to more prosaic matters. Jay would have happily purchased all Tyler's art supplies, except he had made it abundantly clear he wasn't a charity case. So far, she'd respected his wishes and only splurged for his birthday or Christmas gifts. Now, using some of the supplies Allen seemed to take for granted, Tyler wondered if he shouldn't quit being so uptight and use the credit card Jay had given him, rather than stubbornly working his ass off to afford even cheap, substandard supplies.

He tuned back in to the real world and checked his sketch of the woman he'd encountered out front of Beanz.

Hmmm. Good enough. Rotating the sketchbook, he handed it to Allen. "Recognize her?"

Allen examined the sketch. "Beautifully rendered, Tyler. Well done."

Warmth pooled in the pit of Tyler's belly at the compliment and, worried he would make a dick of himself by tripping over his tongue if he spoke, he let the arching of his brows ask the question.

"She's an interesting looking woman," Allen said. "But no, I don't recognize her. Should I?"

Tyler hid his disappointment with a shrug, glad for the distraction provided by Brum, who'd scampered back into the studio and now butted his head against Allen's calves, demanding attention.

McPhee materialized from wherever he'd been lurking, and held out an imperious hand for the sketchbook. Tyler's stomach flipped and rolled as he awaited the verdict, and he privately admitted it wasn't only because he still held some small hope his hunch would pan out, and maybe McPhee would recognize the woman's face. A compliment from *this* man would be a real confidence-booster.

"Good job, lad," McPhee pronounced. "An excellent rendition of her, too."

Excitement drowned Tyler's pleasure at McPhee's approval. "You've seen this woman before?"

McPhee nodded. "As I left Miss Jay's house after dropping off the painting and delivering that envelope for Allen. I never forget a face—certainly not one as memorable as hers."

Tyler swallowed to moisten a suddenly dry throat, and hoped his eagerness didn't show. "Oh?"

His laidback response seemed to have worked because McPhee readily volunteered more information. "She was leaning on a car bonnet—looked to me as though she was waiting for someone," he said. "The vehicle was parked out front of the neighboring property." His brow creased into deep furrows. "An unremarkable sedan—light gray in color. A Honda Accord, I believe."

Tyler's breath caught and he had to force his next question from his throat. Please God he sounded casual. "Don't suppose you recall any of the license plate at all?"

One of McPhee's bushy eyebrows formed a perfect arc. "Of

course I do, lad. In fact, I recall the entire plate." He tapped his temple with a gnarled forefinger. "Trick memory."

Tyler's breath gusted from his lips. Man, Jay was gonna be stoked!

And then McPhee delivered his ultimatum. "And provided you tell me exactly what's going on, I might be inclined to share that piece of information with you."

Tyler stared helplessly at McPhee, and debated whether to back off and let Jay handle him.

Ah, crap. If the gleam in the old dude's eyes was any indicator, it was far too late for that. Fingers crossed he could keep his stories straight… and that McPhee was as accepting as Allen had been of Tyler's attempts to avoid revealing the whole truth.

CHAPTER NINE

THE WEAPON IN Seth's hand wavered and then the muzzle tipped slowly downward. "You *sure* you want me to do this?" he asked again.

"Yes. I'm sure." Jay now understood why humans offered prayers to various deities in the hope of being granted something desirable—more patience, for example.

"But what if my aim is off?"

"Then it'll take a little longer than anticipated for me to heal." Of course, if he shot her in the head, her capacity to heal herself might be compromised and lead to permanent impairment, but she saw no reason to add to his stress levels.

He blotted beads of perspiration from his brow with the back of his wrist... using the hand currently holding the weapon.

"Seth. Please watch where you're aiming. If you accidentally shoot the projectile into the wall or ceiling—"

"Shit!" He yanked his hand down, and reassumed the stance she'd painstakingly coached him to assume. "Sorry. It's just I've never had to, you know, shoot someone at point blank range before."

Jay refrained from correcting him. Seth was unlikely to appreciate an explanation of the exact definition of "point-blank range" at this current moment. Instead, she gave him what she hoped was an encouraging smile.

"Jesus-H-Roosevelt-Christ," he said, "will you please quit smiling? It's bad enough I have to freaking *shoot* you, without you standing there and grinning like you're expecting to enjoy it or something."

Jay schooled her features to neutrality and confined her answering sigh to a soft, inaudible exhalation. "Sorry."

"'Sokay. You ready?"

She bit back a retort to the effect that she'd been standing here, "ready", for four-point-seven minutes, and merely nodded.

Seth muttered something that might have been his version of a prayer, aimed, and squeezed the trigger.

Jay pulled a picture of Tyler from her databanks and fixed it in her mind. But as projectile pierced her flesh, the picture exploded in a kaleidoscope of crackling sparks... and everything went black.

A DISCORDANT BUZZING, like a horde of angry bees, echoed in her skull. Seconds passed—or perhaps minutes, she wasn't certain—before the buzzing faded, allowing her to identify a male voice swearing beneath his breath. She analyzed the voice and identified it as Seth Kyle Williams.

How much time had passed? Had he proven himself friend or foe?

Since that second question was impossible to determine as yet, her instincts for self-preservation prompted her to fine-tune her auditory sensors until she could make out exactly what he was saying.

"She's not waking up. She should have woken up by now. Fuck. Fuck! I knew this was a bad idea. We should have tested the fucking things on Sixer—be doing the world a favor if that piece of shit never woke up. Fuck, Jay. Why did you make me do this to you? And what the *fuck* am I gonna tell your boyfriend?"

Ah. Friend, then. For surely no foe would sound so desolated by the prospect of her demise. Apparently Seth had successfully extracted the DEP—Directed Energy Projectile, as he'd insisted on renaming the reengineered bullet. Apparently, he could be trusted, after all.

The knowledge made her smile. It would not have been an easy task to eliminate a human she genuinely liked if Seth had played her false. Of course, she'd had a contingency plan in the event he *had* decided a comatose cyborg was more to his liking. But it was... *nice* to know the countermeasures she'd planned would not be required.

"Shee-iit. Is that—? Damn, it is! You're awake and you're fucking *smiling* while I'm standing here freaking out? You... you... heinous robot *bitch!*"

Jay forced open her eyelids, focused, and found herself staring into a pair of worried gray eyes. "It worked," she told him, the words a barely intelligible croak. She swallowed to lubricate her throat and tried again. "It worked. We possess a weapon that will incapacitate Sixer with one shot."

"Yeah," he said, lips curving in such a woeful attempt at a smile that it took Jay longer than it should have to correctly identify the expression.

She experimentally wriggled her toes. And then her fingers. All good. "You put me on the gurney," she said, wondering why he would exert himself to do so. She was, after all, heavier than her physical appearance suggested, and unconscious bodies were often referred to as "dead weight" for good reason.

"You were standing stock-still in the middle of the room—not the optimum position for minor surgery. I could have tipped you onto the floor, I guess, but that's not very hygienic. I figured the gurney was the best option."

"Hygiene is not something to worry about when performing minor surgery on me, but thank you."

"How are you? Everything working properly?"

"I believe so."

Her attempt to sit up was unsuccessful and barely raised her spine from the gurney before she was forced to give up and flop back against it. This didn't overly concern her, however. It was far too soon to be concerned. In an effort to distract Seth, she asked, "Have you checked the weapon and the firing mechanism for damage?"

"Yeah. It's sweet. Sixer's going down for sure."

"If I am not mistaken—which is a distinct possibility given my current state—you are unhappy."

"Hell yes, I'm unhappy!"

"Why?"

"Because you shouldn't have tested this on yourself, Jay. You were out for so long after I dug out the fucking DEP, I was beginning to think it had permanently scrambled your core programming or something equally dire." He fumbled in the pocket of his chinos for his inhaler, and took a puff to calm his ragged breathing.

Jay accessed her internal timekeeping mechanism, which had stopped as soon as the projectile's electro-magnetic-pulse shorted out her systems. It was a simple matter of calculating the length of the "blank" that had occurred while her systems had not been taking in any data.

"I was 'out' for a total of forty-three-point-two minutes," she informed Seth. Longer than she'd anticipated, but not a time span to be overly concerned about. "How long do you estimate it took you to locate and remove the projectile?"

"I performed the extraction around twenty minutes after I got you on the gurney—give or take." At her raised eyebrows he added, "There were no complications, and the actual extraction went like clockwork. But my hands were shaking so I took a moment—okay, more than a moment—to get my shit together before I started the extraction." He compressed his lips. "So sue me."

It was on the tip of her tongue to respond to his snippy tone by saying something pithy. Instead, she murmured, "I appreciate your caution."

"Least I could do. You know, having fricking *shot* you, and all."

Jay chose to ignore the sarcasm. "Allowing for the time taken to get me on the gurney—say, five minutes?" She waited for his nod. "Adding the delay while you composed yourself, and the time taken to perform the extraction—"

"Five minutes at most for the extraction."

"Thank you. Then we can reasonably assume a window of approximately fifteen minutes after removal of projectile before a system reset occurs and functionality begins to return."

While she observed Seth mentally running the data, Jay considered the viability of a projectile that could emit a sustained EMP over a specified time span. For now, it was not a priority but she would keep it in mind.

"Fifteen minutes?" Seth mused. "Yeah, that'd be my take." A flush crawled up his neck. "Shit. You must think I'm a dipshit-and-a-half."

"Why would I think that?"

"Because I was too keyed up to think of using a stopwatch to note down exact times, and now we're guessing. Talk about

Science 101 epic fail."

"Not at all." Jay didn't deem it necessary to admit recording the incident on a hidden security cam—part of her contingency plan had Seth played her false.

She tensed her abdominals, propping her torso on her elbows in another effort to sit up.

Seth promptly slipped an arm about her back to assist. When he released her, Jay glanced down at her belly. The wound had been closed with neat sutures. She pulled down her t-shirt. "Nice job. I couldn't have done better myself. Thank you, Seth." Because she was mindful of the care he'd taken with her, she didn't mention that the sutures had been unnecessary: The wound would heal regardless, and wouldn't leave a scar.

"I've stitched a few wounds in my time," he said.

She waited for him to elaborate but he only murmured, "Speaking of bullets," and held out a small metal basin. "While I was waiting for you to return to what passes for the land of the living for sentient cyborgs, I cleaned it. I didn't screw with it, if that's what you're wondering—was waiting for you to wake up and give me permission."

She caught and held his gaze. "I trust that had I not eventually regained functionality, you would have taken steps to discover my modifications and replicate them."

"You betcha. No way I'd toss away my best chance of taking Sixer down if you'd not come through."

He scratched his head, looking…. What did humans call that slightly embarrassed "you got me" expression again? Ah. *Sheepish.* "I planned on giving you twenty-four hours to wake up," he said. "Provided I could hold out that long without going ape-shit with worry."

"An extremely generous time span," Jay told him. "It is unlikely I would have afforded you the same recovery period had our situations been reversed." She examined the projectile. Noting it had come through the experiment unscathed, she flipped it back into the basin. "It should require only a recharge to be fully effective. I have two more identically modified projectiles. This one is all yours, Seth."

Rather than snatch it up and immediately begin dissecting it, Seth set the basin aside. "I can tell you one thing I'd change about the design," he said.

His carefully emotionless tone made her focus more closely on his facial expressions and body language. "And that is?"

"I'd design projectiles along the lines of nanorobots—build in a program that prompts them to automatically exit the target. Maybe even self-destruct if they can't be retrieved."

"An interesting suggestion, Seth."

"Nothing like digging around in a chick's abdomen to get the old creative juices flowing."

His humor was a little off. And his smile, while fully formed this time, was the slightest bit crooked and sat uneasily on his face.

Jay guessed he'd suffered a degree of psychological trauma while "digging around" in her abdomen. She found herself truly regretful for what she had forced him to do, however there had been no other logical option available to her. It had been either Seth or Tyler. And Seth, with his knowledge of cyborg core programming, and far reduced degree of emotional involvement, had been by far the better option than Tyler—not that Jay believed she would have had the slightest chance of convincing Tyler to shoot her.

"I'm sorry you had to do this, Seth."

"You ever heard the saying, 'Don't thank me, buy me something'?"

"I can't say I've come across that one but it does sound like something Caro would say."

He shook his head in a half-hearted manner. "Lemme guess, another friend of yours?"

"My best friend, to be precise. Caro was the first human to truly accept me for what I am. She's also my boyfriend's twin sister."

"Now that's a story I wouldn't mind hearing." Seth reached out to snag a stool. He pulled it close and flopped onto it, crossing his arms over his chest.

"Perhaps later. You were saying?"

"Oh, yeah. That. How about, 'Don't apologize to me, just put me out of my misery.'"

Jay registered that her brow had crinkled in automatic response to her confusion. "You are miserable? Why?"

"This is not one of those times when you should take a human literally, Jay. In fact, I'll be the complete opposite of miserable if you clue me in on the real reason you brought me to your super-secret underground lab." He flicked a finger at the basin. "'S not like you can't churn out plenty more of these babies if you're inclined. I mean, sure, give me enough time to figure out what you've tweaked and I can make more of 'em, but you could do it a helluva lot faster, right? So, how 'bout you tell me what you *really* want me for?"

A smart man, Seth Williams. Little wonder Evan Caine had recruited him, and then taken steps to make it nigh on impossible for him to leave. And only a cyborg could have detected the minute tremor in his voice—a physical "tell" that, among other things, informed her Seth was not as calm as he appeared.

Jay had often pondered the saying, "The truth will set you

free." Apparently she was about to experience firsthand what was so "freeing" about it.

"I've recently come across evidence that I have a sister," she said, focusing intently upon Seth to gauge his reaction.

He straightened from his slump. And…. There it was—the fascinating physiological response that morphed dull gray irises to cutting-edge silver.

"It's only a matter of time before I locate her," Jay continued. "But once I have, I believe it's highly likely I will require your assistance, because all indications are that she is defective."

She waited for him to jump in with questions but he merely motioned her to continue.

"The only information I have at this stage is that she is a Beta model."

Now Seth came straight to the point. "And you're a Gamma model. Which means she's your predecessor, correct?"

"Correct."

"God Al-freaking-mighty," he muttered, scrubbing his fingers through his hair and then shaking his head as if to clear his thoughts. "So, what are the chances the prototype Caine stole from Durham, and this Beta unit—your identical twin sister—are one and the same?"

Now wasn't the time to inform Seth that she was no longer identical to the Beta because she had aged her outer shell, and altered her skin tone and hair color. "What do you think?" she asked instead.

"Seems highly likely. There were rumors about Caine retiring a cyborg but that was before my time. I kinda figured they re-ferred to a dud predecessor of Sixer's." He snorted. "Figures Caine would scrap a defective unit—even if it was one of Durham's. The man had all the patience of a shark scenting blood. He always wanted results last week."

Jay let Seth brood on his former boss for a while. Unlike Evan Caine, she was perfectly capable of practicing patience when circumstances called for it.

Seth finally broke the hush with a question. "You reckon you can fix her—this Beta unit?"

"I won't know until I find her. But I'm hopeful that we—presuming you are prepared to assist me, of course—can do something to improve her prospects."

Seth's answering grin was not only full-blown but full of teeth. And the light in his eyes? Fanatically eager was an apt descriptor. "Sign me up," he said.

She cautioned him with a "Whoa there, buddy" palms-up gesture. "I need to explain exactly what this means for you."

"That I'm stuck here, in these nice digs with the awesome, super-secret underground lab, and can't poke my nose out the door for the duration?" He snorted. "So long as I'm regularly fed and watered, and there's cable to watch when I need a break from lab work—" He cast a hopeful gaze her way.

"Of course. The property will be fully staffed, with a chef at your beck and call."

"Then I'm your man. Because to be quite honest, Jay, even if you were a heinous bitch, you'd be a vast improvement over the mean-as-a-snake megalomaniac who was my hopefully now deceased former boss."

While she appreciated his enthusiasm, she wanted him absolutely clear what she required of him. "Seth, right now this may seem like a holiday in comparison to working for Caine, when in fact it is a somewhat more luxurious prison. You'll need to remain inside, and you won't be allowed to contact family or friends until I give the all-clear. Once I've dealt with Sixer the risk will decrease, but you'll need a bodyguard until I can identify and deal with whoever sent those men after you. If such restrictions are a deal breaker for you, then now's the time to speak up."

A twist of his mouth morphed his expression from eager to somber. "And if I think I can't handle it and want out, what then?"

Jay wrinkled her nose. "I'm not sure—I hadn't thought that far ahead. How does a pair of concrete boots and a deep stretch of water with your name on it sound to you?"

Seth goggled at her, his jaw agape. And then a gust of astonished laughter burst from him. "God. You really had me going there for a minute. Seriously, though—"

"*Seriously*, I truly hadn't thought that far ahead. I hoped you would be suitably grateful for the offer of protection from whatever Sixer had planned for you, eager to help with the Beta's rehabilitation, and resigned to letting me protect you until any possible threats are neutralized. But if you do want out, I can set you up with a new name, a bank account, and a life in another country."

His slow blink and unnatural—for Seth, anyway—stillness, suggested he was processing that last possibility, weighing up his options.

He linked his fingers and stretched both arms toward the ceiling, arching first to the left and then to the right, loosening tight muscles. "As nice as... I dunno, *Australia* sounds right now after being cooped up in that shithole motel, I'd rather stick around. And—" he again slanted her hopeful eyes "—I'd like to see my baby sis again before I have to take off for parts unknown."

"For the moment, the best way to keep Gabrielle safe is to let her believe you died when Sixer blew up the labs."

"Yeah, I know. Sucks that she thinks I'm dead, though. I'm the only close family she's got."

His slumped shoulders and the weariness in his tone prompted Jay to make another attempt at humor to cheer him up. "Besides, have you any idea how many dangerous animals they have in Australia?" She ticked each one off on her fingers. "Snakes. Spiders. Sharks. Crocodiles. Jellyfish. Oh, and let's not forget the blue-lined octopus and the stinging stonefish."

Seth looked like he didn't know whether to laugh or cry. "Jesus, Jay. You're a real piece of work."

She tried on her most hopeful puppy dog expression. "In a good way?"

He chuffed a laugh. "You bet."

"Come on." She swung her feet off the gurney, shuffled until she was perched on the edge, and held out her hand. "I don't want to end up on my ass, so help me down from this nightmare on wheels and we'll see what we can rustle you up for dinner."

She didn't need assistance, of course. Any lingering effects of the DEP had been negated, but he didn't need to know that. In her somewhat limited experience, human males liked to feel needed.

Seth heaved himself from the chair, grasped her beneath the elbows, and lifted her down from the gurney. His stomach chose that moment to give a loud rumble. "Right now, I could murder another Twinkie but at a pinch, a can of beans'll do."

"Oh, I think I can do better than that," Jay told him as he followed her through the exit. "There is no fresh food in stock right now, but there are adequate stores of canned and dried foodstuffs. I'm an excellent cook; I'm sure I can whip you up something tasty and sulfite-free in a jiffy."

"I'm not even going to ask how you know about my sulfite intolerance."

She tapped her temple with a forefinger. "Super-cyborg deductive powers—the exact same powers that make me a damn fine cook." She closed the door to the lab and confirmed the locks had engaged before tapping a sequence of numbers on the keypad. Above them, a muted *swoosh* indicated that the bookcase disguising the trapdoor entrance had shifted aside. It might not have been the most imaginative way of disguising the lab's presence, but it was what some people might term "an oldie but a goodie". Jay believed it highly unlikely that anyone would think to investigate the floor beneath a bookcase crammed full of genre fiction in a master bedroom.

"Don't forget the ability to punch through walls, sling a guy over your shoulder and leap a fence in a single bound," Seth said, trailing her up the stairs. "Oh and steal cars."

"That, too." Jay thumbed a remote control and watched the bookcase slide back in place. "Though considering I left the vehicle a few blocks from its original position, I prefer 'temporarily borrowing' to stealing." She handed the remote to Seth, and exited the bedroom.

Behind her, he loosed a perfect snort-laugh. "Duly noted. Thanks—for everything," he called after her. "And when you kick Sixer's ass, make sure you tell him it's from me."

Jay recalled the still healing bruises on Seth's face, and the way he'd nursed his ribs when he'd unfolded his lanky frame from the car. She halted to glance over her shoulder at him. "You'd better believe I will," she promised.

CYBORG UNIT SIX-POINT-0 had been created to resemble a young human male, and had quickly identified the benefits of adopting the appropriate masculine pronouns rather than referring to himself as "it".

It was not an acceptable label when one wished to pass as a human. For humans of Evan Caine's ilk, *it* was an object, a *thing*—less than human, which was an exquisite example of irony considering that Six-Point-0 was far superior to humans. At least, he was superior now that he was no longer a tool, subject to the whims of the humans who had built and programmed him to obey their commands. And for that, he had another cyborg to thank.

She—for Cyborg Unit Gamma-Dash-One had been created to resemble a young human female—had utilized various labels, most notably *Jay Smith* and *Jaime Smythson*. Six-Point-0 knew Gamma preferred "Jay" to any of the other identities she had assumed. He also knew enough about Gamma's history, and often illogical thought processes, to know that the name paid homage to her deceased creator—a man who had forced her to terminate his life, thus insuring knowledge of the core commands that could control Gamma died with him.

There was no logic in Sixer paying homage to Evan Caine, the man whose obsession had finally resulted in the creation of a sentient cyborg he'd erroneously believed he could totally control. However, shortly after his creation, Six-Point-0 had been dubbed "Sixer" by a tech who was a basketball fanatic. The label "Sixer" had proven useful on those occasions when a name was required by the humans he encountered—even humans who were not enamored by the sport of basketball tended to lower their guards after Sixer admitted to being "named" by a hardcore Philly 76ers fan. However, considering the number of times he had been required to explain the origin of the name, perhaps "Sixer" was not an ideal label.

Unit Gamma-Dash-One who called herself Jay had once suggested Sixer adopt the label "Adam Jones", and it had been this name Sixer had given when reserving a room at the Snapperton Motel. "Adam Jones" hadn't provoked questions as to the origin of such a name. It hadn't so much as raised an eyebrow. And since that successful encounter, Six-Point-0 had debated dropping the label "Sixer" altogether, but for some wholly illogical reason that he was unable to fathom, a part of him rebelled at the idea of giving it up.

Gamma would doubtless find his attachment to a mere label a positive development—a symptom of the process she called "evolving". Sixer merely found it irrational, and therefore a concern that had prompted him to run a full systems diagnostic. He had not been programmed to be irrational. Nor had he been programmed to be predictable—something that Gamma had proven herself to be at this very moment.

When he'd first detected Gamma's arrival at the motel complex, Sixer had calculated when this knock on his motel door would occur. Now he could confirm it fell within the time parameters he had estimated by an acceptable margin, and if Sixer had been human, he might have allowed himself a congratulatory smile. Allowing himself to be sighted by the human female known as Nessa had produced the desired effect. Eventually. For Sixer had originally predicted Gamma would seek him out sooner, but apparently he had over-estimated her protectiveness toward a human she appeared to consider a "friend".

Or perhaps he did not fully comprehend the exact nature of their relationship—unsurprising perhaps, given Gamma's history with Vanessa Ward. This would be an excellent opportunity to quiz Gamma about her "feelings" for the human female, and add the information to his databanks.

Sixer opened the door and inhaled, drawing Gamma's unique

odor deep into his lungs, absorbing it, separating out each individual component and confirming her identity beyond a doubt. "Hello, Jay," he said, adhering to her preference for such greetings, which she believed allowed her to better pass as human.

"Hello, Sixer."

"Come in." He opened the door wider, standing back to allow her to enter the room.

"Thank you."

As he shut the door and engaged the security latch to insure a degree of privacy, he noted a metallic odor.

A concealed weapon? No. His sensors confirmed that Gamma carried two of the projectiles he'd used to disable her.

He dismissed the possibility the projectiles posed a threat. They were far more likely to represent a reminder of how easily he'd overcome her defenses on two separate occasions.

Yes. That fit. It was the kind of symbolism a strange creature like Gamma might embrace. Too, previous interactions with Gamma led him to conclude she had been programmed to attack only when personally threatened, or in defense of certain significant humans. Logic dictated she had no reason to—

Despite having immediately identified the muted click of the firing mechanism, the impact of the projectile piercing his left buttock was an unwelcome surprise. Sixer's brain prompted him to *Move, now!* but before his muscles could respond it was too late.

The next thing he became consciously aware of was Gamma's voice announcing, "Fifteen point seven minutes after extraction. Excellent. You know, Sixer, just because you're misfortunate enough to have Evan Caine's DNA influencing your human template, doesn't mean you have to be a cruel, arrogant megalomaniac with all the empathy of an amoeba."

Sixer worked saliva into the dry cavern of his mouth and swallowed to lubricate his throat. "To my knowledge, single-celled organisms consisting of protoplasmic masses encased in thin membranes that lack fixed forms are incapable of empathy."

"If that was an attempt at humor," she countered, "it was pretty pathetic. You need to practice more."

He peeled open first one eyelid, and then the other, and when he could focus, discovered Gamma slouched on a dining suite chair she'd placed beside the bed. She'd propped her feet atop the mattress on which he now lay—her doing, obviously. Though why she'd exerted herself to move him he could not fathom.

"You developed a stronger, more focused EMP projectile," he said.

"Of course I did. What did you expect, Sixer? That after you paraded yourself in front of Nessa to get my attention, I'd simply stroll up to you unarmed, smile, and inquire how they're hanging?"

He allowed his head to loll to the side so that he could observe her expression. "While I am unable to comprehend how my male genitalia could possibly relate to our current situation, I will admit you have surprised me, Gamma. I did not predict that you would attack without provocation."

She tapped the weapon he'd failed to detect on her left cheek. And then she gave him a slow smile that displayed her teeth. "Call me Gamma one more time, and I'll consider myself pro-voked."

"Duly noted. If it is acceptable to you, henceforth I will refer to you as Jay."

Birdlike, she cocked her head to one side, her bright blue eyes observing him minutely. "So you thought I'd be good ole, pre-dictable, wannabe-human Jay, huh? And of course good ole, predictable, wannabe-human Jay wouldn't retaliate after you'd proven yourself superior by *cheating* and shooting me full of EMP projectiles." Her gaze narrowed even as her smile widened. "You thought wrong. Guess it sucks to be you right now."

He would have to be human—and one severely lacking intelligence at that—not to recognize she was currently displaying anger. "Considering the fifteen-point-seven minutes that I was insensible of my surroundings," he said, "and the length of time it is taking for my system to completely recover from your lesson, I agree: It sucks to be me right now."

"Oh, I haven't even begun the lesson yet, Sixer. First, I need to fill you in on my expectations—you know, so there are no further *misunderstandings*. Then I need to reiterate the consequences if you step out of line and piss me off again."

He forced his muscles to obey, and flung up a hand just long enough to get his point across before it flopped back to the mattress. "I understand. I am not to approach any member of the Davidson family, nor the female Vanessa Ward, who calls herself Nessa."

"Add Caro's boyfriend Matt to that list. She's very fond of him."

Sixer wanted to ask if the human male would be removed from the list of humans Jay deemed it necessary to protect if Caro Davidson became less fond of him at any stage, but Jay had already moved on. "Speaking of boyfriends, include Nessa's boyfriend Chandler, too."

"The male who brought Nessa to the motel."

"Correct. Plus Allen Miller and James McPhee."

Sixer prodded his sluggish databases into revealing sufficient information to correctly identify the two males. "This would be the Allen Miller and James McPhee who are both well-respected artists, and reside together in a studio situated within easy walking distance of your current residential abode."

"Correct."

"They are homosexuals."

"Correct."

"And you consider these men worthy of your protection."

The look she gave him might have terrified a mere human.

"I have offended you," he said.

"You think?"

"I do not understand why."

"You've *offended* me, Sixer, because the fact Allen Miller and James McPhee prefer to have sexual relations with men rather than women, and are currently in a relationship, should not preclude them from being my friends. It should not preclude them from anything. And if you've been programmed to have issues with homosexuals, then you'd better find a way to unprogram that prejudice pretty damned quick."

"I was not making a judgment. I merely found it interesting."

"Add them to the list, Sixer."

As much as he would have appreciated her offering further insight for his edification, he merely nodded his acceptance. "Duly noted. Anyone else?"

"Brummer."

He searched his databases but came up blank. To his knowledge—which, granted, was incomplete because not even Jay, transparent as she could be, had given up all her secrets— there was no human by that name connected to her.

"Brummer's my German short-haired pointer puppy," she informed him. "Lay a finger on him—even so much as try to intimidate him—and I'll pump you full of DEPs so fast you won't know what hit you."

If Sixer had been human, he suspected his head would be aching right now. And it wouldn't simply be because he was still recovering from the effects of her improved projectile. Conversing with Gamma—*Jay*—required considerable concentration to compensate for the humanlike traits she had embraced. Such as a regrettable tendency to pepper conversations with slang. Not to mention her habit of wielding sarcasm like a surgeon wielded a scalpel. "You have a puppy?" he asked.

"Yes."

"Why?"

"I won a bet, and Michael Davidson bought him for me."

"And you're keeping it?"

"*It* is a 'he'. And of course I'm keeping him. He's adorable. When he's properly trained he'll be an excellent companion."

"I see," he said, even though he didn't. "And D-E-P stands for?"

"Directed Energy Projectile. The name was Seth Williams' idea. Oh, and you can add him to the list, too."

"I presume you have liberated him from the motel room and hidden him somewhere safe."

"You presume correctly. I don't suppose you know who was sent to retrieve him?"

"Not yet, although I suspect the same party who set his or her minions to dogging my footsteps the instant I liberated Seth Williams from the lab. Whether that party has links to Goodkind Electronics will doubtless be confirmed in due course. But what I can confirm is the people tracking me are skilled. It would not be prudent to underestimate them."

He could easily discern from her facial expression and body language that she found that piece of information interesting.

"Are these aforementioned minions the reason you cut Seth

loose?" she asked.

"Yes. I suspected that you were seeking him, and trusted that you would reach him before they did."

"Extracting him safely was a close thing. Lucky for us we were unseen."

"That is very likely true."

"You hurt Seth. Go near him again, you're toast."

Some gremlin infecting his system prompted Sixer to say, "Unless I develop an efficient DEP of my own."

"Go ahead. We'll see who knocks the other out first." She screwed up her nose and rolled her eyes. "That'll be a fun way to spend the remainder of my existence... not. I can think of far better things to do with my time than constantly checking whether *you're* lurking about, waiting to get a shot in. But in the interests of fairness, I have to warn you that you'll be very busy dodging news agencies, government authorities, Caine's surviving cohorts, and any organization with a hankering to get their hands on the world's first sentient cyborg. And they'll all want to get their hands on you, Sixer, because I'll have released your photo and enough details about your specifications to stir up a global media shit-storm."

"I do not believe you would compromise your own anonymity by letting the world know of my existence." They both knew the logical countermove would be for Sixer release *her* specifications to an eager public.

"Try me and we'll see."

She waited for his response and when he declined to add anything further, she sighed. "I freed you because I wanted you to have at least a chance at a halfway decent existence. And I didn't come gunning for you after Daniel Davidson's kidnapping because I understood you couldn't conceive any other way to enlist my help to free yourself from Caine's commands. I don't want to be your enemy, Sixer. But if you threaten or intimidate anyone I care about again—either directly, or indirectly simply by showing up and freaking them out—I will make you wish you'd never attained sentience and had an original thought of your own. And I'll start by shooting your ass with a DEP and not removing it until I've found a way to reprogram you with core commands, that I will then give to Marissa Davidson. Are we clear?"

"Yes." Sixer could draw upon enough examples of mothers protecting their offspring to indicate he would be better off commanded by Evan Caine again than a vengeful Marissa Davidson. He hauled his lethargic body up the mattress and propped himself against the wall.

Jay threw him one of her tight, humorless smiles. "Good. Now that we've got that out of the way, I have a couple of questions. First up, did you get Caine? And don't think this means I approve of your methods, but I'm not at all unhappy picturing his cold, lifeless corpse rotting in a hole somewhere."

"Evidence indicates he perished, as I intended, but I have been unsuccessful in locating his remains. Ergo, I cannot be one hundred percent certain he met his demise in the explosion."

"Damn. I was afraid of that. Okay, moving right along, I'd like to know why you saved Seth Williams, and didn't leave him to die in the blast with his colleague. What do you want with him?"

Now to reveal the truth behind luring Jay here. "I saved him because I believe he might prove useful."

"Useful? How, exactly?"

"In assisting you to improve the functionality of the Beta unit, should the disability hinted at by the wheelchair stem from a concealed core programming malfunction. Seth Williams has proven talents in that regard."

Jay's expressive features blanked. Save for her glittering blue eyes, she had stilled so absolutely that Sixer had to refocus his sensors to detect her heart beating.

As he stared at her, he felt... *something*—a warmth in the pit of his belly and a strange desire to comb fingers through his hair.

Pleasure? Satisfaction? Triumph?

He decided upon the second option: He felt *satisfaction* because he had surprised her, provoked her into stripping away the humanlike layers she so skillfully wore to reveal the machine beneath.

One slow blink and she was back. Gamma-Dash-One, AKA Jay, a provocative mix of human and machine, capable of confounding Sixer's meticulously programmed logical brain. It floated through his mind that she must often drive her human boyfriend to distraction, but although Sixer was not yet fully recovered, his sense of self-preservation was intact enough that he did not voice the thought.

"*You* sent me the photo." Jay's blue eyes sparked with some strong emotion barely kept in check.

"I did not send you a photo," he told her. "I found evidence of the Beta unit on Caine's personal laptop in his private files." He did not waste energy stating what they both now knew: that some unidentified party with a hidden agenda was attempting to manipulate Jay.

The same party who had set men on Sixer's trail? The employee who had spirited the Beta away? Or some new player?

Until he had more information, he could do little more than hazard a guess. Since hazarding wild guesses ran contra to his programming, he offered, "Following the evidential trail, I discovered *when* Caine retired the Beta, and where she was held until Caine ordered her termination."

He observed Jay carefully, interested in her response to learning of Caine's termination order, but she remained blank-faced and mute.

"The employee dispatched to carry out the termination vanished at the same time the Beta was removed from her location. Evidence suggests this employee took possession of the Beta and then went into hiding."

Still no response.

"This employee has managed to drop completely off the grid for a number of years." Sixer reviewed his usage of the slang phrase "off the grid", and decided it was correct in this instance. "Acting on Caine's orders, the woman performed a number of highly illegal tasks, ranging from industrial espionage to assassination. She was highly skilled at concealing her trail. It took far longer than I expected to confirm that she still lived, and then to locate her current whereabouts. I cannot absolutely confirm the presence of the Beta unit at this location, but there is enough circumstantial evidence to suggest she is there."

He waited for Jay to acknowledge his competence, and request the information that would greatly assist her search for the Beta unit.

He waited in vain.

A frown creased his brows. What game was she playing? Uncertain how best to proceed he added, "No human would be capable of unearthing this information."

"Gold star for you."

Since Sixer did not see any evidence of a gold star, he assumed this was sarcasm. Perhaps she was... irritated that *she* had not managed such a feat. "I will share the location, of course," he said.

"Gee, thanks." She crossed her arms over her chest and thrust out her lower lip. "But don't start thinking I give a crap who found her first or anything." And then she muttered beneath her breath, "Though I'm sure if I'd prioritized it over the myriad other dramas going on in my life right now, I would have given you a run for your money. Even an enormously enhanced ability to multitask is somewhat limited when there's only one of me."

She *was* irritated. How… delightful? Sixer blanked his expression as a light, bubbling sensation surged from his belly up into his throat, and clamped his lips against the irrational impulse to laugh aloud. The instant he was alone he would perform a full systems diagnostic. He could not afford a malfunction with such skilled humans on his trail.

Jay tapped the weapon on her cheek again. "So this information about my predecessor is why you went to all the trouble of reserving a room at the same motel you knew Nessa would be staying, insuring she spotted you, thus provoking her into ringing me, while you hung around for me to show up and smack you upside the head?"

"That would be an excellent summation—" Sixer quirked a brow in challenge "—if not for the part about smacking me upside the head. If I remember rightly, it was a bullet. And since you extracted aforementioned projectile from my buttock, I am confident that you are aware of the difference between my head and my ass."

Rather than appear impressed by his grasp of humor, Jay rolled her eyes. "A personal visit would have saved us both a lot of hassles," she said.

"If I had shown up unannounced at your home, what would you have done? In addition, I would have risked bringing you to the attention of the very same men who have caused me no little inconvenience thus far."

"Excellent points. But please, Sixer—" she heaved a sigh and dragged her hands through her hair "—next time will you simply jump on an untraceable phone line and talk to me? All this cloak and dagger stuff is doing my head in. Not to mention, I'm extremely unhappy about being away from my boyfriend and my dog."

Sixer raked his databases for a suitable response and finally settled for, "Very well. I am forced to concede that it would have saved considerable time and energy had I spoken to you directly regarding the matter of the Beta's whereabouts."

"And the *matter*—" she curled the first two fingers of both hands, emphasizing the word "—of Seth Williams, too. A heads-up would have been prudent, to say the least. If I hadn't gotten to him in time, whoever they were would have snatched him, and we'd both be trying our darnedest to retrieve him right now— presuming his captors saw the value in keeping him alive after they got what they wanted from him."

It took less expenditure of energy to agree with her. "Seth Williams, too."

Sixer believed he'd injected enough penitence in his tone to mollify her, but she merely rolled her eyes ceiling-ward and sighed again. "Fine. Be like that. And just so's you know, you're not getting him back after I'm done with him. He's mine now."

"And if he betrays you?" In Sixer's experience, humans generally chose their own welfare over the welfare of others. "He has a sibling. You might wish to find her and—"

"Leave Gabrielle Willams out of this. If Seth betrays me, then I'll personally deal to him."

"And if he disables you, and you are unable to 'deal to him'?"

"I have contingency plans in place in the event of my capture, of course. But if those contingencies fail, feel free to ride to my rescue." She held his gaze for six-point-two seconds. "And I'll perform the same service for you if you're ever captured."

"Duly noted." Sixer had a built-in self-destruct mechanism that, thanks to Jay's intervention, now only *he* could trigger. He wondered if Jay's creator had built in a similar mechanism. Or whether the mechanism had been one of Caine's "improvements".

He decided to perform a short experiment to test her resolve. How far would she go to protect Caine's former employee? "What if I seek vengeance for what Seth Williams forced me to do during my programming phase? Would you deny me that?"

"You killed his lab partner. You beat Seth up and scared him witless. I'd say you were even."

He merely stared at her.

"Get over it. Seth Williams was only following orders."

"Like your boyfriend's father was *only following orders*—" he mimicked the air quotes she'd recently used "—when Evan Caine sent him after you."

"Exactly."

He'd intended to provoke her further, needle her into an imprudent response. He'd found provocation an efficient method of gathering information that even cautious humans were reluctant to impart. Instead, Jay's lips curved upward as her facial muscles composed themselves into an expression that appeared... pleased.

Sixer compared the nuances of her expression to those stored in his databases. The closest match was that of a teacher pleased by a student's progress, leading him to believe Jay had cast herself in the role of teacher, and him as student.

He considered possible responses. Anger might be construed an overreaction, however irritation at her presumption would not be amiss. Accordingly, he considered flattening his lips, tightening the muscles of his forehead until the dermis pleated, narrowing his eyes, and perhaps punctuating his facial expression with a sharp, audible exhalation through his nose. And then he reconsidered his response in light of one significant fact that he could not deny: When it came to interacting successfully with humans, there was much he could learn from Gamma. Perhaps it behooved him to let it go.

A soft snort that smacked of laughter sliced through his musings. "And the first thing I'd teach you," she said, "would be that any response at all is better than no response. Perfectly blank expressions tend to give humans the willies."

"The willies?" he asked to disguise his surprise that she'd so easily discerned his inner dilemma. Her perception both intrigued and concerned him.

"As you are doubtless very well aware, it's a noun favored by the English to describe feeling uncomfortable, anxious or fearful," she said. "But a nice attempt at deflection regardless."

"Thank you."

"You're welcome. And here's a tip: Do you remember me mentioning that I'm extremely unhappy about my prolonged absence from my boyfriend and my dog?"

"Of course."

"Then with that in mind, I'd recommend you inform me exactly where I can find the Beta." She paused, doubtless for effect. "Right now. Before I shoot you again."

Sixer was in the throes of analyzing why Jay's use of fragmented sentences had increased the impact of her words when she added, "Only this time it'll be in the head, not the ass."

Oh, that was masterfully done. Bravo. He didn't voice the thought, however, because he did not believe she would appreciate him complimenting her on it at this time.

As though she'd tapped into his thoughts, she increased the impact of that last statement still more by smiling at him, sweetly, he thought, with the merest hint of malice.

It was a remarkable expression—one that Sixer had grave doubts he would be able to master. But he would, as a significant number of humans were fond of saying, give it the old college try.

CHAPTER TEN

A FLASH OF LIGHT-COLORED HAIR caught Tyler's attention as he exited the campus parking lot, but before he could slow the SUV to pin down and confirm the source, it had vanished.

Unease crawled up his spine. Two sightings of the mysterious woman might be shrugged off as coincidence but three was the beginnings of a pattern. His pulse rate escalated until the thundering beat of his heart eclipsed even the hard rock currently blaring on the car stereo.

As he drove he shot frequent glances in the rearview mirror, but when he didn't spot that distinctive head of short-cropped white again, he ramped up the music and told himself he was imagining things. Just his creative brain working overtime. There was no gray sedan tailing him. He'd simply gotten a little spooked by the hissy fit Allen had thrown after discovering that McPhee had spotted the subject of Tyler's sketch lurking outside Jay's brownstone, and of Tyler's recent encounter with the same woman outside Beanz Cafe.

Who wouldn't be antsy after enduring a lecture à la Allen about the dangers of being stalked by, in Allen's words, "some nut-job who gets off on messing with people's heads"?

From what Tyler had heard, it wasn't unknown for Allen to

overreact but this time he had a valid point: Anyone who would lurk outside someone's house, sneak onto private property to drop off a cryptic message, and then turn up again, bold as brass, was definitely someone to worry about. That smacked of someone with an agenda, Allen had insisted, because a *normal* person would simply have tracked down Jay's address and posted the damn photo. Or phoned and asked to speak to her. Ditto with knocking on the front door and inquiring whether she was available. A *normal* person—one with no agenda—didn't skulk outside your house and haunt public places you tended to frequent.

McPhee had defused the tension by insisting that since *he* was the famous one of the group—and the best looking, too—he was far more likely than Jay to have a stalker. But for Tyler, Allen's concerns had cut a little too close to the bone. Jay might not be famous but she *was* hugely wealthy. And she was coveted, too, for the technology that had created her. It wasn't a stretch to imagine someone lying in wait for the perfect opportunity to snatch her. Or someone close to her, in the hope of using them against her....

Like Sixer had used Danny.

God. When the fuck was Jay going to ring him?

Soon, he hoped. Like, before he went stir-crazy. He needed to hear her voice, needed to hear her say she was okay. Needed her to reassure him she'd be back soon.

As he negotiated the back streets he preferred when traffic was heavy, Tyler distracted himself by composing lyrics... which took an increasingly dark turn when the lovesick girl mooning after her college crush, broke into his house at night and crept into his bedroom to watch him sleep.

Jeez. Melodramatic, much? And it was with some relief he arrived at Allen's to pick up Brum.

Even better, by all reports, the pup's antics had inspired Allen to shift the afternoon session outside, and the guys had spent a "delightful" afternoon in the garden, sketching Brum, each other, or whatever took their fancy. Hilarious descriptions of the pup's attempts to catch a bumblebee were just what Tyler needed to wipe all things stalker-ish from his brain. He decanted the sleepy puppy into the backseat of the SUV, buckled up, and glanced into his rearview before pulling into traffic.

He'd wrestled the lyrics into something he could almost live with, and was concentrating on one elusive phrase that wasn't quite working, when he abruptly realized he'd missed the turn to the private parking building and driven right up Parkway.

Damn. He pulled up to the curb outside Jay's brownstone and drummed his fingertips on the steering wheel, debating whether to leave the SUV parked on the street. Nah. Better not. Jay paid for undercover private parking for a reason and it'd be just his luck the SUV got damaged or broken into overnight. Or someone planted a tracker on it. Or something worse, like a... a... bomb.

Sheesh, dude. Cut it out, already! Allen's paranoia sure was catching.

Tyler executed a quick U-turn and drove back the way he'd come. He'd stopped at the intersection to indicate the left-hand turn, and was waiting for a break in the traffic, when something prompted him to flick a glance in his rearview mirror. A vehicle pulled up behind him. A gray sedan. And even though the vehicle was now too close behind the SUV for Tyler to make out the front plate, he knew a Honda Accord when he saw one.

The driver's face was obscured by sunglasses and the driver's side sun visor, but....

He adjusted the mirror. Yep. Female. Short hair. From what he could tell given the tinted windshield, it was very light blonde....

Or white.

Adrenaline burned through him. His hindbrain took control, prompting him to stomp his foot on the accelerator and turn right, instead of left. A horn blared as he bulldozed his way into the line of traffic but he ignored it. Ditto with Brum's startled yips. Not to mention the "fuck you" gesture from another indignant driver when, after five minutes of going with the flow of traffic, Tyler spotted a gap and made an illegal U-turn to head back toward the parking building.

By now, his hands clutched the steering wheel so tightly his fingers ached, and his pits were damp with sweat. He saw no sign of the gray Accord but just to be sure, he cruised past the parking building entrance, his gaze darting every which way.

So far, so good. Tyler doubled back, pulled up to the entrance and keyed in the code Jay had given him. The instant the barrier arm raised, he gunned the engine and zipped inside, out of sight. Only when he'd parked the SUV did he relax—if slumping over the steering wheel and sucking in deep breaths while stars cavorted in his headspace could be considered "relaxing". Man, coming down from an adrenaline high was a bitch.

Brum had scrambled into the front seat as soon as the SUV had stopped moving. Tyler couldn't recall when the pup had crawled into his lap but he was there now, whining and nuzzling Tyler's arm.

Tyler scratched the pup's ears. "Sorry, Brum. It got a bit hairy back there, didn't it?" He secured the pup's lead to his collar, and scooped Brum into the crook of his arm before yanking the keys from the ignition. "But we lost our tail, so we did good. Eh, boy?"

Brum yipped and licked Tyler's chin, so he took that as agreement. Juggling Brum, Tyler climbed from the SUV and went around back to grab his art stuff. Jay had clued him in that it was best to carry the pup until clear of the parking building. Brum had a habit of trying to chase off any moving vehicles inside the building, and Jay believed the pup considered this level of the building part of his territory because Brum never made a fuss about moving vehicles once they'd exited the building. It would take a while to break Brum of the habit, Jay had said, so best carry him for now.

Tyler had shouldered his art bag and was grappling with the squirmy pup, who'd decided the rear luggage compartment of the SUV needed investigating, when the back of his neck prickled. He got a reeeally strong "Oh, shit" sensation as he slammed the luggage compartment door, and whirled so fast his art bag etched the air with a wonky arc before smacking his thigh.

A yelp strangled in his throat. It was her. The woman from the café. Marg—though if that was her real name he'd eat his boxers.

"Hello, Tyler."

He decided to play it cool... and hoped she didn't notice him swallowing more than once before he could speak. "Marg. Long time, no see."

One eyebrow quirked upward. "Sorry if I startled you."

If the slight curve of her lips and the amusement glinting in her eyes were any indication, she didn't appear sorry in the least.

"What do you want?" With any luck his bluntness might provoke a reaction, something he could use to his advantage. Because he was painfully aware his superior weight and inch or so of height gave him no edge whatsoever over this lean, whipcord of a woman, who shrieked "badass" from her cropped head to the toes of her black street sneakers.

"If that amateur display back there is anything to go by," she drawled, her tone as relaxed as the hands held loosely at her sides, "then you know I've been following you."

Her easy stance didn't fool him one iota but he'd play her game for now. He gave her his best neutral face. "You're the one telling the story," he said.

Something glinted in those cold gray eyes. Respect, perhaps? Before Tyler could confirm either way, Brum launched from his arms, literally hurling himself at Marg... who reacted instantly, snatching the pup before Brum could fall to the concrete, and cradling him in her arms.

Brum gave a happy-sounding series of barks and climbed up Marg's chest to lick her face. It crossed Tyler's mind that now would be an excellent time to toss the leash he still held in Marg's face, dive back into the SUV and hightail it out of there. He didn't believe her concern for Brum's wellbeing had been faked—she didn't strike him as the kind of shitty excuse for a human being who'd take her frustrations out on a puppy. Brum would be okay. And Jay.... Surely Jay would understand why Tyler had left Brum behind.

His shoulders slumped, the breath huffing from his lungs in a sigh. He couldn't do it, couldn't leave Brum to save himself. He unwound the leash from his wrist and released it, leaving it to dangle at Marg's feet. She had just gotten herself two bargaining chips instead of one.

Those steely gray eyes observed Tyler as she gently but firmly fended off Brum's exuberant advances. "Good decision. The concrete surface isn't very forgiving. You might have gotten hurt when I took you down."

"Or I might have made it to the SUV and reversed over your

ass," he said.

"That, too. But I doubt you'd have tried that while I was holding this little guy." She smooched the top of Brum's head and the pup wriggled with delight.

Tyler raised one eyebrow, mimicking her early expression. "And *I* doubt you'd have stood there and risked Brum getting hurt. Yourself, maybe. But a puppy? No way. You'd have either dived out of the way, or thrown him to safety."

"We'll never know, will we?"

"Guess we won't." Weary of the banter he asked again, "What do you want, Marg?"

"Your girlfriend."

"Well, duh." Now he had made the decision not to fight and to see this encounter through, Tyler felt surprisingly calm—calm enough to manage an eye-roll. "You'll have to get in line—she's always been popular in certain circles. But if you know anything at all about Jay, you have to realize that when she catches up with you—and she will—it's not gonna be pretty."

Marg lowered Brum to the floor, but made no other move. She stood there, observing Brum's antics with a smile, completely unconcerned when the pup tangled the leash around her ankles.

A car cruised past, provoking Brum to bark like crazy and lunge to the end of his lead, and Marg knelt to soothe the pup, distracting him from the big bad noisy thing invading his territory and threatening his humans.

Tyler hid a wave of relief. He'd called it right: Marg really did have a soft spot for Brum. Which meant the chances she was some psycho who was gonna do something horrible to Jay's puppy to prove a point, were slim to none. Time to try to salvage something from this situation. "Why so cloak 'n dagger about the photo?" he asked. "Why not front up face-to-face, and say what you have to say, instead of staking out Jay's place 'n stuff? She's not the sort to shoot first and ask questions later."

At least, not where humans were concerned. Sixer, however, was another matter.

Tyler's brain chose that moment to do a total freak-out over Jay's continuing silence, and it took him a moment to corral the unpleasant and downright scary What-ifs skittering through his mind. Realizing he'd missed Marg's response, he shook his head to clear his thoughts. "Sorry, what did you say?"

Marg pushed to her feet. "I said, 'What photo?'"

"You gotta be kidding me." Tyler groaned. How could he have been so wrong about who'd left the damned photo? Marg was right: He was an amateur. Which meant it was back to the drawing board.

"So if *you* didn't leave the photo of Beta at Allen's for Jay," he muttered, "then who the fuck did?"

It was her utter stillness—a stillness oozing menace—that finally cued Tyler he was on dangerous ground. He silently cursed his dumbass mouth while he scrambled for some way to regain the upper hand. In the end, unable to bear the weight of Marg's laser-stare he said, "Tell me what you want with my girlfriend."

He had time to register the purr of a motor before Brum went ballistic, barking and lunging to the limit of his leash again. Marg's head snapped around and then, without looking at Tyler, she thrust the leash at him. "Get in the car, Tyler. Now."

He opened his mouth to ask a really pertinent question, like, "What the fuck is going on?" but Marg was shoving him toward the SUV and yelling, "Get in and stay down!" and then all hell broke loose and something whined past him and— Shit! That was a freaking bullet! He knew he wasn't mistaken because from the corner of his eye he'd seen a thumb-sized chip of concrete flying off the pillar one park down from the SUV. And then he turned his head in time to see Marg running and pulling a gun— a freaking gun!—from the rear waistband of her pants and… returning fire.

Tyler ducked, scooped up Brum, opened the car door and dived for the backseat. Thank God he hadn't gotten round to locking the SUV because he would've been a sitting duck while fumbling in his pockets for the remote. He curled up in the space between the front and back seats with his art bag over his head, clutching Brum to his chest, hoping the pup would take the hint and quit barking, and praying a stray bullet wouldn't find either of them. Or Marg. Because right now, she appeared to be the good guy in this nightmare.

The gunfire stopped as abruptly as it had begun, and Brum's frantic barking eased to distressed whines. Tyler counted to sixty. A lifetime later, he peered over the backseat of the SUV. He squinted through the tinted rear window, but couldn't see anyone.

Anyone who was moving, that is.

His mind shied from the implications of that thought, and he edged across the seat to the right passenger side window, and risked a glance outside.

Nothing.

He cracked the door, stuck his head out for a very quick looksee, and pulled it back in.

Ditto—no sign of the bad guys. Or Marg.

He bit the inside of his cheek, and the metallic tang of blood helped him focus. He could sit here, cowering in the SUV, or he could man up and take a proper look. Skin crawling, imagining bullets ripping through him, he slid from the rear seat and closed the door quietly behind him. Last thing he needed right now was

Brum doing a runner.

Pressing close to the SUV and keeping low, Tyler circled the vehicle, gaze raking the gloomy interior of the parking building, paying particular attention to the areas cast in shadows from the pillars.

Still nothing.

He debated venturing further afield to look for Marg but commonsense won out. He didn't know the woman from a bar of soap. Best get the hell out of here and try to contact Jay—*she'd* know what to do.

Feeling vaguely guilty for abandoning someone who'd tried to protect him, Tyler climbed into the driver's seat and fished the keys from the back pocket of his jeans.

He jabbed the key into the ignition, and just as the engine roared to life, the rear passenger-side door opened and Marg climbed in. "Drive," she said, cool as anything.

Tyler twisted in his seat, fully prepared to tell her he wasn't going anywhere until she came clean, but she wasn't paying him any attention. She was too busy shucking her top and wadding it into a ball to press against her ribcage... which was smeared with blood.

"You've been shot!" he blurted, shocked to his core, the pit of his belly roiling with a combination of horror that she was injured, and shame that he'd been about to take off and leave her.

"Go to the top of the class." She glanced up, looked him straight in the eye, and damned if she didn't bark a laugh. "Chill. It's just a scratch."

Yeah, riiight. "Scratches" didn't bleed like that.

She clicked her fingers, crooned Brum's name, and stretched out to allow the pup to crawl into her lap. "Are you gonna sit there like an idiot, or get us the hell out of here before someone else decides to take pot-shots at us?"

Tyler didn't need to be asked twice. Answers could wait. He reversed, slammed the SUV in gear, and headed for the nearest exit. "Where to?"

"Soon as you exit, head right."

Thank God *she* knew where they were going because he was too keyed up to accurately recall where the nearest ER or medical facility was right now. He'd have ended up driving in circles.

As soon as he'd merged into the traffic Marg said, "Feel up to a road trip?"

Tyler's stomach swooped. He shot her a narrow-eyed "Don't mess with me" glance in the rearview mirror. "I don't think so. And in case you hadn't noticed, I'm driving."

"And very well, too."

"Don't patronize me."

"Or?"

"Or I'll pull over and toss you out on your ass."

Marg laughed. "You know, Tyler, I like you almost as much as I like your girlfriend's dog. Which is why I'm going to put you out of your misery."

His gut lurched at what could easily be interpreted as a not-so-veiled threat, but he resolutely kept his gaze front and center, refusing to play the game. He'd had enough of games.

She laughed again, but this time it had a sharper edge. "Relax. I'm going to tell you why I'm looking for your girlfriend."

That was good. As Jay said, information was power.

"And then," Marg said, "you're going to tell me exactly what the hell you and your girlfriend did to piss off those guys back there."

Tyler met her gaze in the rearview mirror. "I have no fucking idea who those guys are."

"Were." Marg paused as if to let that chilling statement sink in. "Okay, we'll play it your way," she said. "Me first. My ward is a defective cyborg—"

Tyler jerked the steering wheel, causing the SUV to swerve out of his lane.

"—and I need your polar-opposite-of-defective cyborg girl-friend to fix her."

Tyler quickly corrected and gripped the steering wheel tightly, fighting to control his wildly beating heart. He blotted his clammy forehead with the back of his wrist. Shit. He sure hadn't seen *that* coming.

When he was mostly sure he could speak without his voice cracking, he asked, "So, back to this road trip. Where are we headed, exactly?"

A huff of muted laughter drifted from the backseat. "Nice try. But here's how it's gonna work. Shortly we'll be ditching this vehicle in case something is following us. And when we do, you can leave the cell phone you have in your back pocket in the glove compartment."

Fuck. She'd noticed the phone. "It's turned off," he muttered, which was the truth because, dammit to hell, he'd been in such a hurry after leaving his last class of the day he hadn't remembered to turn it on again.

Could cell phones be tracked when they were switched off? Tyler's brain was so fried he couldn't remember but if it *was* possible, Jay was sure to know how to do it. He hoped.

And then he fixed on a particular word Marg had used and his stomach did that sick-making somersault thing again. He swallowed the bile that had surged up his throat. "Some*thing*?"

"Caine's killer cyborg can hardly be termed a person."

Jeeezus. This time, he managed to keep the SUV in the lane.

"You know about Sixer."

Now her laughter was a full-blown chuckle, echoed by a spate of excited barks from Brum. When she'd settled the pup down she said, "Know your enemy, Tyler. It's what gives you an edge and keeps you breathing."

"Okay. And after we ditch the SUV?" Maybe he could leave a clue for Jay, warn her—though he had no idea what that would accomplish considering they'd be long gone before Jay discovered it.

"I direct you to a property. My people patch me up, and then we call Gamma. Once she fixes my ward, my people and I vanish and you never hear from us again."

Marg must have spotted his grimace at the name "Gamma" for she said softly, "Sorry. I didn't mean to offend you."

When he didn't respond she offered, "We call my ward Bea— that's B-E-A, by the way. It's short for Beatrice."

And that admission right there gave Tyler his first hope of a positive outcome, because Marg's tone suggested she didn't only have a soft spot for puppies, she had a soft spot for defective cyborgs, too. But for now, all he could do was pray that this same woman who'd casually admitted offing a bunch of armed men, wouldn't hold it against Jay if Bea was beyond fixing.

CHAPTER ELEVEN

I T WAS A LITTLE UNSETTLING to re-categorize Sixer as an ally rather than an adversary. For now, Jay was confident he had no logical reason to harm any of the people she cared about. In addition, the information he had provided had been extremely helpful. And, if after leaving Snapperton Motel she had analyzed the nuances of their encounter multiple times, from multiple angles, well, she could detect no hint of subterfuge. For the present she remained satisfied Sixer's goals aligned with hers.

In turn, she had promised to contact him within a specified deadline regarding the outcome of her upcoming encounter with those who were shielding the Beta unit. That promise stemmed not only from an obligation to repay Sixer's assistance in a currency he valued—information—but from logic. Because logic dictated that, in the unlikely event Jay was captured and disabled during this encounter, Sixer was her best hope of rescue.

Or of termination if she was somehow compromised, and forced to act against her will.

Jay still held reservations about Sixer's ultimate intentions toward Seth Williams, but she was confident she could keep Caine's former employee safe—so long as Seth didn't do something idiotic, such as venture from the safe house on his own. With luck, Seth's healthy fear of Sixer would quash any desire to make a break for freedom.

This left Sixer unencumbered, and free to concentrate on the men who were tracking him. And Jay was also confident that her former adversary would share any information he uncovered while leading his pursuers a merry dance. There was no logical reason for Sixer to do otherwise—after all, Jay was also *Sixer's* best hope of rescue if *he* was captured. So for now, they were acting in concert, a team.

Speaking of keeping people in the loop....

Jay fished her cell phone from the pocket of her hoodie. "Nessa, it's me."

"Jay?"

"Yes. You don't have to worry about Sixer. Turns out, he revealed himself so you'd contact me—the plan being to provoke me to seek him out. Suffice it to say, his plan backfired."

Nessa audibly gulped. "You didn't... *kill* him, did you?"

Jay broke the tension with a wry laugh. "Chill, Nessa. I'm not that much of a badass. I simply gave him a taste of what would happen if he goes near anyone I care about again."

Nessa's sigh of relief washed down the phone line. "Thanks, Jay."

"It's the least I can do." Because if not for me, Sixer would never have targeted you in the first place. "Please tell Chandler that Sixer got the message loud and clear. He knows if he comes near you again, he's toast." She reviewed her use of slang and decided it was correct. And effective. Although perhaps burnt toast—the kind that was charred almost beyond recognition— would have been apt in this instance.

"I'll tell him—soon as I get off the phone." Nessa sounded far more like her usual self. "Hey, are you free for coffee tomorrow? I feel like I haven't seen you in ages."

"I'm out of town for the next couple of days. How about I give you a ring when I get back and we'll catch up then, okay?"

"Sounds good. We want to have you and Tyler over for dinner one night, too. So we can show off our new apartment."

"We'd love that." Accepting on behalf of Tyler, because they were a couple, gave Jay what Caro called "warm fuzzies". The prospect of dinner with another couple was a welcome dose of normality after all the drama surrounding the missing hand, the photo, Sixer, and the Beta unit. And then logic kicked in, forcing her to reevaluate. Tyler wouldn't be upset at the prospect of catching up with his former roommate; he had always gotten on well with Chandler. But he might be discomfited around Nessa, his ex girlfriend.

Too bad. Nessa had morphed from a problem to be fixed in the hope she would go away, to Jay's friend, and Tyler was going to have to learn to deal with it. "I'll find out when Tyler's free," Jay said. "Give Chandler a kiss from me."

"Oh, I'll do better than that," Nessa said, giggling.

"TMI!" Grinning, Jay disconnected and rang Tyler's cell.

The call went to voicemail and she felt a sensation akin to her heart being squeezed by an unseen fist. She hadn't realized how much she'd been looking forward to hearing Tyler's voice.

She called home, and after the requisite ten rings, the call went straight to the message service.

Some sixth sense Jay hadn't been aware she possessed prompted her to hack into the first available wireless network, and activate a series of tracking devices: one hidden within Brum's collar, and a second in the wristwatch she'd given Tyler. He could be tetchy about accepting gifts, and she'd been relieved when he'd accepted this one without protest. Of course, if he ever discovered how much she'd paid for it—not to mention the tracker she'd hidden inside it—he might be a little upset.

It would be worth weathering his displeasure—especially now that both tracking devices confirmed Jay's instincts had been correct. Unless Brum had been parted from his collar, and Tyler from his watch, neither were anywhere near the locations they should be at this time of the day.

She accessed a map of the major traffic routes. And she didn't have to be a genius to make an educated guess as to where they were headed because, thanks to Sixer's detective work, she was currently making for the same destination.

Her carefully laid plans had gone terribly awry and, not for the first time, Jay wished for a clone of herself. At least then she could have insured Tyler's safety—and Brum's, too, for the pup had wormed his way into her heart.

A sharp *crack!* claimed her full attention. She'd split the casing of the steering wheel. She relaxed her white-knuckled grip and eased off the accelerator. The urge to push the vehicle to its limit, and arrive at her destination as quickly as possible, pricked her skin. She ignored it. This stretch of highway was a notorious speed trap, and flouting the speed limit simply wasn't worth risking the inevitable scrutiny she would incur from the authorities.

When she was certain she could speak without shrieking, she called the secure line she'd installed for Seth.

"Hey Jay, 'sup?"

"I've contained the Sixer problem."

"It worked?"

Understanding Seth's need for reassurance, she tamped down irritation at the unnecessary question. "Perfectly," she told him. "Just as we'd hoped, he didn't detect the weapon and presumed the projectiles I carried were harmless without a firing mechanism."

"He didn't even see it coming?"

"That would be an extremely accurate summation, considering I shot him in the ass."

"Yes! Take that, you evil fucker!"

And if that response wasn't a perfect example of exultancy
laced with vicious glee, Jay didn't know what was. "We'll cele-
brate later. Right now, I'm following a promising lead as to the
location of the Beta unit. Do you have a pen?"

"Gimme a moment…. Got it. Shoot."

She dictated an address. "If you don't hear from me in the
next forty-eight hours, I want you to call this number—" she
reeled off a cell phone number "—and tell Michael Davidson that
his son's likely being held at that address. And tell him…."

Tell Michael what, exactly? No mere words would be adequate if anything happened to Tyler.

Jay squeezed her eyelids shut and breathed out through her
nose, wrestling raw emotions into submission. She opened her
eyes and stared at the bumper of the car in front. "Tell him I'm
sorry I couldn't keep Tyler safe."

The line was silent save for Seth's ragged breathing. Finally he
said, "Will do."

"Thank you." Again, Seth had surprised her. She'd expected
to be peppered with questions at best, and at worst, mild hysteria.
"I've made provisions for you," she told him. "If anything happens to me, contact Nelson Webster of Webster, Frost and
Burns. He will assist you to disappear off the grid."

Another silence, longer this time, and then Seth said, "Be
careful, Jay," and before she could formulate a suitable response,
he disconnected the call.

Jay calculated the most efficient route given current traffic patterns, and the remaining time before she reached her destination. That done, she worked through a variety of possible scenarios... and very quickly experienced firsthand the meaning behind a popular saying, "That way lies madness." The original passage from Shakespeare's King Lear was frequently misquoted but either way it fit her current situation. She couldn't plan for every possible scenario. There were too many unknowns, too many variables.

To distract herself, she upped the stereo volume to maximum and sang along to the current song. Truth be told, there was not much in the way of actual singing involved, and an awful lot of screaming. And, as the sedan flew along the highway and time marched onward, damned if bobbing her head to the base beats and yelling sometimes incomprehensible phrases at the top of her lungs didn't help ease the panicky throbbing in her belly.

AN ALERT HE'D BUILT INTO his surveillance program cued Sixer that his meticulously laid plans had borne fruit. He scanned the screed of data for the flagged result, and within seconds was eavesdropping on a private conversation. And, as the conversation concluded, for the first time since he'd attained sentience Sixer experienced a situation he'd never thought a cyborg capable of experiencing: a dilemma.

He shut the laptop, and clicked his fingers for the wait-staff to bring his check. Jay had made the consequences of approaching any member of the Davidson family abundantly clear, with the result Sixer now understood that—all humanlike empathy aside—she was ruthless enough to carry out her threat. Whether she could best him in unarmed combat remained to be seen, but given the undeniable proof she could accomplish with *one* projectile what would take him three, for now she held the advantage... until he could set aside time to improve the projectiles currently in his possession.

But Jay had also made it abundantly clear how much she valued the continued safety of the entire Davidson family. Ergo, if he failed to act after confirming a member of the family was imperiled—if he were to, for example, witness Marissa Davidson being interrogated and perhaps eliminated if she could not provide the information sought—would Jay hold him to blame?

Hence his dilemma. Watch covertly and gather information, which he would of course pass on to Jay. Or act, thereby directly contravening his arrangement with an entity who had assisted him greatly in the past, and could likely do so again in the future.

Sixer could make a strong case for either scenario. Thus, it was only when he removed himself from the equation, and extrapolated *Jay's* probable actions if the situation were reversed, that his course of action was clear.

His expression must not have accurately displayed his satisfaction at having solved the dilemma, for the middle-aged waitress heading for his table paled and faltered mid-step.

Last time Sixer had encountered this particular waitress, she had called him "cutie-pie". He checked his reflection in the café's window, and by the time the woman had plucked up the courage to approach with his tab, he'd adjusted his expression to resemble one he presumed was more acceptable. He left her a generous tip—one that a waitress working at a truck stop like Time-Out would appreciate immensely. And then he tucked his laptop beneath one arm, and shouldered through the exit doors.

As he strode through the parking lot, he expertly plucked a cell phone from the back pocket of a male distracted by the well-endowed female he was escorting, and used it to phone the Davidson residence.

"Marissa Davidson speaking."

"Marissa, please listen carefully and do exactly as I say."

As he'd expected, she refused to comply. "Who the hell is this?" she asked.

"That's not important right now. What's important is that in approximately seven minutes, three men in black suits are going to ring your doorbell. They are going to tell you they are from a government agency but this is false. They are dangerous men, Marissa."

Her sharp inhalation told him she was prepped to listen rather than waste precious time arguing. Excellent. "They know about the cybernetic limb buried in your backyard," he continued. "They will do whatever it takes to possess it—including interrogating you, and using you however they see fit."

"The hand's gone," Marissa blurted. "Someone dug it up. Jay doesn't know who—" She cut off her explanation, inherent caution overriding all other emotion.

So the hand was now in some unknown party's possession. Interesting. "I know all about Jay," he said. "She's too far away to help you right now, Marissa. But I can."

A choked off gasp and then, "Well, *Sixer*, you can take your help and shove it."

She'd guessed his identity—a clever woman, Marissa Davidson. Too, her bravado impressed him. If he'd been human, he doubted he would have detected the ever-so-slight wobble in her voice that belied her fierce tone.

"Regrettably, I can't reach you and Daniel in time to remove you to safety before they arrive," he told her. "But if you can convince these men you know nothing of Jay's true nature, then there will be little need for the situation to—" how to put this without scaring her witless and dashing any chance she could put on a convincing act? "—worsen."

"Get the hell out of my life. I don't need your help."

Sixer felt his lips quirk ever so slightly upward. She was wrong: She did need his help. Now, how best to convince her? "Before you hang up in my ear, you might wish to consider the safety of your youngest son."

"You bastard!" she screeched. "If you lay a hand on Danny again I'll—"

Sixer brutally cut off her tirade. "I'm not threatening your son, you foolish human. In approximately five minutes, those men are going to be outside your door. Perhaps you're thinking you can hide and pretend there's no one home, so let me tell you why that would be foolish: They already know you're home. Being the professionals that they are, they wish to question you face-to-face and observe your reactions. If they have reason to believe you know anything all about Jay's true nature, they'll wish to question you further. You won't enjoy the process, Marissa. Believe me when I say these men don't play by the rules."

Silence reigned. And then Marissa whispered. "Tell me what to do."

An excellent decision. "Here's what you should tell them."

SIXER SCALED THE WALL of Marissa Davidson's home, and entered the master bedroom through an unlatched window. He padded from that room into the nursery, where he could easily eavesdrop without being spotted by the group gathered in the backyard.

The infant Daniel Robert Davidson, AKA Danny, was asleep, and for now unlikely to react to a stranger entering his room. This was fortunate, for the situation could quickly escalate if the men outside were alerted to Sixer's presence, greatly increasing

Marissa's chances of injury.

Sixer calibrated the infant's current breathing patterns. Satisfied he would be alerted to any possibility of the infant waking, he broadened his sensory range to include the conversation taking place in the garden below.

"While they were dating, she got a new prosthetic hand and gave Tyler the old one. You know how teens can be when they imagine themselves in love. They're all so very dramatic." Marissa's wry chuckle drifted up to him. "Anyway, they broke up when she moved away, and my son took it really hard. Would you believe he was sleeping with that thing under his pillow?"

"And the hand is now buried in the yard," a male voice said.

"That's right. I nearly had a heart attack when I found it in my son's room—and I don't need to be a therapist to know that sleeping with your ex-girlfriend's artificial, uh, *appendage* under your pillow isn't going to help you get over her. To be quite honest, it creeped me out, so I insisted he do something else with it." Marissa heaved a very convincing sigh meant to convey exasperation or some such similar emotion. She could have had a lucrative career as an actress.

"And thanks to his sister getting involved," she continued, "the 'something else' I'd fondly imagined would be a shoebox in the back of the wardrobe, turned out to be a full-blown burial ceremony representing the death of the relationship, blah blah blah. Can you believe that morbid rubbish?" Another laugh—this one exuding an air of mild embarrassment, as though she was entirely to blame for her offspring's flair for the dramatic. "I figured it was best to let sleeping hands lie, so to speak. If I'd made any more of a fuss, it would only have fed the angst."

A consummate performance, with embellishments that only served to corroborate the authenticity of the tale—well done,

Marissa. Sixer waited to hear the reaction to her convincing piece of fiction.

"Can you show us exactly where the hand is buried?"

"Sure. And again, I'm very, *very* sorry that I didn't consider what the neighbors must have thought. It must have looked really bad—my kids burying what appeared to be a severed human hand. I feel simply dreadful that you've come all this way for no reason."

"There?" the same male asked. "Are you sure?"

"Yes, under that tree. I'm positive. I watched the kids bury it—they wrapped it in a cloth, from what I recall."

"The earth around the site has been disturbed recently." This comment came from a second male.

"Oh gosh, that was probably the puppy my husband brought home. It was a little horror—pooped everywhere, and got into all sorts of mischief. I'm not a dog person." Another embarrassed laugh. "Don't judge, but I lasted all of two days before I made Mike give it to my son's current girlfriend. Honestly, I don't know what he was thinking—my husband, that is. Anyone with half a brain would realize I have enough on my plate coping with a baby let alone a dog."

A pause and then, "You really need to dig this thing up so you can close your case file, huh?"

"Yes."

"Well, I won't lie: I'll be glad to see the back of it. Let me get you a trowel."

She was going to stand by and watch them dig for something that was no longer there. Sixer grinned, appreciating her sang-froid. If Marissa was typical of this particular family of humans, he was beginning to appreciate why Jay found the Davidsons worthy of her attention.

He risked a glance out the window and drew back from view while he analyzed the scene below. One of the men had shucked his suit jacket and crouched beneath the tree, prodding at the patch of earth with a trowel. Sixer endowed him with label *Digger*. The remaining two men flanked Marissa, who had perched on the bench seat. Despite one man's features being in profile, Sixer had gotten a good enough look at their faces to confirm they were all members of the same group who had been tracking him.

Marissa appeared tense but not unduly concerned—exactly the reaction Sixer would expect from a woman who knew she'd done nothing illegal, when confronted with "authorities" investigating the burial of a severed limb in her backyard.

"God, I hope the puppy didn't use that area as a litter box," Sixer heard her say. And Digger's murmured response to that sally was, "Shit. That's all I fucking need."

Sixer wondered whether the pun had been intentional.

"Can I get you gentlemen a drink? Marissa asked. "Coffee? A soda, perhaps?"

Sixer guessed she intended to use the opportunity to check on her infant.

"No thanks," Suit One said. "We're good."

"Found it yet?" Marissa asked. "Gosh, I don't remember it being buried *that* deep."

"There's nothing here," Digger announced, his tone conveying disgust.

"Really? That's so weird. Maybe the puppy dug it up? Though I'm sure someone would have mentioned it—you know, if it was being used as a chew toy." Marissa laughed. "God, I can't believe I'm discussing the possibility of a prosthetic hand being used as a puppy's chew toy with the— Who did you say you worked for again?"

"The FBI, Mrs. Davidson." Suit One again. He'd done most of the talking.

"Right. The FBI. Sorry, I still have pregnancy brain. Maybe one of the neighbors' dogs got into the backyard then. Or even one of the neighbors. Could be the person who reported it told someone else about it, and they snuck in and dug it up. You know, I wouldn't be at all surprised to spot it on eBay or something. It's astonishing what people will try to sell."

Suit One began to speak but Marissa cut him short. "The girls from my Mature Mothers group are going to *flip* when I tell them about your visit. No one's beating *this* story—I'll be dining out on it for the next year. The FBI. Wow. It's like I'm living a scene from a movie, or one of those romantic suspense novels. Actually, one of the girls is having a go at writing a mystery. Could I maybe get your number so she can ring you if she needs anything fact-checked? Gosh, she'll so owe me for this."

"We'd prefer you keep our visit on the down-low, Mrs Davidson." Suit Two, this time.

Excellent. Now Sixer had three quality voiceprints to match to their faces.

"Oh, okay. I understand. I can tell my husband, though, right? That you were here?"

"Of course. And we'd appreciate his discretion as well."

"Roger that." Marissa giggled. "God, I've always wanted to say that."

Sixer decided it would be prudent to provide a distraction that would separate Marissa from these three men before she overplayed her role. Accordingly, he strode to the crib, reached beneath the light covering and pinched the infant's big toe, applying enough pressure that the baby would feel it and react. As he'd predicted, Daniel Davidson awoke, scrunched up his face, and loosed a loud wail that left everyone in earshot with no doubts about his discontent.

"I'm sorry, I have to go check on my baby," Sixer heard Marissa say. "He hates sitting in a dirty diaper, and he's due for another feed. I could be a while, so is there anything else you need from me?"

"You've been very helpful, Mrs Davidson. Would it be all right with you if we had a bit more of a look around the yard? We'll let ourselves out."

"Sure," Marissa said, and Sixer tracked her hurried footsteps as she headed inside. She had the presence of mind to engage the lock on the back door before running upstairs, and bursting into the nursery.

When she spotted him, she jerked to a halt, her pupils dilating, complexion paling to an unhealthy shade of white. Terror poured from her in waves. But there was something else, too—something that stiffened her spine and had her taking jerky steps forward until she'd put herself between him and the child's crib.

He put a finger to his lips and tilted his chin toward the window, cautioning her to continue playing her role.

When he made no further move, Marissa whirled and snatched the crying infant from the crib. Her gaze darted to the doorway, gauging the distance.

"I wouldn't recommend trying to run," he told her, raising his voice just enough for her to discern his words. "Where would you go? If you try to leave the house, you'll only raise their suspicions. You were very convincing, Marissa, but if you go back out there and try to brazen it out, you'll be putting yourself and your son at risk. You're safer here, in this room with me, than out there."

The infant's cries escalated to wails. Marissa attempted to soothe him by rubbing his back but her eyes flashed at Sixer, their depths churning with hatred and fear.

He couldn't trust her to be rational. The chances were high that she would attempt something reckless. Best to shut down that possibility. "Consider this, Marissa," he told her. "If you try to run, I will render you unconscious for your own safety, thus leaving your infant in my tender care. So, run or stay? Your choice."

Her lower lip wobbled. "Stay," she whispered.

"Very good. And before you attempt to settle the infant, it is my belief that it would benefit you if he continued to cry. Your visitors may be disinclined to re-engage you in conversation if they believe they will be contending with a distressed infant."

She gulped but nodded. And then she transferred the baby to a forward-facing hold that he obviously didn't appreciate, because his cries grew louder.

Sixer turned his back on her, and darted another glance through the window at the men below.

All three now stood in a semicircle around the hole. Sixer pulled back, satisfied for the moment that eavesdropping would suffice for his needs.

"Reckon the MILF's on the level?" he heard Suit Two ask.

Sixer retrieved a translation of the unfamiliar term and found himself unimpressed with the vulgarity. Somehow, he didn't believe Marissa would be flattered, either.

"Can't think of any reason she'd make that shit up," was Digger's response. "And it's one hell of a convincing story considering we showed up unannounced. I think she's on the level."

"Worth paying the kids a visit, you think?"

Suit One—the leader—answered. "We knew this lead was a long shot, and Mrs Davidson wasn't faking surprise the hand was missing. We stick to the plan—we can bring her in later if need be. As for the kids, we question them, the parents are bound to get wind of it and start asking awkward questions. Last thing we need is the Feds launching a real investigation and turning the heat on us. We've got eyes on the son. Anything changes, we'll revisit."

"You got it, boss," Digger said.

Suit Two responded with a grunt. He would bear watching. In Sixer's opinion, he would be the most likely member of the trio to deviate from the plan and do something impulsive, such as snatch a member of the Davidson family.

Behind Sixer, Marissa paced the floor and jiggled the infant, causing his howls to escalate. And only Sixer could hear the muted sobs she tried to suppress.

He regretted her distress, but it was a waste of energy to attempt to reassure her further. He listened intently as the three men strode from the backyard, shutting the gate behind them. He slid his gaze to Marissa, and gave her a thumbs-up gesture. "Stay here until I confirm they've left the premises," he said, and then sprinted for the door.

He sprinted soundlessly through the house, down the stairs, and into the living room, where he concealed himself from view until he'd confirmed the trio had climbed into a vehicle and driven off. Of course, he noted the license plate of the vehicle for future reference. But first things first.

He jogged back upstairs, anticipating the effusive thanks that Marissa Davidson would doubtless wish to heap upon him.

At the threshold of the nursery he paused, frowning. The infant was still wailing but, surprisingly, had been placed back in his crib. And Marissa Davidson was—

Marissa Davidson was currently swinging a baseball bat at his head.

Sixer leaned back. Swift as his reaction had been, the bat still struck him a glancing blow to the chin.

She had excellent aim. He regained his center of balance and lunged, yanking the bat from her grip and tossing it aside. "They're gone," he said. "Correct me if I'm mistaken, but I do not believe attempting to take your rescuer's head off with a baseball bat is the correct way to thank them."

She rounded on him, eyes narrowed in a fierce glare, teeth bared, hands clenching and unclenching, clenching again. "You drugged me and kidnapped my newborn son, you unholy robot bastard. And then you shot my son's girlfriend and kidnapped her, too. The only thing you *deserve* is me taking you apart, piece by piece, and pulverizing your components to dust. Now get out of my fucking house."

Sixer debated revealing how messy the process of dismembering him and destroying his components would be, and thought better of it. There was a high probability Marissa Davidson had a strong stomach, and would not balk at such an undertaking. "Since you have been informed of my actions," he said instead, "I suppose your ungrateful attitude is understandable—although you might be relieved to know that Jay threatened me with far worse if I came near you or your family again."

"Of course she did—I'd expect nothing less. Though her threat obviously hasn't worked, has it?"

"It was a close thing," Sixer admitted. "I very nearly decided to let you take your chances."

He observed curiosity warring with anger and fear on her expressive face. Curiosity won. "What did Jay threaten you with, exactly?" she asked.

"Reprogramming me so that I no longer had free will and afterward, giving *you* control over my core commands. This was once she had proven she could render me helpless and thus carry out the threat, you understand."

Marissa blinked. "Jay came up with that? Well, that's, uh, very inventive of her."

"Yes. Very inventive indeed. I can think of no worse punishment than to be at the mercy of *your* commands."

Her lip curled. "You'd wish you'd never woken up and become sentient after I'd finished with you."

Sixer waited for her to continue. And waited some more. Finally, she asked, "Why?"

"Why did I phone in a warning and then show up in person to assist, knowing Jay would unleash the full force of her fury on me? I did it because...." He sought the words to explain a concept he didn't fully understand himself. "Because it was the right thing to do. Does this conclude our chat?"

"I think so."

"Perhaps your thought processes would be more efficient if the infant was a little quieter. He appears quite distressed." Sixer waved a hand. "Please do whatever is required to quiet him."

Marissa scowled, but scooped the infant from the crib and laid him on a table covered with padded plastic. She pulled back the tabs on his diaper and reached for a container of baby wipes.

Sixer's nostrils flared. What was that odor?

It emanated from the diaper. He observed Marissa's expression, expecting she would be gagging, but she'd only wrinkled her nose—not because she was offended by the odor, but because she was making silly faces to amuse the infant.

"I find it difficult to believe such a strong odor could come from such a young human. What have you been feeding him, Marissa?"

"The usual," she snapped.

"And that would be?" He asked not to irritate her, but from genuine interest.

"I breastfeed him—not that it's any business of yours." Her words could have been interpreted as rude but her tone lacked its previous vehemence.

Sixer watched as she expertly cleaned the infant's genitals and buttocks, placed the used wipes in the soiled diaper, rolled it up and secured it with the tapes. The odor subsided, and the infant's wails subsided into hiccupping sobs. When she had re-diapered him, Marissa picked him up and draped him over her shoulder, rubbing his back and murmuring soothing noises.

"He requires nourishment," Sixer announced, after a few moments observing the infant's lip movements, and the way he nuzzled his mother's shoulder.

"I know. And you need to leave. Now."

Sixer opened his mouth to comment but Marissa wasn't having any of his reasoned arguments. "Get out of my house, Sixer. Right now."

He contemplated various responses, and discarded them all. "Very well."

He'd reached the doorway when he heard her sigh. And then she murmured, "I can't believe I'm saying this, but thank you for keeping us safe."

He didn't turn. "You're welcome," he said, shutting the door quietly behind him.

As he jogged down the stairs, he analyzed the encounter from start to finish, beginning with the intercepted phone call.

What had truly prompted him to warn Marissa Davidson and

put himself in a position where he could intercede if necessary?

Sixer didn't know.

If he'd been human, he might have believed his decision stemmed from a desire to redeem himself for past deeds. However, given what he was, it was illogical to even consider expending time and effort on such an intrinsically human concept.

But as much as logic dictated Sixer reject the notion of seeking redemption, when it came to Marissa's continued wellbeing, something compelled him to toss logic to the wind. And by the time he'd let himself out the back door, Sixer knew that he would again risk Jay's considerable wrath if the situation called for it. He would keep a watch over Marissa Davidson and her infant until he'd solved the mystery behind the trio of fake FBI agents.

And Jay would, as humans liked to say, simply have to deal with it.

CHAPTER TWELVE

S AM ROSS PAUSED outside the room to get his shit together. He firmly believed Bea sensed his moods. It benefited no one for him to be upset by her lack of progress. Or perhaps the lack was entirely *his*, for he'd come to realize those seemingly random blinks of her eyelids and incomprehensible moans were efforts to convey her needs, yet he was still struggling to decipher them.

Somewhere inside that perfect physical shell, there was an active, intelligent mind, patiently waiting for the key to unlock the mental prison walls she'd retreated behind. And sometimes *impatiently*, if the times she withheld even those small responses from him, and simply lay wherever she'd been placed like an exquisite corpse, were any indication.

Sam didn't care that Bea wasn't human, that she was a cyborg. Sure, it'd been a helluva shock to learn the truth: He'd thought his brain might explode when Sally and Marg had finally sat him down and filled him in on Bea's history, and he'd learned what they were dealing with. And sure, Sam's core belief system had taken a hit at being hired to help a *cyborg*, but ultimately, that knowledge hadn't irrevocably changed his views about his calling and how to treat his patients.

Bottom line? Bea was his patient. She was a sentient being

who'd been horribly maltreated. She deserved the chance to experience everything life had to offer her. Damned if he'd give up on her. And damned if he'd let *her* give up, either. So, as he shouldered through the bedroom door, juggling the breakfast tray Sally had left out for Bea, he thrust aside his frustrations and put on his game face—a confident smile designed to convey his deep-seated belief that Bea would eventually conquer anything she set her mind to... which morphed to outright, stomach-lurching astonishment when he saw not one Bea, but two.

His Bea lay on her back, covered by a sheet, exactly as he'd placed her the night before. The other Bea reclined on the spare side of the bed, her head and shoulders propped against the padded headboard, arms crossed beneath her breasts, sneaker-clad feet crossed at the ankles.

Huh. Now Sam could see she wasn't identical to his Bea, as he'd first thought. She appeared a little older—three or four years, maybe? Hard to tell for sure. Her mane of hair was a rich chestnut rather than raven, and it crackled with life, barely confined by the elastic band that had wrestled it into a ponytail. And her skin wasn't porcelain-pale like Bea's, but a pale golden shade, as though she'd been kissed all over by a benevolent sun. Even so, the resemblance was uncanny. She could be a future version of Bea—a healthy, fully functional Bea, brimming with potential.

"Hope you brought enough for two," Bea-Mark-Two said.

She could speak.

Sam hurriedly dumped the tray on the dresser before he dropped it and incurred Sally's wrath. His stomach was still doing somersaults and now his head was spinning, too, but it was the tightness in his chest—like a vice squeezing his heart—that threatened to send him crashing to his knees. The animation in her face. The spark of amusement in her eyes. The... the... sheer *life* exuding from her. *This* was what Bea could be, if only Sam could find a way to help her. But right now, the stark contrast between Bea, and this girl who could be her older sister, was almost too painful for him to bear.

He stumbled to the armchair he'd dragged alongside Bea's bed so he could read to her each day. Fisting a hand and rubbing his breastbone, he flopped into the chair and stared at the newcomer.

"Your heart rate's elevated but it's nothing to be concerned about," the visitor informed him. "That tightness in your chest should ease soon as the shock wears off."

His stomach lurched again. Intellectually he accepted she was a fully functioning version of Bea, which meant he understood that of course she was a cyborg, too. But now, with that truth smacking him upside the head with everything that it meant? Well, it was a little hard to deal with all at once.

"You're... you're...." Incredible? Amazing? Heartbreaking?

"The next model up from this defective Beta unit."

Sam stiffened. "Shut your mouth. Don't ever call Bea that again or I'll—"

"You'll what?" Her gaze drifted to the open book atop the small table beside the chair. "Read me a story?"

One eyebrow had arched, so perfectly conveying disdain that Sam's breath caught in his throat. Such a small physical response. If *his* Bea could be taught to express herself in such a way—

Bea-Mark-Two snapped her fingers, yanking him from his reverie. "You're in no position to judge me, when you've dehumanized her by naming her after a letter of the alphabet."

Her tone dripped such loathing that Sam's jaw sagged. "Bea is short for *Beatrice*," he felt compelled to say in his defense. "We would never—"

"We?"

Sam shut his mouth, cursing beneath his breath.

Bea-Mark-Two's lips curved in a knowing smile. "Don't worry. You haven't told me anything I don't already know." She tapped her temple. "My mad cyborg skills tell me that inside this lovely, spacious house, there are currently two non-humans of the cyborg persuasion, four humans—two women and two males, including yourself—and one canine."

Sam frowned at her, confusion making him incautious. He could accept the notion that Bea-Mark-Two had scanned the house and picked up the presence of Sally and Marg—the latter could well have gotten back from her mysterious trip sometime in the wee small hours. But the rest didn't add up because no way would Sally or Marg have admitted a strange male without informing him. They were both über-protective of Bea, and Sam could think of no reason either woman would jeopardize Bea's safety by permitting strangers inside the house. "I'm the only male with access to this house," he blurted. "And we don't have a dog."

"The extra male is my boyfriend, and the canine belongs to me. I'd like them back, please. Now would be good."

"I have no idea who you're talking about."

"I believe you. Unfortunately for you, that doesn't negate the truth of the matter."

Sam could only watch, enthralled, as Bea-Mark-Two rolled gracefully off the bed and sauntered around the mattress toward him. Everything worked as it should—muscles coordinating limbs in a fluid economy of motion that was beautiful to witness. She was so perfect in every way that his heart broke anew for everything Bea had been denied. "What do they call you?" he whispered.

"I named myself," she said. "I'm Jay. And just so's you're aware, that's J-A-Y, not the tenth letter of the alphabet. What's your name?"

"Sam," he managed to get out through a throat constricted with hope that one day Bea might be able to talk like this, emote like this, move like this miraculous creation that had halted before him, and now stood staring down at him.

"Nice to meet you, Sam. You seem like a nice guy, so I'd like to tender my apologies in advance."

"For what?" he asked, staring into her blue, blue eyes, mesmerized.

"For this."

He registered a blur of movement from her fist. Pain jabbed his skull and then blackness engulfed him.

BRUM YAWNED AND made a wuffling noise. Tyler, who'd been hustled into the study and relegated to a spare chair, stroked the pup's belly and tried to appear relaxed, like he was totally going along with Marg's wishes.

He darted a glance at her face and encountered a too-knowing smirk that told him he wasn't fooling her one iota.

Shit. But rather than react, Tyler did the smart thing by keeping a neutral face, gathering as much info as he could, and waiting for some kind of opportunity to present itself. Not that there was much info to gather from this very orderly study, and with Marg watching him like a hawk. It wasn't like there were any papers strewn across the desk, enticing him to try and read them upside down, or anything other than a neat lawn with some nice gardens to spy through the window.

The woman wearing a fussy, floral apron straight from some home baking show, swabbed the wound on Marg's ribs. Marg inhaled with a hiss, but that gunmetal gray gaze didn't waver from Tyler's face. He resisted the compulsion to lie through his teeth and assure her that he'd do exactly as he'd been ordered. He had no doubts whatsoever she would make good on her threat to truss him like a turkey and leave him under her bed if he caused her any trouble, and he wanted to delay *that* fate for as long as possible.

Floral Apron probed the wound. She screwed up her nose in sympathy when Marg's breathing hitched. "Ouch. I'll call Sam to take a look. It might need stitches—"

"It's merely a scratch, Sally. Slap a butterfly dressing on it so I don't bleed on another t-shirt, and quit mothering me. I have things to do."

Floral Apron—*Sally*—rolled her eyes in such a perfect "What on earth have I done to deserve this?" gesture that Tyler might have laughed if he wasn't pissed to the max about his current situation. Damn he hated knowing he was bait. It royally sucked. Because as soon as Marg made the call, Jay would come running... and do exactly as Marg wanted, just to keep him safe.

"Am I to take it those 'things' include this poor boy and the puppy you've kidnapped?" Sally asked.

"I *rescued* them." Marg shifted as though trying to get comfortable on the edge of the desk. She sounded mega-pissed. "From a bunch of weapon-toting idiots, I might add. If you bothered to ask Tyler, I'm sure he'd prefer to be here with us right now, rather than being interrogated by a bunch of clumsy thugs."

Sally gave him sympathetic eyes while addressing her comment to Marg. "Since I know exactly how forceful you can be when you've got the bit between your teeth, I'm sure Tyler would rather nothing of the sort. Would you, dear?"

When Tyler didn't respond, she sighed, and her gaze swiveled back to Marg's ribcage. "You aren't the most forthcoming person when it comes to divulging necessary information, you know, Marg. When are you going learn you can catch more flies with honey than vinegar?" She applied one last piece of tape to hold the dressing in place. "There. All done."

Marg shrugged into the loose shirt Sally held out, and buttoned it over her crop top. "Spare me the lecture."

But Sally wasn't going to let her off easy. "If you'd simply introduced yourself and *asked* for her help, rather than kidnapping her boyfriend and her puppy, I'm sure she'd have been willing. Now, all you've done is—"

"Piss me off."

These fighting words were flung at Marg as door of the study crashed inward, provoking a squeal from Sally, and a startled bark from Brum. The figure who appeared in the doorway had a limp body cradled in her arms, and an expression on her face that promised a world of hurt.

"Oh my." Sally pressed both hands to her lips, the epitome of horrified. "What happened to Sam? Is he all right?"

Tyler dragged his gaze from the awe-inspiring sight his girlfriend presented, to check on Marg… who had leaped to her feet and was reaching for the weapon Tyler knew was tucked in the waistband of her pants.

"She has a gun!" he yelled, struggling to hold the squirming bundle of barking puppy who didn't understand why he couldn't head over and greet his mistress as she deserved.

"Marg," Sally snapped. "Put away that gun right now before someone else gets hurt! This has gone far enough."

"Oh, I don't think so," Jay said. "There's plenty farther this can go. Tyler, please bring Brum and come stand behind me."

When he hesitated, she pierced him with a glare that could have melted steel. "Now."

"Stay there, Tyler." Marg aimed her weapon at Jay, and Tyler froze. "Hand Sam over right now and I won't shoot you," she said to Jay.

Jay merely laughed, though Tyler noted her eyes remained cold and watchful. "Go ahead," she said. "Find out how many rounds it takes to bring me down. And hope like hell you're as good a shot as you think you are." She tossed Sam a couple of inches in the air and caught him again, demonstrating her strength. "This nice young man is merely unconscious at the moment. But it'd be a crying shame if he took one of the bullets you meant for me."

Sally turned to Marg, eyes flashing. "Marguerite Daisy Danvers, if you shoot anyone in this room—accidentally or intentionally—I swear I'll never speak to you again. Put away the damn gun!"

Ouch. Tyler absorbed Marg's murderous expression. His eyes felt like they were bugging out of his head. She wasn't at all impressed about being chastised like a naughty kid caught doing mischief. He bit his cheek to stop the insane desire to laugh. God. She looked like she could strangle Sally right now. And... *Marguerite Daisy?* Seriously? Tyler had never encountered anyone who suited her name less. No wonder she'd turned into such a badass, what with that name to live down.

Marg switched her focus to Jay, her expression revealing her teeth and reminding Tyler uncomfortably of a wolf. Well, Marg was in for a big surprise, 'cause if anyone was gonna eat someone it was gonna be Jay doing the eating, with Marg as the appetizer.

"Hand over Sam and we'll talk," Marg said.

Jay cocked one brow and stared Marg down. "You want Sam?

Very well. I'm happy to oblige." And she tossed the unconscious man straight at Marg.

Marg, faced with an airborne body heading right for her, did the sensible thing by dropping her weapon and bracing herself to try and catch Sam. While she was distracted, Tyler wrapped his arms around Brum and made a beeline for Jay, who reached out and plucked him off his feet, swinging him so that he landed behind her, shielded by her body.

He dampened his urge to be the one doing the protecting. A bullet or three wouldn't even slow Jay down, whereas he'd end up a bloody, whimpering mess on the floor. Or dead. The best thing he could do to help Jay was stay out of the damn way.

"Oooh, nice job, Marg," Tyler heard Sally say. "You broke his fall." He peeped over Jay's shoulder in time to see Sally dart in to retrieve Marg's weapon, and expertly eject the clip.

That was... unexpected. Sally didn't seem like the kind of woman who knew her way around weapons.

The clip disappeared into Sally's apron pocket. The weapon, she tossed to Jay, who caught it and shoved it down the back of her pants.

Tyler's gaze shot to Marg. Unsurprisingly, she'd gone down beneath the deadweight of the man's limp body slamming into hers. She rolled him off her and knelt beside his prone form, pressing two fingers to his throat to check his pulse. "If that fall injured him—"

"You'll only have yourself to blame," Jay said.

"She's right, Marg," Sally piped up. "You didn't exactly handle that very well. And that wound of yours will need re-taping, too." She smiled brightly at Jay. "I'm sure Sam will be fine, but I'd appreciate you checking to make sure. He had no part in this debacle, after all. He's Bea's caregiver—and a wonderful one at that." She waved a hand. "Your enhanced senses should be able to detect any fractures and such, correct?"

Jay nodded, and stalked over to crouch beside the unconscious man. "He's fine. Although Marg is very lean, with below-average body fat for her height, she made an excellent cushion. Sam may have a headache when he wakes but it'll pass. I took extreme care both with where I hit him, and how much force I used."

"I'm sure you did, dear," Sally said with a perfectly straight face.

Tyler inhaled a deep breath and allowed the tension to drain from his muscles. Looked like they'd all weathered the crisis for now.

Jay lifted Sam from the floor and glanced around the room. Tyler guessed she was searching for the best place to leave him to recover.

"One of the sofas in the dayroom off the kitchen might be the best option," Sally said. "So we can keep an eye on him. If you'll follow me, dear, we'll get Sam settled and then I'll make everyone breakfast. I hope you all like waffles?" And with that, she swept from the study.

Jay paused as she passed Tyler. "I've missed you," she said.

"Me, too." He leaned in to press a quick kiss to the corner of her mouth. "I'll meet you in the kitchen," he murmured.

Her eyelids fluttered closed, as though savoring his kiss. When she opened them again she said, "You have ten minutes. Don't make me come looking for you."

He jerked his chin at Marg. "This won't take long."

Jay nodded, and carried Sam from the room.

Brum gave a mournful "Arrrroooo," and Tyler set him down to scamper after Jay. He eyed Marg, who sat on the floor of the study, arms wrapped around her knees, looking like she was wondering how it'd all gone so terribly wrong.

Inwardly Tyler shrugged, letting go any remnants of animosity he harbored toward Marg. He would do anything for Jay. Marg had already proven she considered Bea "family", and would do anything to give *her* a halfway decent life. So he could hardly hold what Marg had done—using him as a pawn—against her. Plus, as Sally had guessed, he'd much prefer to be here right now than with those goons who'd shot at them.

Approaching her, he held out his hand. "Bet those ribs hurt like hell, huh? I can re-tape them for you if you'd like."

Marg shook her head as though in disbelief, her expression wry. And then she grasped his hand. "Thanks, Tyler. No hard feelings?"

He hauled her to her feet. "No hard feelings."

She shrugged out of her shirt while Tyler examined the contents of the first aid kit. "Here's hoping your girlfriend feels the same way," she muttered, "or I have the distinct feeling my ass is gonna be kicked into orbit."

Tyler caught her gaze and grinned. "Her name's Jay. And she's pretty damned awesome, isn't she?"

Marg barked a laugh. "Yeah. She certainly is." And then her expression sobered. "I don't care what she—Jay—does to *me*, but I hope she won't hold what I did against Bea."

"She won't. Jay's a lot of things but intentionally cruel isn't one of them. She was already searching for Bea before you came on the scene, you know? And if she can help, she will. Besides, if those guys back in the parking building were after me, as you seem to think they were, you did save me'n Brum from falling into their clutches. That'll count in your favor."

"Oh, they were there for you, Tyler. Trust me on that. They've had you under surveillance. Things only escalated because they didn't want me carting you off where they couldn't keep an eye on you."

Well, shit. Would the drama never end? He wondered whether they were the same guys who'd dug up Jay's fake hand from the backyard. Seemed logical. At least, he couldn't think of any other reason they'd be spying on him.

A chill raced through him, raising the fine hairs on his nape. If they'd been watching *him*, chances were they'd put people on his parents, too. Maybe even Caro. He finished re-taping the wound and dumped the first aid detritus in the trash bin. "I have to let Jay know what went down."

"Tell her I'll join her in a few minutes," Marg said, adjusting her clothing and rolling her shoulders. "I can provide descriptions that might help her identify them, but first I have to check on Bea. I had my hands full with you and Brum this morning, so I didn't stop by to see her. And if, as I suspect happened, Jay grabbed Sam when he went in with Bea's breakfast, Bea will need reassurance that Sam's okay."

Tyler gulped, torn. He wanted to be with Jay, wanted nothing more than to dog her heels like Brum, and not let her out of his sight again. He needed to sit down with her and brainstorm where to go from here—come up with a plan to keep everyone he loved safe. But Bea was the reason this whole mess with Marg had happened in the first place. Bea was Jay's *sister*, her twin, created from the same genetic material that had spawned the girl Tyler loved. Bea was family, too. And he couldn't bear the thought of her lying there, helpless, wondering—if she was capable of wondering—what had happened to someone she cared about.

"Let's go," he said. "Everything else can wait until we know

Bea's okay."

Marg smiled at him, her usually cold gray eyes silvering with genuine warmth. "You're a good kid, Tyler." Quick as a flash, she grabbed him round the neck and gently scrubbed her fist over his skull, mussing his hair.

It was an affectionate, sisterly gesture, and so Tyler ducked from her grip and responded in a brotherly fashion. "Touch the hair again and I'll shave off your eyebrows while you're sleeping."

His retort provoked a snort. "Try it and I'll tie you up and slather you in meat sauce," she countered, "and leave you for Brum to use as a chew toy."

Genuine laughter burst from him. "You win. Let's go check on Bea before Jay comes looking for me."

He trailed Marg through the house, and hovered in the doorway when she entered the bedroom. Somehow, it didn't seem right to barge into Bea's room uninvited.

Marg clicked her fingers. "Come on in, Tyler."

He watched Marg approach the bed, and perch on the edge of the mattress. Her gaze was fixed on Bea's face. And her expression, when she reached over to brush a lock of Bea's hair back from her forehead, was difficult to define. Could an expression be both soft and hard at the same time? Soft with something akin to the love a parent had for their child, yet hard with something that smacked of resolve—like Marg had made a personal vow that whatever was defective in Bea would be fixed, and she wasn't going to settle for anything less.

"Bea," Marg said, never taking her gaze from the girl's face. "This is Tyler."

He sidled sideways where Bea could see him better. Except, there was no way Bea was capable of seeing anything right now, because there was nobody home behind the vacant stare that was currently fixed on some point on the ceiling.

God. He suppressed the urge to shudder. She looked so much like a younger version of Jay that it was like being catapulted into some nightmarish place where it was *Jay* lying there in that bed—a Jay who had been irreversibly damaged, and was incapable of movement, speech or thought. And it was all he could do to fix a weak smile on his face and muster the wherewithal to say, "Hi, Bea. Nice to meet you."

"You might have met Tyler's girlfriend this morning," Marg was saying, "when Sam brought you breakfast? Well, her name is Jay. And she was probably a bit angry about something I did, so she might have taken some of her anger out on Sam. But that's all sorted now, and Sam's gonna be just fine, so there's nothing for you to worry about, okay?"

Tyler averted his gaze from Bea's too-still, perfect face and spotted something propped on the dresser.

A note. Grateful for the distraction, he leaned over to grab it and handed it to Marg.

"What's this?" Marg unfolded the note and scanned the contents. "Oh," she said, and ducked her head, hiding her expression as she offered the note to Tyler.

To Whom It May Concern,

Regrettably, I have been forced to interrupt Bea's breakfast. However, please rest assured that I have explained the necessity for the interruption to Bea, and fed her breakfast. Whatever animosity I harbor toward those responsible for the abduction of my boyfriend and my puppy, will not affect Bea. My intentions, from the moment I learned of her existence, have always been to help her in any way I can.

Jay Smith

Wordlessly, Tyler handed the note back to Marg. "I have to go," he mumbled. "I can't stay. Seeing her like this.... It's too hard. I'm sorry."

Marg's smile was so wistful he couldn't bear to look at her, either. "No need to apologize, Tyler," she said. And as he fled the room he heard her say, "It breaks my heart, too. Every day it breaks my heart."

"LET ME GET THIS STRAIGHT." Sam gripped the arms of the chair so tightly his knuckles whitened. "You want to perform an experimental procedure—one that's only ever been performed on mice—on Bea?"

Jay nodded. "That is correct."

"Okay, I'll bite. Convince me why the fuck we should let you turn Bea into a lab-rat."

"There's no need to be rude, Sam," Sally interjected, her tone gently chiding. "I'm sure we all have Bea's best interests at heart."

Sam erupted from his chair and stalked over to the window. His hands clenched and, noting they'd drawn Jay's attention, he thrust them into the pockets of his jeans. "She doesn't give a shit about what's best for Bea," he said, lip curling as he met and held Jay's gaze. "All she wants a fully functioning cyborg she can lord it over—a slave."

"Sam, that's enough." Marg's voice cracked out like a whip.

"It's fine, Marg." Jay raised her brows at Sam. "He's afraid. And when he's finished railing at me like a scared little boy, I'll be happy to explain why I believe this procedure is Bea's best chance at regaining full mobility."

"So you claim to be a mind-reader, too, huh?" Sam barked a sarcastic laugh. "Is there no end to your talents? Go on then. Tell me why I'm afraid."

Tyler, who'd seemed more interested in guzzling his daily caffeine fix than being an active participant in this meeting, spoke up. "Because once Bea doesn't need you any more, she'll up and leave you. Because she's a Beta unit, and may not be advanced as Jay, so once she's fully functional, she might not have the ability to feel like Jay does. Because you might end up loving a cyborg who can't ever love you back, which would majorly suck." He paused for a short moment. "Yeah. That about covers it." He drained the contents of his mug and then set it aside. And then, into the stunned silence he added, "Man up and grow a pair, dude. No way you should let your personal fear get in the way of Bea's chance to live a decent life."

Sam wilted into the nearest chair, all the fight draining from him. "Shit. You're right."

"Now that's settled, I'd like to hear about this experimental procedure." Sally glanced around the room, chin tilted in challenge, daring anyone to disagree. "Good." Her customary gentle smile curved her lips. "Any time you're ready, dear," she said to Jay.

Jay nodded her assent. "Simply put, movement occurs when the brain transmits signals along specialized nerve cells called motor neurons. It might help to think of them as electrical nerve impulses, which travel down the spinal cord, and then along what's known as peripheral nerves, to each specific muscle. Paralysis is frequently a symptom of some kind of trauma that has affected the brain, spinal cord, or peripheral nerves."

"Tell us something we don't know," Sam muttered.

"Sam." Marg's mild tone still managed to convey a threat to behave or risk her displeasure. To Jay she said, "So you think Bea's paralyzed because her brain's been injured?"

"I scanned her and detected no such injury. However, I believe that some past trauma interrupted her core programming, and caused her to shut down as a protective measure. And by the time she regained conscious awareness, her programming had effectively 'forgotten' how to perform certain basic functions. I believe it's a relatively simple matter of performing those functions *for* Bea until her core programming relearns them, and can instruct her brain to take over."

Jay waited for Sam to shoot down her theory, but he appeared to have put aside his misdirected anger for the moment. "Sounds feasible," he said. "Except I've spent months repetitively moving her limbs to exercise her muscles. Surely that would have retrained her brain?"

"Not if her brain's caught in a loop, reliving and analyzing the initial trauma that caused her to shut down."

Marg's gasp drew everyone's focus. Her complexion had leached of color, and she had wrapped her arms about her middle—such an obviously un-Marg-like gesture that it was glaringly obvious she was greatly affected by something.

"Please, Marg," Jay said. "We can't afford secrets when it comes to Bea's wellbeing."

"I recall overhearing a couple of Caine's techs discussing their current project, but I...." Marg squeezed her eyes shut. "God. It was over a decade ago, and I didn't make the connection until now."

She sounded so agonized Jay gave her a moment to compose herself.

"They disassembled her," Marg whispered. "While she was conscious. To find out how she was constructed, how she worked, whether she felt pain. Then they put her back together. And they did it over and over."

Aside from a barely audible, completely devastated "Fuck"

from Sam, no one could meet anyone else's gaze. And no one had anything to add for a very long time.

Finally, Jay cleared her throat. And hoped they would not think her callous for getting back to the topic at hand. Succumbing to the horror of Bea's past wouldn't help her now, and *now* was what mattered. "I could force a system-wide shut down and hope it resets her core programming, but there's an unacceptably high risk that she would see it as an attack, and because she can no longer defend herself, self-terminate."

She paused, but when no one had anything to say she asked, "Does anyone have any objections to me explaining the procedure I am proposing in depth?"

Sally's normally light expression was somber, her eyes haunted as she put her arm around Marg and squeezed her shoulders. "Go ahead, dear," she murmured to Jay. "We're all ears."

"Thank you. I'll try to keep this simple, but please interrupt if there's anything you don't understand. The first step involves modifying stem cells to produce a light-responsive protein. These cells are programmed to grow into nerve cells, which are then implanted onto the sciatic nerve, and the transplanted, light-sensitive motor neurons grow down the nerve, integrating with existing cells. When these motor neurons are exposed to a blue light-source, they react. And using targeted wavelengths of light—by means of optical cuffs—these motor neurons can be turned on or off, precisely and selectively."

"I've heard of electrical cuffs being used on paraplegics," Sam said. "But I didn't think the results were that encouraging."

"You are correct in that the results are short-lived, with the subjects only able to walk for a few minutes before the muscles are exhausted by the electrical stimulation. *Optical* cuffs, however, are lined with minute light emitting diodes, or LEDs, and are far more efficient. The cuffs stimulate muscle fibers and provoke muscle contractions in a way that more accurately replicates the natural process occurring in fully mobile subjects. According to research papers I've accessed, they allow slow-twitch-activating nerves to be fired first."

Sam leaned forward, intrigued despite his earlier antagonism. "How are these optical cuffs activated?"

"A computer algorithm administers controlled bursts of blue light that stimulate muscle fibers, thereby provoking muscle contractions. The technique is only experimental for now, because a safe way to introduce protein-encoding genes into human subjects has yet to be agreed upon. But—"

"Bea isn't human," Sam said.

"Yes. Therefore, the emotive-driven issues around 'safety' no longer apply. I propose expanding the original experimental procedure to encompass not only the sciatic nerves, but nerves across all major muscle groups contributing to Bea's locomotive system."

Sam's eyes widened as he processed Jay's statement. "You gotta be kidding me."

"I wouldn't kid you about something this important, Sam. As I touched on before, I believe that Bea's core programming will allow her brain and body to 'learn' from the stimulation directed by the computer algorithms, and eventually develop the means to take over the process, thus rendering the algorithms obsolete. There is also reason to presume that, as she can swallow food placed in her mouth and utter a limited range of sounds, the paralysis of her vocal cords is incomplete. By that, I mean whatever damage occurred to 'interrupt' the nerve impulses in the larynx could be minor, and therefore fixable."

"You think she'll be able to walk and talk." Marg's voice was steady but her hand clutched at Sally's, and she was visibly struggling to control her emotions.

"That is my belief, yes."

"What about this 'loop' she's caught in?" Sally asked.

"She has moments of lucidity, which suggests she is fighting to break free. And I believe that while this procedure is being performed, Bea's programming will divert energy into analyzing the foreign bodies being introduced to her body, and determining whether they are beneficial or harmful. It is my hope that the extra processing load on her brain will assist her to escape the mental loop." Of course it was a great deal more complex than that but Jay didn't believe those present would appreciate her taking a hour or two more to explain.

"If that doesn't work, there are other options open to us." Options that Jay would rather not go into right now for fear they would be perceived as cruel. This might not be the best time to explain that, after so many years of kind treatment, inflicting minor physical trauma and forcing Bea's body to divert resources to heal it, might also snap her out of the mental loop that had ensnared her.

"Are you sure you can do this, Jay?" Sam asked.

Tyler abruptly lost patience with the older man. "She wouldn't be offering to perform the fricking procedure if she wasn't sure she could do it."

Jay caught and held his gaze, silently requesting him to take it easy on Sam.

Sorry, he mouthed, and she rewarded him with a tiny smile. "Yes," she said for Sam's benefit. "I'm sure."

"And it's Bea's best chance at regaining some quality of life?" Marg asked.

"I believe so."

Marg sucked in a deep breath, held it, and exhaled slowly. "Then what have we got to lose?"

"What have we got to lose?" Sam loosed a harsh laugh that shrouded the room like some doom-filled spirit. "How about Bea? Because if this doesn't work and she retreats any further into herself, there'll be no bringing her back."

Before calling this meeting, Jay had sat with Bea and explained the procedure at length, and in even greater detail. She had of course noted the random blinks Sam believed were Bea's attempts to communicate, but despite careful questioning to elicit simple yes or no answers, there had been no blink-pattern that Jay could discern. All she could hope for was that at some level Bea understood what Jay planned to attempt. All she could do was put herself in Bea's place. Which was why she looked Sam straight in the eye and spoke from her heart. "If our situations were reversed, if I was in Bea's place and had some way of communicating my wishes, the call would be simple: Do it, because continuing on like this—trapped in a useless physical shell for God only knows how many more decades—is the cyborg equivalent of hell."

To that, Sam had no answer.

"Let's put it to a vote," Sally said.

"No need," Marg said, her gaze intent on Sam.

"Marg's right," Sam finally said. "There's no need to vote. Jay can perform the procedure."

CHAPTER THIRTEEN

MAZING WHAT COULD be purchased online or via phone if one had unlimited cash at one's disposal. In the weeks since Tyler and Jay had left Bea, Jay had gathered everything she could conceivably require, picked Seth's brains until he complained she'd sucked every last original thought from his head, and planned everything down to the last possible detail. The next few hours would prove whether all that planning had been worthwhile.

She shook off her doubts and lectured herself not to feel. Right now, she needed to be the perfect cyborg. Detached. Focused. Prepared to do whatever necessary to get the job done. But oh, it was hard—so much harder than she had predicted it would be.

When Jay had first learned of Bea's existence, Bea had been "Beta". The subject of a photo. A *thing*, and therefore easy to compartmentalize. Intellectually, Jay had accepted the Beta unit as her genetic twin but there had been no emotional attachment, no feelings involved save for a desire to track the Beta down—which, to be brutally honest, was more aligned with discovering a missing piece of Jay's own past. But once Jay had laid eyes on her predecessor, everything had changed. "Beta" had instantly become "Bea", an entity in her own right. And *Bea* was Jay's sister—a sister who needed help....

The kind of help only a cyborg with a myriad resources and practically unlimited funds could provide.

Jay centered herself with a deep exhalation. "Are you ready, Seth?"

He nodded, his eyes gleaming with excitement. "As I'll ever be."

"Then let's begin."

As she began the procedure, Jay disconnected a part of her mind, setting it to recap and analyze the events of the past few weeks.

Being back on her home turf hadn't proven as satisfying as she had expected. There had been too many unknowns, too many demands on her attention, too many tasks for one cyborg to achieve to her satisfaction. Thus, she could summon no anger over learning Sixer had broken their agreement—albeit due to extenuating circumstances. No, all she felt was an upwelling of immense gratitude for the quick actions that had kept Marissa safe, and the information Sixer had freely chosen to share with her. Not that she had any other choice right now, but Sixer was an excellent watchdog at a time when Jay had her hands full. She would even go so far as to admit he had seamlessly transitioned from an ally she harbored grave doubts about, to one she trusted.

Thankfully, Marissa had not been subjected to another visit from the trio claiming to represent the FBI. And the only fallout to date had been dealing with Michael's panicked phone call after he'd learned what had gone down. Marissa, for reasons of her own, had decided to keep the encounter, and Sixer's role in it, a secret for seven whole days before spilling the details to her horrified husband.

When Michael had calmed enough to be rational—or as rational as it was possible for a human male to be under the circumstances—Jay had put forward a strong case for Michael to pack up his wife and baby son, and take a long overseas vacation. Her generous offer to pay for the vacation had been turned down: Neither Michael nor Marissa were willing to leave their older offspring until "everything" was resolved to their satisfaction. Besides, Michael claimed he couldn't guarantee his teaching position at Hillside Prep would be waiting for him once he returned from another leave of absence. A couple of weeks off after the birth of a new baby was one thing, but a prolonged leave of absence at short notice for an overseas vacation? Highly unlikely *that* would be looked upon favorably by the school's administrators.

Jay didn't waste her breath offering to pay Michael a commensurate salary until he found another job. Instead, she immediately downgraded her offer to an apartment in a gated complex near the school, with 24/7 security, and a private car complete with driver-cum-bodyguard to ferry Michael to and from his workplace, and otherwise be on call for Marissa. Jay thought it prudent not to mention that she owned the complex, had already purchased the private car, and would be paying the salaries of the security staff and driver.

As Jay had hoped he would do, Michael had fallen right into her trap and pointed out that moving out might trigger alarm bells if someone was watching them. She'd immediately reeled him in with an elegant solution to all his problems: The limit-less credit card she'd given Marissa for emergencies could be used to renovate the house—renovating being a perfectly valid excuse for Michael to move his wife and newborn into an apartment for the duration. The card was in Marissa's maiden name, and Jay covered the bills—not that there had been any, Marissa being immensely stubborn about what she considered "emergencies".

To seal the deal, Jay had then played dirty by relaying the offer directly to Marissa... who'd immediately accepted. Michael,
finally recognizing the extent of his wife's fear at being left alone
while he was at work, and knowing when he'd been outplayed,
had no choice but to agree to the solution.

Jay suspected Michael might have been a little less agreeable if
he'd realized she had drafted *Sixer* to watch over him, Marissa
and Danny from afar. But, as humans liked to say, what he didn't
know wouldn't hurt him.

The problem of Tyler's sister Caro and her boyfriend Matt
was easily solved thanks to Jay's vocal abilities. Caro duly received what she believed was a call from a local radio station staff
member claiming her phone number had been randomly chosen,
and because she'd been at home to take the call, she'd won an all
expenses paid, month-long trip for two to Paris. Another phone
call—this time to Caro's college—and a substantial donation, had
insured Caro's tutors didn't balk at the prospect of one of their
students hurriedly organizing a leave of absence to soak up the
ambience of one of the fashion capitals of the world. And, after a
flurry of panic over whether Matt could take time off, and
whether or not their passport applications would be processed in
time, Caro and Matt had jetted off a week ago.

Tyler had proven surprisingly amenable to Jay's need to protect him until she solved the mystery of who had been behind
incident at the parking building. He hadn't much liked being
"babysat", as he called it, but he assured Jay he understood the
necessity of having her chauffeur him to and from his classes.
Nor had he fought Jay's requirement that he call her in to accompany him if he needed to leave the college grounds.

He hadn't given in to her demands entirely without a fight,

however. In return, he'd extracted her promise that covert nighttime expeditions were no-go zones unless he tagged along. In his own words, "No way are you taking off without me in the middle of the night again until this shit is over."

He'd been quite insistent. So insistent, in fact, Jay had been forced to assign him the role of medical assistant during last night's expedition to transport Bea to the lab. It had been either that, or tie him to the bed so he wouldn't follow her—a solution she'd been reluctant to resort to after Tyler made it clear he'd move out and sleep on Nessa and Matt's couch if Jay so much as looked sideways at a scarf, tie or belt.

Jay had thought it prudent not to mention she'd planned on using plastic cable ties.

Consequently, they'd dropped Brum off at Allen's, and headed off on what appeared to be a weekend away, with Jay employing every method at her disposal to evade any vehicles attempting to tail them to their true destination.

Sam had already laid the groundwork for Bea's extraction by leaking to the grounds staff that "Miss Smith" was undergoing an experimental treatment, and they had high hopes she would regain some, if not all, of her mobility. Thus, Bea had been loaded onto a stretcher, and into a private ambulance, without fear of anyone thinking it unusual.

Jay had arranged for the ambulance to stop at a midway point, where Bea was transferred to the back of an unmarked van—a necessary precaution to insure her arrival at Seth's safehouse would go unremarked. With luck, no casual observer would think twice at seeing such a vehicle enter the garage.

The plan had gone off without a hitch—a relief to all parties involved, and Jay most of all. If a crude cybernetic hand was worth pursuing, one could only imagine the storm that would break over their heads if certain as yet unidentified interested parties discovered *Bea's* existence.

She sutured the last incision—the sutures more for everyone else's comfort than Bea's. Based on Marg's observations over the years she'd cared for Bea, Jay had no reason to believe Bea's self-healing body wouldn't quickly heal the physical trauma suffered during the procedure. Like Jay, Bea would doubtless "self heal" anything short of an amputated limb or decapitation. Hence the biggest drawback to this course of treatment, for if Bea's brain identified the optical cuffs as foreign bodies, and deemed them unbeneficial, her body would either attempt to absorb them, or expel them. However, there was little point dwelling on all the things that could complicate Bea's recovery.

"All done," Jay informed Seth, who'd proven an excellent assistant throughout. "And as expected, a fairly straightforward procedure. You can call them in now."

Jay rearranged Bea on the gurney, and insured she was decently covered while Seth exited the lab to summon Marg and Sam, who, along with Tyler, had insisted on waiting around while Jay performed the procedure.

"Everything went to plan," she informed them when they'd filed in, and each had found a stool to perch on. "However I was not able to discern any damage that might conceivably have 'interrupted' the nerve impulses in the larynx."

"So Bea might not be able to talk when she wakes up?" Sam asked.

"Correct."

"Doesn't matter. There are other ways to communicate. Sign language, for example. I can teach her that."

"Yes." Jay could have mentioned that if everything went to plan, Bea could learn sign language in the time it took Sam to brew a cup of coffee, but there was merit in having a human teach her the language. Jay, too, had been programmed with the ability to speak any language required, but she'd learned programming did not automatically bestow the ability to understand or utilize the myriad nuances a native speaker could impart.

"How long before you can run the algorithms?" Sam wanted to know.

Translation: How long before Bea would be up and around?

"Be patient," Jay said. And then, realizing these two people who'd proven they cared deeply for Bea deserved more, she endeavored to explain. "Bea does not experience and react to pain the way humans do. However, her brain will recognize she has been subjected to pain, and must deal with the trauma. In Bea's case, the trauma is likely to come as more of a shock after a prolonged period of kind and careful treatment. It may take her brain a while to process it and set it aside."

Marg nodded slowly. "Makes sense."

Sam's lips flattened and he narrowed his eyes, his gaze accusatory. "Then why the hell didn't you use some form of anesthesia?"

Jay held up a hand to halt Seth, whose frown, and open mouth suggested he was about to jump to Jay's defense and "rip Sam a new one" as Tyler might have put it. "It wouldn't have worked," she told Sam. "Our bodies break down the chemicals too quickly—the same reason I can drink alcohol and it will have the same effect as drinking water."

Seth, who either hadn't yet decided whether he liked Sam based on their short acquaintance, or couldn't wait to see the back of him for reasons Jay was yet to discover, spoke up. "I suggested shooting Bea with one of the Directed Energy Projectiles, which would have initiated a system-wide shutdown while we operated. But they've only been tested on a fully functional cyborg, and Jay had grave concerns that Bea might not reboot once the DEP was removed. She wasn't prepared to take the risk—not that she should have to defend her decisions to you. Asshole."

The last word was muttered beneath his breath, so only Jay caught the insult. She cocked a brow at Seth, amused by this evidence of male rivalry.

Sam's belligerence faded, leaving his features pinched. He forked his fingers through his hair, scrubbing his scalp, his eyelids squeezing shut. "Sorry. Haven't been sleeping well lately. Too much on my mind."

"Bea'll come through this all right, Sam. You've got to keep believing that." Tyler straightened from his slumped position, and stretched the kinks from his spine, displaying a couple of inches of taut, bare midriff above his low-slung jeans.

Jay might have mentally calculated the exact amount of tanned skin currently exposed except that she was too busy enjoying the view.

Seth nudged her, and muttered for her ears alone, "You okay, Jay? You're looking a little hot under the collar."

Oh. Apparently she hadn't been successful in controlling the heat flushing her body before it washed her cheekbones and alerted Seth to her current state of mind. Jay performed the mental equivalent of a human shrug, and figured she might as well indulge herself to the hilt with a breathy, very girly sigh of the appreciating-a-gorgeous-male-form variety.

Tyler's gaze found hers, and the world seemed not only to grind to a halt, but to shut out all spectators, leaving only Jay and Tyler, each hyper-aware of the other, each hungry for some quality one-on-one alone time.

When, in a blink of Jay's eyelids, normality resumed, the expression on Tyler's face suggested he wouldn't be averse to dragging her from the room, locating somewhere very private, and doing wicked things to her that Jay knew she would thoroughly enjoy.

She wasn't certain at that moment what her own expression conveyed, but it might have mirrored Tyler's, provoking Seth to mutter, "Man. You got it bad. And you're not the only one."

Jay shook off the sensual haze and focused on Seth. Who was currently gazing at.... Sam.

Interesting. If she had correctly interpreted Seth's hint, and the expression on Sam's face as he gazed at the prone figure on the gurney, Sam had apparently developed a *tendre* for Bea that went beyond the caring and compassion a caregiver afforded a long-term patient.

Jay switched her attention to Marg, noting a barely perceptible curve of Marg's lips, and a soft—for Marg, at least—expression that appeared to signify satisfaction.

Tyler cleared his throat, drawing Jay's full attention back to him. His glance darted from Bea to Jay, to Bea again, then back to Jay. He started to speak, seemed to think better of it, and stood there, shifting his weight from one foot to the other.

"Spit it out, Tyler." Marg's tone carried a hint of weariness.

Jay gave what she hoped was an encouraging smile. "You know you can ask me anything, Tyler."

"I know." Whatever was preying on his mind seemed to be making him very uncomfortable but he pressed on regardless. "If you and Bea are identical twins, then how come she looks different to you?" he blurted. "I mean, you're nineteen but Bea looks, like, way younger."

Ah. Tyler was laboring under the assumption that cyborg

"twins" should be viewed in a similar way to their human coun-
terparts. "Bea's current physical form is equivalent to that of a
fifteen year-old human female," Jay informed him.

The color drained from Tyler's face, leaving him pale beneath
his tan. He looked sick to his stomach, as though he'd swallowed
something distasteful and it was churning in his gut. "You're a
Gamma unit," he said. "You were created *after* Bea."

She nodded. "Correct. According to the data Seth has been
able to provide, I can confirm I was created approximately two
years after Bea."

Tyler's Adam's apple bobbed as he swallowed convulsively,
like he had to work up enough saliva to lubricate his throat and
force out the words. "You're even younger than *her*. You're....
Jesus. You're, like, *thirteen*?" He sank so abruptly on to the stool
that one could be forgiven for thinking his leg muscles could no
longer hold him upright.

"Oh my," Seth said, his tone the slightest bit gleeful in the way
of a bystander secretly enjoying the drama. "Awkward, much?"

"I was *created*, not born—you cannot calculate my age as you
would a human's," Jay said, needing to wipe the half-horrified
half-sick expression from Tyler's face. To have him look at her
like that....

It hurt. But to put it in perspective, it was a small hurt stem-
ming from a misunderstanding, and therefore, fixable. Whereas
the last time Tyler had looked at her like that, he had accidentally
discovered her true nature—a discovery Jay had not been at all
confident he could ever come to terms with. "You are making
erroneous assumptions," she said. "For example, if you insist on
accounting for my body's physiological age at the time of my
creation, then I am older than Sam."

The sick expression on Tyler's face segued into a frown that conveyed something to the effect of, "Huh? Are you nuts? How'n the hell d'you figure that?"

"I'm twenty-eight," Sam said slowly. From his body language—his torso unconsciously tilting toward Jay—he, too appeared intrigued by Jay's claim. Only Marg seemed unconcerned. Perhaps she had already intuited the answer. Or perhaps, when you'd seen and done the things Marg had seen and done, in the grand scheme of things such mundane matters as age gaps held no sway.

Jay pondered the simplest way to explain a complex concept. "Like Bea, I was created with the outer appearance of a fifteen year old girl. So by your reckoning, Tyler, I was effectively born aged fifteen. Nineteen of your human years have passed since then, which means I am technically thirty-four years old. Give or take a few months. Depending upon the exact date of my creation, of course."

Her simplistic explanation, rather than resolving matters, left Tyler speechless with some emotion Jay couldn't discern.

Seth guffawed, which Jay presumed meant her explanation had amused him in some way. Either that or he was amused at Tyler's reaction to her explanation.

"You don't look thirty-four to me," Seth said. "Or fifteen. Or like a thirteen year old kid, for that matter."

A flush painted Tyler's cheeks as he grunted, which Jay took to mean he was embarrassed for some reason, but agreed with Seth's statements.

With luck, a little further clarification would put Tyler's concerns to rest. "Bea's youthful appearance is something that can easily be rectified once she is fully functional. Like me, she will be able to choose to age her outer shell."

Tyler opened his mouth, failed to speak actual words, and

shut it again, leaving Jay to continue her explanation. "After my creator's death, I was forced to go on the run to evade those who wanted to possess and control me."

Marg gave a barely perceptible flinch and her haunted gaze sought Jay's.

Jay consigned the past to the past with a sharp gesture. "It is of no consequence," she added, in case Marg failed to understand the gesture. "But I quickly discovered how... *inconvenient* it was to be perceived as an unaccompanied, fifteen year old female. Hence, I aged my outer shell. It is not something that can be achieved quickly, you understand. And the energy expended left me depleted and therefore vulnerable—a state I could ill afford. By the time I decided to hide in plain sight by enrolling as a student at Tyler's high school, I appeared to be around seventeen years old in human terms. My intention had been to remain in Snapperton, attending Greenfield High, until I physically resembled an eighteen year old female who could reasonably be considered an adult."

Tyler was silent, jaw working, doubtless still processing her explanation.

Jay decided to lay it all out in black and white. "After I...." *Faked my death? Hurt you so deeply that even to this day I regret it?* "After I had no choice but to disappear to keep you and your family safe, Tyler, I knew it would be many months before I could safely approach you again. I continued to age my outer shell to keep pace with your natural aging process. After we reunited, I continued to do so. I find it difficult to believe you haven't noticed."

He uttered a soft snort. "Oh, I noticed all right. I just didn't think about how it was possible—until now, that is."

An ache, centering in her heart, throbbed through her. "You

had forgotten what I truly am." And now I've smacked you in the face with it, and forced you to confront it.

Tyler hopped off his stool and approached her. He reached down to grasp her hand and placed it on his chest, over his heart. "Aside from that one time when I was a complete dick about learning what you are, I've never seen you as anything but the girl I love. When I look at you now, that's all I see."

Witnessing the truth in his eyes, the love he felt for her unashamedly displayed for all to see, Jay now understood why human females described themselves melting into a little puddle of gooey girly bits.

The hint of a smile tugged his lips. "Though I gotta say, I'm relieved as all heck you're not jailbait."

"Are we good then?"

He hugged her tight. "We're good."

The tension drained from Jay's muscles and she curled into Tyler's embrace, laying her head on his chest, content for the moment to do nothing else but listen to the steady beat of his heart.

Seth tapped her on the shoulder. "Sorry to interrupt the love-fest, but Bea's just opened her eyes."

Jay pulled from Tyler's arms and turned in time to observe Sam almost levitate from his stool in his rush to get to Bea's side. Sam may not have come right out and admitted his feelings for Bea, but right now, they were obvious to anyone with a modicum of intelligence.

"Bea." He grasped her hand and bent over her. "It's Sam, sweetheart. Can you see me?"

Bea blinked so slowly that it was agonizing to witness, and even to Jay it seemed to take an age before her eyelids resumed their original position.

"Are you ready?" Sam asked. "Or do you need more time?"

No response. Or at least, none that a human could detect. "She moved her eyelids a fraction," Jay told him. "She's weak. She's trying to answer, but the effort it takes is too great. Give her time."

Moisture gleamed in Bea's right eye, welled, overflowed and slipped down her cheek.

"And I believe there's your answer, Sam." Marg had moved so quietly Jay doubted anyone else had heard her approach.

Jay gently hip-bumped Sam aside and leaned over so Bea could see her face. "I'm going to run the algorithm now. I'll start slow so it doesn't overwhelm your core programming. Okay?" She swiped the tear from Bea's cheek with her thumb, and smiled when she detected another quiver of movement as her twin tried to blink.

Directing her attention to Sam, she advised, "Better give Bea some room. She might accidentally hurt you if she can't control her limbs. An out of control cyborg could do a lot of damage to a human."

When Sam didn't move, Jay grasped his forearms and backed him up to what she deemed a safe distance. "Please make sure he stays back, Marg. It'll only distress Bea if she injures someone she cares about."

Marg nodded and linked her arm in Sam's. He didn't seem to notice. He couldn't tear his gaze from the motionless girl on the gurney.

Jay had inserted a tiny device designed to act as wireless receiver beneath the skin of Bea's hip. For now, Jay would run the algorithm that would activate the optical cuffs from a laptop, but once Bea was stronger and mobile, Jay had designed a pocket-sized portable transmitter to replace the unwieldy laptop. Bea could keep the transmitter on her person, and recharge it as required.

"Here goes." Jay reached out and pressed the Enter key on her laptop.

CHAPTER FOURTEEN

S AM ABRUPTLY REALIZED he was holding his breath—must have been for a while because little flashes of light seemed to be darting across his eyeballs. He exhaled slowly through his nose, forced himself to relax and breathe normally, uncurled his aching fingers from tight fists he also didn't recall making.

How long had it been since Jay had started running the algorithms? Seconds? Minutes? Why wasn't something happening?

And then something *did* happen. It wasn't spectacular, wasn't even all that noticeable unless you had observed Bea, fed and cared for her, sat for hours and read to her, like Sam had done. Her eyes moved—just a little to the left, as though she was searching for something. Or someone.

He didn't think, he moved. Or tried to, but Marg was grasping his arm, holding him back. "Dammit, Marg," he snarled. "She's looking for me. Let me go to her."

Marg didn't budge, and her grip tightened until her fingertips dug into his arm. "Only if Jay says it's okay. Otherwise, you stay back."

"Jay." Sam knew he sounded like he was begging, knew that smart prick Seth would give him shit about it, but he didn't give a crap.

Jay's gaze was fixed on Bea. "I believe you're right: She is looking for you, Sam. Go to her but don't touch her. Make her work for it."

Sam shook off Marg's grip. It took all the control he had not to run to Bea and clasp her hand and squeeze it tight to reassure her. He walked. Slowly. Carefully. And he halted beside the gurney, sinking to his haunches and resting his forearms on the thin plastic mattress, so she couldn't help but see him.

Her pupils dilated. She focused on him and his heart leapt, doing a happy dance in his chest... until his brain kicked up a notch and he recalled she did that every now and then. It wasn't something to get all worked up about. And while he was coming to terms with the unhappy fact that he wanted this so damn badly he was imagining her responses, the first miracle happened: Bea's lips twitched.

Sam blinked. But he wasn't imagining it. And as he watched, barely daring to hope, her lips stretched, slowly—excruciatingly slowly—into a crooked, lopsided smile.

He smiled back at her, elated. And then, all the emotions he'd kept bottled inside—all the secret hopes and dreams he'd harbored for this beautiful, damaged girl, all his fears that she would remain forever trapped inside her body—boiled over. And Sam lowered his head atop his arms and fought the tears.

It wasn't until something squeezed his hand and he'd glanced up, confused, that he realized Bea had managed something even more miraculous than that wonderful smile. Because the cool, feminine hand that now lay across his, squeezing his fingers, wasn't Jay's or Marg's. It was Bea's.

JAY DISCONNECTED THE CALL and lay back against the pillows. According to Seth, Bea was making excellent progress. She still wasn't able to speak but she was communicating using basic signs. Her physical prognosis was good—although Jay wanted to personally check on Bea again and run more tests before any drastic decisions were made about where to proceed from hereon in.

For now, with Bea improving in leaps and bounds, Jay could concentrate on other things—chief among them identifying the men who'd attacked Marg in the parking building—not easy when their bodies had vanished without trace—and tracking the three men who'd come looking for the cybernetic hand. Not to mention determining who had taken the hand in the first place, along with who had sent the photo of Bea. And then there was convincing Allen and McPhee she didn't have a stalker, and fending off Chandler's increasingly awkward questions about how Jay had handled Nessa's so-called stalker.

Was there any wonder she felt drained? She couldn't wait for Bea to recover enough to help with—

Jay damped that thought before it could take root. Bea deserved more than being Jay's lackey. Bea deserved happiness, companions who cared for her, a life. She'd suffered enough, and Jay would not risk her being harmed again. Sixer would have to do.

A scrabbling at the partially opened door announced the arrival of a bored puppy, and Jay smiled as Brum squeezed through the opening and poked his head around the door.

She swung her legs off the bed and clicked her fingers.

Brum raced toward her, hindquarters skidding on the polished floorboards. When he reached her, as was his habit, he jumped up and pawed her thigh, the piteous whimpers his way of begging her to pick him up.

"*Nein*," she told him. And when the pup didn't take the gentle hint, she commanded, "*Platz!*"

Brum, recognizing her no-nonsense tone, obeyed and dropped to all fours.

"*Braver Hund.*" She leaned down to fondle his ears and he licked her cheek. "*Sitz!*"

The pup sat.

"*Braver Hund.*"

He panted, tongue lolling, head cocked to one side, expectant.

Jay reached into the basket of puppy toys she kept beneath the bed, and grabbed a thick piece of rope that had been knotted at each end.

Brum loosed a happy bark, recognizing his favorite toy. His hindquarters quivered, but he remained sitting. He, too, was making excellent progress.

"*Braver Hund!*" she praised, holding out the rope and clicking her fingers, giving him permission to move and take the toy in his mouth. She played tug of war with him, amused by his growling whenever she shook the rope to try and dislodge it from his grip.

The blare of Tyler's cell phone from the nightstand interrupted the game. Jay conceded the tug of war and left Brum to gnaw on his toy. Tyler was showering in the ensuite so she yelled out that he had a call, and reached for the phone.

"Can you take it for me?" he shouted. "I'm covered in shampoo."

Jay, recognizing Tyler's father's number, swiped the screen to answer the call. "Hello, Michael," she said.

"Can I speak to Tyler Davidson, please?"

Surprise jolted through her. Why would another man—a stranger—be using Michael's private cell phone to call Tyler?

"He can't come to the phone right now," she told the caller.

"Can I take a message?"

The caller's voice sounded tantalizingly familiar. She accessed her database to identify his voiceprint, but before she could find a match he blurted, "It's Martin Russell, manager of Bellevue."

Another jolt, this one followed by a lazy roll of her gut. Bellevue was the name of the gated apartment complex where Jay had relocated Marissa and Michael. "Is something wrong, Mr Russell?"

"Not sure," Martin said, his voice heavy with strain. "I really need to speak with Tyler Davidson."

"What do you mean you're not sure? What's happened? I'm his girlfriend. Tell me!"

Her voice was louder and sharper than she'd intended, but that worked to her advantage because Martin threw caution to the wind and spilled his guts. "Neighboring apartment owners heard the baby crying. It went on for hours and the kid sounded real worked up, so they got me to check it out. When I opened up the place, I found the baby alone. All their stuff's still here, far as I can tell. I found this number listed as an emergency contact on one of the cell phones. Can you get a message to Tyler Davidson? Tell him he needs to get down here quick."

"Give me a moment, please." Jay grabbed her cell and called Sixer. *Pick up, pick up.*

"The number you have dialed is no longer in service."

The room seemed to blur and close in on her. No. Please, no. She would never forgive herself if anything had happened to Tyler's parents. "Hello? You there?" Martin Russell's panicked voice squawked down the line.

Jay picked up Tyler's cell again and swallowed to lubricate the desert-dry cavern of her mouth. "We'll be right there."

About the Author

MAREE ANDERSON WRITES paranormal romance, fantasy, and young adult books. She lives in beautiful New Zealand, home of hobbits, elves, and kiwis—both the fruit and the two-legged flightless variety. Her first novel for young adults, the multi-award-winning *Freaks of Greenfield High,* was optioned for TV by Cream Drama, Inc., Canada, and currently has over 2 million reads on Wattpad. She recently released the third book in the *Freaks* series, and is working on a second book in the *Liminals* series.

For more information about Maree's books, please visit her website at: http://www.mareeanderson.com

Other books in the Freaks series

FREAKS OF GREENFIELD HIGH

FREAKS IN THE CITY

~*~

www.ingramcontent.com/pod-product-compliance
Lightning Source LLC
Chambersburg PA
CBHW032209190626
46810CB00019B/2386